Parsons' Mill

Parsons' Mill

Timothy Lewontin

University Press of New England
Hanover and London

UNIVERSITY PRESS OF NEW ENGLAND
Brandeis University
Brown University
Clark University
University of Connecticut
Dartmouth College
University of New Hampshire
University of Rhode Island
Tufts University
University of Vermont

Printed in the United States of America
Designed and produced by
Christopher Harris /Summer Hill Books
Perkinsville, Vermont

Library of Congress Cataloging-in-Publication Data

Lewontin, Timothy.
    Parsons' Mill.

    1. Sawmills—New England.   2. Sawmill workers—New
England.   I. Title.
TS850.L45   1989   674'.2'0974   88–40521
ISBN 0–87451–479–7

5 4 3 2 1

The events described in this book are
based on personal experience. All
names and locations have been changed.

Contents

Parsons' Mill

"The great drawback to this sort of thing in America," continued Mr. Arbuton, "is that there is no human interest about the scenery, fine as it is."

"Why, I don't know," said Kitty, "there was that little settlement round the saw-mill. Can't you imagine any human interest in the lives of the people there? It seems to me that one might make almost anything out of them. Suppose, for example, that the owner of that mill was a disappointed man who had come here to bury the wreck of his life in—sawdust?"

—WILLIAM DEAN HOWELLS,
A Chance Acquaintance, p. 76

Driving By

here at the bottom of the front page of the *Haddam Courant*, the sole journal for a prosperous and progressive Vermont community of ten thousand guarding the confluence of the North and Connecticut river valleys, read a plain little advertisement:

Wanted:
Sawyer to train
Henry Parsons Mill

It was such a simple and attractive statement, so matter-of-fact in its nature, but it contained just the hint of opportunity for which I longed. Absent were the usual requirements that find themselves a permanent place in the consciousness of every job seeker. There were no "experiences required," nor résumés to be submitted, not even a letter of recommendation was asked for. The simple phrase, "to train" implied that all such conventional specifics were irrelevant.

I knew where the mill was and had passed it many times. It sat atop a small bluff around which one of the back roads into town wound sharply. Driving by on my way into town I would slow down in order to accommodate the hazards of the road's bend. As I did, I got a panoramic glimpse of its buildings and yards, the logs piled up high in front, and occasionally, some old hand performing tasks that made me wonder at the deep and dark processes occurring within. With its gray clapboard siding, its six-over-six sash windows, and its lean brick smokestack the mill had an order and simplicity, a self-containedness, that gave it the imaginative promise of a child's toy model.

In summer, the logs piled in their long rows twelve and fifteen feet high were adorned with water sprinklers. Spray drifted lazily back and forth across these small hills, giving the logs the appearance of having been cultivated there, as if someone were just waiting until they were ripe, so they could be picked and processed. I had seen the old hands in their green khaki pants, shirts, and caps hosing logs down with more water and rolling them into a dark recess of the mill. But I did not know the reason behind these peculiar baptisms, nor did I have any idea what became of those logs afterwards. It was probably curiosity about these matters, as much as it was a need for work, that drove me to get a further glimpse of the workings of that mill, and I took the advertisement for a "sawyer to train" as my invitation.

I was not long out of college, married, and unable to find satisfactory employment. My wife Amy and I had gone to school in Boston together and had emerged just as the economy nosed into recession. Jobs of any sort were quite scarce, and it was a difficult time to be on one's own for the first time, whether one posessed a newly minted certificate of higher education or not.

One of the peculiarities of the time was that every personal advantage could easily be turned to disadvantage. People were "undereducated," or "overeducated," without experience, with too much experience. It mattered not, because whatever job one sought, it seemed meant for someone else.

I was not from Vermont, couldn't properly say that I'd grown up there. But I had spent a number of summers there as a child and had developed a feel for the place that can only come from childhood. Well, I mean, an adult can spend twenty-five years in a place and never feel he understands it, never quite feel that it's home. But a child spends a year or two—even a few summers—and it remains with him his entire life. That was how I'd gotten the idea that if I wanted a chance folks up in Vermont might be willing to give me one.

If I had to say where I'd really grown up, I suppose it would be the Midwest. No, not in the midst of an enormous field of corn and wheat, but in Chicago, that enormous city on a lake. More specifically, I'm from the south side, or sout' side, as the working people put it. This latter distinction is an important one, because the south side is the dirtier, more desperate side of town, whereas the north side is the one you'll see in the travel brochures, with its "gold coast" and its bohemian prosperity.

But of course for me, locality was a bit ethereal. I'd grown up under the protection of the academic world, my father being a scientist who lived in a world of molecular structure and differential equation. The university to which we were attached formed the nucleus of a small middle-class oasis, which was surrounded by ghetto on three sides and by that beautiful lake to the east. I went to a private school nearby, where my peers' parents were all the more prosperous variety of humanity—doctors, lawyers, businesspeople, academics—and there was always an implied and comfortable assumption that someday we would follow suit.

It was a peculiar world in many ways. We were supported by a world of abstract ideas, while surrounded by a world as violently real as could be. At night shots were fired, and sometimes you knew the people killed.

Now, years later, Amy and I were out in the world, alone together, as they say. All that abstraction came back to haunt us. No longer protected, we had spent two years moving about the old mill towns of western Massachusetts, where it was cheaper to live than Boston, trying desperately to establish some sort of stability. She got a decent job with the civil service for a while, and I worked as a handyman and jack-of-all-trades. But that life was cut short when the Republicans in Washington decided to cut the "fat" out of the budget, and Amy lost her job.

Down, but not out. Sitting in a dead mill town on the lower Connecticut River—a bastion of former Yankee greatness. Vast mills of red brick surrounded by elaborate networks of canals, locks, dams—all lay silent, deserted. Spectacular fires erupted sometimes, and the whole town would come to attention, first elated at the spectacle and then mourning the loss. One by one, great monuments were being reduced to flat fields of rubble.

So up Interstate 91, straight north up the Connecticut we gleefully escaped. We were traveling the "precision valley," as they had called it in the last century, the technological marvel of its day, following it to where it emerged from the Green and White mountain ranges. Here one might still find vestiges of the values that had illuminated an earlier time. You could hear the locals speaking its language, contemptuous of the flatlanders *down there*, marveling at the desperation.

3

On a bright and sunny Saturday morning in mid-August, with the sky bathing everything in gold and blue, I slowly wound my way along dirt roads towards a self-appointed interview at Mister Parsons' mill. As I drove, I tried to imagine what lay before me and to remind myself to relax and be forthcoming. I really had no idea what to expect from such a place, nor of the people who worked there. From my distant perspective as a passerby, the mill had always seemed inviting. Now that I was accepting that invitation, I fell victim to my own imaginative extremes. I had picked a Saturday to make my application, with the intention of avoiding other employees. It was going to be difficult enough to sell myself to Parsons, and I had no interest in doing it under the stolid gaze of a bunch of cynical millhands.

I crept my little pickup truck into the gravel yard that lay in front of the mill and parked in what I hoped was an appropriately discreet spot. There, at a set of large sliding wooden doors, a tall, lean, creaky-looking figure bent stiffly over some repair work. From the yard he appeared to be vigorously and attentively rotating a screwdriver with the full force of his figure. I slowly made my way across the yard, raising an alarming crunch of gravel with every step I took, but he seemed so intent on his work that he failed to notice me. I came to a cautious halt at ten feet and called out, "Mister Parsons?"

He continued his vigorous concentration on the work before him, merely tilting his head back a bit in order to adjust his focus. I stood my ground, waiting for a response. Finally, continuing to work, and without looking up, the old man said, "I heard you coming."

"Oh . . . uuh . . . well . . . I was wondering whether or not there was any work here right now."

Twisting himself half around while keeping his hands in contact with his work, his eyes focused not on me but on some undefined area over my shoulder, as if he were wondering who else I'd brought along. "No," he said, "I haven't got anything right now." And then twisting back, he returned to his labors.

"Damn!" I thought. "I guess he's filled it then." But there was something slightly promising about the way his voice had risen to a higher pitch as he said the word "now," and so I persisted. "Well," I said, "I saw that you had an advertisement in the *Courant*."

"Yea-ahs," said Parsons, stretching the word out into New Englanderese, as if to say, how *very* observant of you.

"Uuh . . . well . . . do you expect that you might have something in the near future?"

After a moment, the old man stopped what he was doing, carefully put down his tools, and turned to face me. He was tall and very thin, wearing gold-rimmed glasses similar to my own and was dressed in the green khaki shirt and pants that were standard issue for the working stiffs of the region. His age was evident in the wrinkle of his skin, putting him past seventy as far as I could tell, but his silver hair remained long and luxuriant. On his face he wore the kind of constipated expression of someone who has had to stop what he is doing in order to dispose of an annoying fly.

"Well it's possible that I might have something in the near future. What can you do?"

This had always proved a particularly unsettling question for me because it left so much leeway. It would not have done to explain that I could recite passages from memory of *The Wasteland*, and yet it was not an altogether irrelevant fact in an assessment of my capabilities. So I opted for the general autobiographical approach.

"Well . . . I went to college, graduated with an eye towards teaching high school . . . didn't like it much though."

The look of constipation softened a bit.

"After that I worked as a theater manager and then was self-employed as a carpenter for a while."

"What did you say your name was?" Parsons' interest seemed slightly piqued. I told him, and added, "Perhaps you know my father. His land borders on some of yours."

"Ohhh yes," he smiled, "I know your father." His eyes remained narrowed despite a broadening smile. My father had once tried to buy a parcel of woodland that Parsons owned and had been flatly refused. It was a piece of history that I'd hoped to avoid in our little conversation.

But at the moment I supposed that it would have dawned on him sooner or later that he knew my father, and it seemed best to get past the matter.

"Your father's a scholar, isn't he?" The word "scholar" had a special sneering emphasis that was impossible to miss.

"Yes . . . that's right." I tried to sound impatient with this line of questioning. "He's a biologist."

"Yea-ahs," he groaned dryly. "Ever work in a mill before?"

"No."

"Well, this would be kind of an unusual occupation for someone with your backround, wouldn't it?"

Here, I was prepared to be argumentative. "Well, not really. I've got a brother who works as a mechanic, another that's a machinist, and then my third brother . . . well, he's a scholar."

"Oh! *he's* the scholar, eh?"

"Yes," I smiled. "The rest of us just didn't seem to have the right . . . ," and at a loss for words, I tapped my skull.

Apparently Parsons approved of this gesture, because he smiled also. "Well, you've had a good education. Obviously you've got the brains for the job, but have you got the brawn?"

The question had been a rhetorical one, but I started to answer it anyway. "As I said, I've worked as a carpenter. . . ."

"Yes," Parsons interrupted. He looked me over appraisingly. "Yes, you've worked with your hands before." I took this matter-of-fact observation as a compliment. I am of a slim build and don't exactly look as if I've been heaving bales of hay all my life. My hands are well articulated, but they do not have that rough-worked and weathered temper of hard experience. Still, Parsons had seen something of a mechanical intelligence in my figure, and in that simple glance of appraisal had seen the pride I took in my hands.

"Well," Parsons continued, "you certainly have an interesting family, but I really don't have anything right now."

It occurred to me that he might be thinking that I was only after a summer job, so I suggested that perhaps it might be a good idea if I were to call on him again in the fall.

"Yes, that *might* be a good idea." But his tone implied that he considered this merely theoretical, and was not about to commit himself to approving it. Instead, he moved abruptly off to attend to some garden hoses attached to faucets on the side of the mill.

I didn't feel that our interview had really come to a satisfactory conclusion and thought that at the very least he ought to have a copy of my phone number. So, keeping a respectful distance, I paralleled his movements. And seeing that I had not yet given up, he guessed what I was after.

"Well," he cried impatiently, "have you got a telephone where you live?"

I scribbled my name and number on a scrap of paper and handed it to Parsons, who stuffed it in his shirt pocket with such dispatch that I felt certain that I'd merely witnessed the first leg in that scrap's journey to the wastebasket. Parsons' sudden annoyance at my presence was now quite obvious, and I stood watching dumbly as he turned to the set of faucets. Using that same vigorous but precise movement of the hands with which he'd manipulated the screwdriver, he began to rotate the four of them in rapid succession. After a momentary hesitation, the garden hoses began to jump and twitch, and I turned around to see the fine spray of seven or eight water sprinklers rising majestically upon the hill of logs behind me. Up they rose, wavering a bit as they climbed higher and higher and began to extend their spray towards me, forcing my hasty retreat.

When I had regained safe ground, I looked over at Parsons. He seemed to have forgotten all about me and was patiently considering the distribution of water over his log pile, occasionally making minor adjustments to the faucets. I smiled broadly and shouted, "Perhaps I'll be seeing you soon."

"Perhaps," he said sourly. But as I turned to go, I thought I caught an interested and bemused look on the old man's face.

7

Baptism

A bout two weeks after my interview with him, I got a phone call from Mr. Parsons. "Yes," he said, "there probably is work for you here." As I came later to learn, the word "probably" was the strongest form of affirmation that Parsons could manage. So "probably" actually meant definitely, and I had the job.

Two days later, I showed up at what I considered to be the ungodly hour of seven in the morning. As I entered the mill, I noticed my coworkers—a disappointing two in number—already sitting and waiting for work to begin. From a tiny office in a corner of the main floor, Parsons emerged and spun around a hundred and eighty degrees to look up at the large clock that hung over his door. After a few minor adjustments to his wristwatch, he turned back towards us. "Gentlemen, we have a new man come to play with us." He grinned slightly, while the others laughed without humor and looked away. They certainly didn't look like the friendliest bunch in the world, but I had expected as much and had come prepared to keep my distance.

The first task Parsons showed me was "trimming dowel." Parsons and I proceeded "downcellar," where we grabbed a large and worn-looking wooden cart on heavy cast steel wheels. It was piled high with hundreds and hundreds of those cylindrical wooden sticks known as "dowel." With an effort that was to become very familiar, we forced the rumbling cart onto the mill's freight elevator, which bounced alarmingly with the weight. "This is a lanyard type lift," Parsons lectured as we rode upstairs. "Not too many of these around anymore." With some pride, he demonstrated how the elevator could be stopped and started at any point by pulling on a thin cable running the entire length of the shaft. "Little tricky 'til you get the hang of it."

Wheeling the cart across the main floor, he took some time to maneuver it into exact position next to the "trim saw." This was an odd, jury-rigged device that Parsons himself had knocked together out of

8

some odds and ends, and of which he seemed even more proud than of the "lanyard type lift." The trim saw consisted of a pair of small, lethal-looking saw blades spinning naked at either end of a long, hinged bar. Its sole function was to trim dowel rods to a specific length. One operated it by sticking a dowel on the arm and pushing the arm through the spinning blades, which were so spaced as to trim both ends of the dowel at once.

The cart we had brought upstairs consisted of dowels intended for shipment to a manufacturer of wooden ladders, who would use them as rungs. Since these rungs would be called upon to support the full weight of a person who might weigh well over two hundred pounds, I was advised that I held the rather serious responsibility of making sure that they were free of such defects as knots, rot, insect holes, and curly or twisted grain. The grain had to be measurably straight and was adjudged as a slope ratio of length to width, known in the trade as "grain slope." The particular dowels in question could not posess a "grain slope" of more than "one-in-seven," meaning that for every seven inches of length the grain could not slope or curve more than one inch from the rod's center.

To consider the qualities of a piece of wood is to consider the use to which it might be put, as I soon discovered. If a particular dowel possessed any serious defect in its grain structure, its use as a ladder rung could lead to a broken neck. Having found such a defect, I was required to decide whether it might be useful for some other purpose, or if it ought to be thrown out altogether. Depending on the nature of the fault, I might trim it to a shorter length for use in a narrower ladder, save it to be turned down to a smaller diameter dowel, throw it in a basket of dowels that Parsons would sell to a furniture manufacturer of less exacting standards, or throw it in yet another basket of material for firewood.

So there I stood, with a supply cart on my right, which by later estimation consisted of over fifteen hundred dowels, and in front of me sat the trimming machine. On my left sat a cart divided into three compartments, onto which I was to load trimmed dowels of various lengths, and around me on the floor sat the various laundry baskets into which I was to dump the dowels intended as firewood or for sale to a furniture manufacturer. In retrospect, the matter was all quite simple and straightforward, and this seemed to be how Parsons viewed the matter, since he took only the briefest moment to explain it to me.

It was his habit to employ an abbreviated jargon, which left the uninitiated dumbfounded by its simplicity, and absolutely mystified as to its meaning. His actual words of instruction to me flowed forth continuously without pause or elaboration, and ran something like this: "Now we trim these down to three sizes: eighteens, twenty-ones, and twenty-fours. They use these for ladder rungs so you'll want to look out for large knots like . . . ," he fished around the supply cart for a few seconds before locating an example, " . . . like this one. You'll also want to watch out for curly grain, insect holes, rot, and we don't like a grain slope of more than one-in-seven. If they're rough like this one, we can turn them down to thirteen-sixteenths. Use this basket for your culls, we'll sell them to the chair manufacturer. And this basket gets used for firewood."

He then turned abruptly on his heels and started to head off to attend to another front.

"Uuh, Mr. Parsons?" I called out, tentatively raising my hand like the class dunce. "What do you mean by 'grain slope'?"

Parsons turned around impatiently and gave me a pitying look, as if it were one of the cruelest tricks that nature could play on a human being that he didn't know what grain slope was. In the mocking tones of a tough old schoolmaster, he proceeded to explain what he clearly considered should be obvious to anyone of normal intelligence. After the issue of grain slope had been sufficiently clarified, I was still left in the unfortunate position of wondering exactly what he'd meant by the rest of his instructions but was totally afraid to ask for further clarification.

Reluctantly, I set to work and soon found that the baskets on the floor were filling up at an alarming rate. I could find a fault or two in every other dowel I picked up, and kept giving Parsons worried looks. Am I doing this right? Are there any more baskets? But Parsons studiously ignored me, the baskets began to overflow, and dowels began to clatter across the floor.

After an hour or so, my two fellow employees, who seemed to spend most of their time running busily from one section of the mill to another, moving carts, riding up and down on the lanyard-type lift, and making cracks to one another, casually strolled over to my area. One of them, considerably older and more ragged looking than the other, peered into the overflowing baskets and said to his companion, "Look perfectly good to me." Then the younger one peered into the baskets and said, "Look okay to me too." The two of them strolled casually away to roll around more carts, and disappeared down the freight elevator again on another mysterious assignment. I found myself wondering if their comments had meant that I was doing "okay," or that the dowels I was throwing out were "perfectly good."

In any event, I was saved by the nine o'clock break. My fellow employees reappeared on the elevator, and one of them shouted, "Break!" He pointed to the clock over Parsons' office, and drew his hand across his throat as if to slit it. The two of them moved across the mill to a sunny area along the wall between the office and the mill's entrance, drew up a pair of upturned buckets, and sat down. I tried to follow suit but was unable to find a bucket not employed for some other purpose. I settled for leaning uncomfortably against a large wooden bench built into the wall.

The two of them, whose names I gathered were Craig and Charlie, continued their mumbled consultations with one another, laughing and casting sidelong glances in my direction. Naturally this made me uncomfortable, and I tried to concentrate on the various odd pieces of machinery scattered throughout the mill. In front of me sat a very large and deadly looking affair with an enormous fifty-two-inch circular blade that I assumed was the mill's main saw. It was equipped with a bewildering variety of knobs, cranks, pedals, and levers that looked as though they had something to do with holding a log in place as it was being cut, but I could not imagine exactly how. And so while Craig and Charlie continued their private ruminations, I tried to show how unconcerned I was by shuffling over to the saw and carefully examining it. Touching a lever here, pulling a piece of sawdust off there, all the while I stood there, I pretended a fascination with the machine, but I was really trying to figure out how long I would last in this atmosphere.

After ten minutes of break, getting back to work seemed like a welcome relief. Parsons arrived on the freight elevator, and with the kind of deliberate shuffle peculiar to people of tremendous energy who find themselves trapped in stiff old bodies, he moved rapidly across the mill to redirect us to the fray. He gave Craig and Charlie an instruction incomprehensible to me but that seemed to make perfect sense to them, and added, "In the meantime I will go through the culls with our new member." Craig and Charlie looked at one another briefly and smiled before heading off to their appointed task.

The "culls," as Parsons called them, consisted of those dowels I had rejected for use in ladders and had saved for the furniture maker. There must have been three or four hundred of these, but showing an amazing patience, Parsons went through each and every one of them, explaining why it would have been "perfectly all right" to use this one for a ladder dowel, or why another should have been trimmed to a different length, or why yet another should have been consigned to firewood. When we had disposed of the culls, Parsons decided that perhaps it might be a good idea to go through the basket of firewood. Two hours later, both baskets on the floor were nearly empty. It turned out that just about everything I'd classified as a cull could have been used as a ladder rung, and that everything I'd thrown out could have been culled, retrimmed, or turned to a smaller diameter. In fact, it seemed that an infinite number of things could be done with a stick of dowel before you had to resign yourself to throwing it out.

As I returned to the work, it came to me slowly, imperceptibly, but quite surely, that when he'd first set me to work, Parsons hadn't told me half of what I'd needed to know in order to do the job properly. This too was Parsons' way. The omissions had been deliberate and were calculated to leave me confused. He'd known I'd make all those mistakes, but still let me blunder along in my unmerry way. I even thought I detected some real pleasure in the old man's face as he saw me wince at the prospect of going all the way back to the beginning and starting again.

By noon, I had been working for five hours and was still only a third of the way through the supply cart. I wondered whether I'd ever get through it, or if Parsons was just having a little fun at my expense and had decided that Sisyphus was my name. It was beginning to irk me that I had to stand alone at a single tedious task all day long, while everyone else got to run here and there, doing this and that, never quite getting the chance to be as bored and frustrated as I now felt.

As I worked my way through this seemingly endless task, and as I got used to it, I developed a simple working rhythm that allowed my mind to drift. In six deft movements of the hands and arms I would grab a dowel, spin it in my hands to look for faults, slap it on the trimmer, push it through the spinning blades to trim it, pull it back, grab and spin it to have a second look for faults, then drop it in the cart. These movements got faster and faster as I counted out the six beats, and I could hum along this way in a kind of pleasantly meditative trance as I grabbed dowel after dowel after dowel. Then some perturbation, or a fatigue either mental or physical, might break that trance, and the rhythm would modulate and slow a bit before I gradually rebuilt my speed. A fault might crop up, and I would come to a complete halt as I took a few seconds to study it and decide whether

12

I should trim it, retrim it, or just drop it into a basket before returning to the start of that six-beat rhythm.

After a while, the cart of finished dowels would begin to fill up, giving me a sense that I was actually getting somewhere. But no sooner did I reach this state of contentment, than would Craig come along and without so much as a glance in my direction start to grab up my finished dowels and tie them up into neat bundles, which he stacked on a pallet on the other side of the room. It soon became apparent that he could tie them up at about ten times the rate I could produce them. I was soon dropping dowels on an empty cart again, and no matter how fast I worked, it remained that way. So instead of concentrating on how fast I was filling up the cart, I decided to derive my sense of accomplishment from the rate at which I could deplete the supply.

Aside from bundling the dowels I'd finished trimming, Craig was also carrying out a variety of other tasks. With assorted wrenches, pliers, and screwdrivers he tentatively probed at a substantial-looking machine that sat directly to my right. Whatever he was doing, it was not terribly familiar to him because he kept stopping to ask Parsons for advice. Parsons would mumble a few words to him, and Craig would come striding back to the machine, probe some more, then light back to Parsons for further mumbled instruction.

In the meantime, Parsons and Charlie were carrying on similar ruminations over a small ripsaw next to Craig's machine. There was much discussion and scratching of heads as the two of them took the ripsaw apart and then put it back together again several different times. The saw was switched on, Parsons would carefully feed a board through, and then measure the result. Shaking his head with dismay, Parsons would switch it back off, and once more the two of them took the machine apart. Finally, Parsons was satisfied with whatever adjustments they were making and started feeding one board after another at a rapid and steady pace. The resulting pieces were blanks about one inch square on the ends by two feet in length, which Charlie began methodically stacking on an empty cart.

Craig had finished tinkering with his machine and set it running. Grabbing a bunch of the blanks that the other two had produced, he began to feed a few of them into the machine. Out came a dowel rod, which he promptly measured and showed to Parsons. After examining it carefully, Parsons gave Craig an assenting nod. Grabbing an even larger bunch of blanks and heaping them in a pile next to his machine,

Craig started feeding the machine at the incredible rate of about one a second. To my horror and amazement, the machine started to deposit them on my supply cart. Out they popped from a tube, like some kind of rectal nightmare. And as they fell onto my cart, mounting ever higher and higher, I struggled valiantly to keep up. But no matter how fast I worked, Craig could feed them through faster. When he'd gained a sufficient lead on my supply cart, he shut the machine down, casually strolled around me, and tied my finished cart up into bundles. By the time I'd even put a dent in what he'd piled onto my supply cart, he'd already emptied the finished cart, and was back producing more for the supply.

This was how the work continued for the rest of that afternoon. Until the moment the first dowel had dropped onto my supply cart, I'd made absolutely no connection between what I was doing and the activities of those around me. It had been an utterly heartbreaking revelation for me, because no matter how hard I worked, my supply cart remained full, while my finished cart remained empty. I stood there in the middle of it all, working furiously just to maintain an equilibrium, while those around me seemed to carry on their work with relaxed and easy attitudes as if nothing could be sweeter than the methodical torture of this "new member" in their midst.

As the first day at Parsons' mill drew to a close, I was having serious doubts about my ability to stand a second.

Floored

4

By nature I am a shy person, and as the next few days of work went by, and I became more and more practiced in the art of trimming dowels, I began to concentrate on the problem of how to break the ice with my fellow employees. Aside from a few bits of mumbled advice from Craig on the qualities of this or that particular dowel rod, there had been virtually no communication between us. Craig was quite young, only eighteen or nineteen I guessed, but he enjoyed the advantage of experience in the ways of the mill and used that advantage to maintain an aura of aloof superiority over me that was nearly suffocating. Charlie was much older and more ragged, but he had a kind of forbidding dignity about him. At break I would make a few attempts at eye contact with him, hoping for the exchange of a word or two. But he just sat there on his upturned bucket, staring fixedly at the floor, taking long hard drags at his cigarette, studiously ignoring me.

It was Craig and Charlie's habit to sit outside in warm weather in order to more fully enjoy their lunches, while Parsons remained sequestered in his office, listening to the noon news on an ancient tube radio. I chose to eat outside but spent the first couple of days in depressed isolation on a large pile of railroad ties well out of sight of Craig and Charlie. By the third day, as I sat there munching away at an apple, I began to berate myself for not trying hard enough, thinking that perhaps I appeared to be the unfriendly one. After finishing my lunch, I strolled over to the others, just as casual as you please, and hovered there for a moment waiting for an invitation to join their company. No such invitation was forthcoming, so after a few moments of uncomfortable silence, I volunteered a weak, "Hi!" They both nodded in return and continued about the business of consuming their lunches.

"God, it's a beautiful day," I ventured.

"Yeah," said Craig.

And then, as often happens in such circumstances, my mind went blank, and I could think of absolutely nothing else to say. Or, if I could think of anything, it seemed so totally banal that I simply could not muster the courage to make myself speak. Apparently they had nothing to say either, and the renewed silence became as deadly as ever. I was by now completely convinced that these two despised me for some as yet unspecified reason. What had I done? Had I taken someone else's job? Was I some kind of a scab? Or was there something in my appearance that offended them? The entire matter remained a mystery to me until I gave up and began to shuffle off.

"Fag!" one of them cursed under his breath.

I stopped dead in my tracks and turned to face my accuser. But the two of them continued to avoid looking directly at me, shooting sly, resentful little sidelong glances at me instead.

"Lord!" I thought. I had certainly faced this one before, but I was burning. I turned on my heel and muttering obscenities headed back into the mill's cool darkness. Back at work, trimming dowels, I grew angrier and angrier at the thought of such closed mindedness. Why did people always have to categorize others? Why did one always have to prove one's loyalties? My pace picked up. Lost in thought, and by now completely used to the task, I lost all awareness of the world beyond me and my trimmer. The others were no longer creating new dowels for me to trim, and I worked with a grim determination to empty the remaining cart and get on to some other task, or get the hell out of that place altogether. Parsons had other ideas. After two-and-a-half days of standing at the trim saw, I had come to the end of the work. Parsons led me "downcellar" to show me several more carts filled to the brim with untrimmed dowels and asked me if I "wouldn't mind" doing these as well. It looked as though there were more dowels on these carts than on those I had already tackled. I was flabbergasted. I could not believe that the old man really meant it and kept looking at his face for some sign that perhaps this was just a little joke that he liked to play on newcomers. But despite the little touches of humor to be seen playing at the corners of his mouth, he appeared to be absolutely serious.

Arriving on the main floor with my new burden, I was starting to boil. Charlie looked up from his work across the mill and shot me a sympathetic glance. "Save it!" I tried to say with a look and pushed the cart off the freight elevator with all the power I could muster. Its wheels clattered and banged as they struck the floor, and it rumbled along uneven floorboards, giving force to my feelings. "Just let anyone get in the way and I'll run 'em right over," I thought.

Although the mill was a noisy place, it was always possible to make yourself heard when you wanted. The trim saw was nearly inaudible as it ran, mixing in with the generalized *shhhh* of many other running blades. But when a dowel was forced, the trim saw had a high pitched shriek that was all its own. If you were gentle in the way you fed it, the sound was gentle also, but to push a dowel through its blades with full force was to make a statement that nobody could miss. As I worked, and my anger increased, my automatized motion took on a savage emphasis. The others now started to regard me with some alarm. But now that I had gotten their attention, I returned it with a defiant and fixed glare.

At first Parsons seemed to enjoy my predicament. He shuffled about, busying himself with this or that, a kind of reddish humor decorating his face. It was becoming clear that this was the old man's idea of fun. Inadvertently, I had run into a contest with him. Either he was going to fire me, or I was going to quit, but I was determined to get the better of the old bastard. Defiant looks had no visible effect, so I started muttering at him from under my breath, punctuating each insult with the thrust of the arms in the motion of my work. The place was much too noisy for my words to be heard, but Parsons could see my lips moving, and he was obviously a man of some imagination.

After a while the treatment began to work. He no longer smiled, the red in his face began to deepen, and I was encouraged to increase the force of my motions and the depth of my obscenities. Parsons now began to strut about with great urgency, making little beelines past me, harassing me, trying to break my spell of anger. Finally he stopped and stood directly behind me so that I was unable to see him. He might have been preparing to bring a hammer crashing down on my skull for all I knew, but I continued my forced pace. On my periphery, I could see that he had decided to sort through my finished cart, looking for mistakes. With an angry and erratic motion he pawed through dowels, sending them clattering to and fro. I slowed a bit, concerned that he might find the evidence he needed to justify his anger against me, and straightened my back, feeling that a confrontation was imminent.

To my surprise, he stopped his impatient search for faulty work, threw a dowel aside, and wheeled around my machine, heading for

17

some distant point across the mill. But no sooner had he cleared my machine than he caught his foot on a looped handle attached to one of the cull baskets and came tumbling to the floor with a mighty crash.

An old person falling is a terrible sight to see. Their bodies no longer have the spring with which the young can defend themselves against the tricks of gravity. Instead they collapse, and fall inwards, their bodies seeming as vulnerable as some grand old building undergoing instant demolition. Despite my anger, my first instinct was to see that Parsons was alive and well. Despite a look of shock that momentarily crossed his face, no serious damage appeared to have occurred. Stunned, and sitting there on his seventy-year-old butt with his legs stretched before him, he looked like some absurd and overaged child playing in the sand at the beach. Looking around as if to find his bearing, he fixed his gaze on the offending basket loop, and withdrawing an unpleasant-looking pocket knife, he focused all his fury against the offending handle as he slashed and tore it away.

It was clear that I could just as easily have been the intended victim of Parsons' slashing fury, and my body tensed instinctually. But with the trim saw and its spinning blades between us, and him still sitting foolishly on the floor, I felt safe. That brief sense of critical danger passed almost as soon as it had come. And though I am not a person prone to violence and am ill-equipped to handle it, I felt a little giddy with triumph. My ears told me the mill had hesitated in its labors, and as I looked up I could see that Craig and Charlie were both watching me with wide-open eyes from across the floor. I gave them an even and prideful look, and then indicating with my eyes the man on the floor, who was by now folding up his knife, I tried to say without words that I was the one who had put him there.

Craig 5

By the end of my first week at Parsons' mill, I had gone through almost every dowel in the mill that needed trimming. Craig had bundled my work into neat packages of fifty, and stacked them on pallets in an ingenious and beautiful architecture strapped in place ready for shipment. Each pallet contained forty-eight bundles of fifty dowels each, and since we'd created four pallets, it was easy for me to calculate that I had trimmed close to ten thousand dowels over the course of four days.

Parsons, who by now seemed to have forgotten our previous acrimony, was in high spirits. He had an order filled and ready to ship and a new man who'd produced it for him without stalking out first. "Looks like we found a good one," he confided cheerfully to Craig as they passed by where I stood finishing off a partial cart. Apparently any trouble that I'd caused was now officially forgiven.

But as the days passed, it became clear to me that the mill was operating at a near standstill. Parsons had us performing "chores," which in his specialized vocabulary meant the variety of essential, yet seemingly unproductive tasks that any organized activity requires. A writer might sharpen his pencils, lay out his paper, and organize his manuscript. Charlie, Parsons, and I swept up, counted stock, and processed those odd bits of wood that were set aside for one reason or another when things had been going full blast. In his official capacity as driver for the mill's small dump truck, Craig collected scrap and delivered it as firewood to a long list of households that were already preparing for the coming fall and winter.

My wife and I were also gearing up for winter. As urban apartment dwellers, we were used to having our needs met (or not met) at the drop of a rent check. Now that we had opted for the country life, the prospects of maintaining our own house in the woods, heating it without the assistance of public utilities, and getting to work without public transportation were cause for more than a little apprehension on our part. On the surface, we had little doubt that we could handle the worst that this sort of life had to offer and considered ourselves quite self-reliant. But even the best-prepared test taker is nervous before the test occurs, and it came as a revelation to me when I discovered that even those who have lived in the country all their lives still feel a peculiar dread at summer's end. Will the wood hold out? Will the car die? Will the wood stove burn the house down? How often will we lose the electricity? Every year, without fail, these questions strike again and again. Those who have long experience in these matters learn ways to get a head start, but they can never be absolutely sure that someday they will not be overwhelmed.

"Ash," said Charlie. "Best to burn it green, that's what they say." It was the first time that Charlie had addressed me directly, and it took me aback a little.

"Umm, is that right?"

"Oh yeah. Burns much too hot if you let it dry." He struck a match, lit a cigarette, and looked ahead philosophically for a moment before turning back to me. "Where ya living?"

"Oh, my wife and I are renting a little house up in Stepney."

Astonishment crossed his face. "You married?"

"Yup. Have been for, oh let's see, uh, five years."

"Is that right?" He paused to consider this new bit of intelligence.

Within a week or two of my start at the mill Amy had acquired a job as a librarian at a small public high school across the river. Jobs for women were scarce in this region, and as she'd always had an interest in working in a high school, the matter came to us as somewhat of a miracle. We were now both to be working, and that thought alone would help to sustain me through whatever Parsons might throw my way. The house we'd rented was tiny and cramped, but the sense of routine engendered by our jobs, and the need to make our household work, was already making for a closeness and sense of purpose that had been under constant stress when one or the other of us had been out of work.

"How're you heating your house?" Charlie asked.

"With wood. Got to. There's electric back up, but I sure can't afford to heat it that way."

"Well," he brightened, "you're in luck working in an ash mill. You can take pretty much what you like for firewood."

"For free?"

"Oh yeah. Probably if you asked him, old Henry'd even let you use the truck. It's one of the benefits of working here." And then pausing for a long drag on his cigarette, and exhaling with a broad smile, he added, "In lieu of any others, that is."

Charlie looked the part of the tough and bedraggled millhand. His glasses rode halfway down his nose, his hair was unkempt, and he seemed to shave only on a twice-weekly basis. His pants were so loose that they sagged precariously on his hips, allowing for a fine view of the upper third of his boxer shorts. Somehow he gave the impression that were it not for the belt he was continually tightening around his waist his entire being would collapse on the floor in a heap. Yet there was something in the thoughtful way he voiced his phrases that betrayed a sophistication way beyond his appearance.

As for Craig, perhaps because I was new, or because I was somewhat older, he was particularly competitive and seemed determined to prove how much more effective he was at being "a man." On even the most temperate days in that late summer, he strode about the mill stripped to the waist, moving with the poised forcefulness of a basketball player, carrying out his appointed tasks with the self-satisfied air of one fully aware of his greatness. "Cooperation" was not a word that had much meaning in Craig's vocabulary, and I soon discovered that it was virtually impossible to work alongside him.

Much of the scrap wood produced at the mill came in the form of long boards that were either too thin, mostly bark, or faulted in some other way that made them useless for anything but firewood. Since most people who heat with wood do so in small stoves, one of Craig's tasks was to reduce the mill's longer scrap boards into serviceable chunks before loading them into the dump truck for delivery. He did this by collecting five or more defective boards, piling them on a little movable bench, and then pushing them through a spinning cut-off blade. The bench was arranged to move into the blade, as well as sideways. Craig had to push the boards through the blade, pull them back, slide the table along a foot or two, and push the boards through again, repeating the operation until he had cut the pile into burnable lengths. This arrangement was further refined, so that as each cut was made, and a group of chunks fell off the blade, they landed on a conveyer belt that carried them outside to the truck. Unfortunately, it had happened early on in Craig's career that he forgot to place the truck where it was supposed to be in order for the entire arrangement to work as it should. In fact, he had forgotten about the truck altogether, and when he went outside to hop in the cab and make his delivery, he found a truckload of wood, but no truck. It was clear that Craig had resolved never to be humiliated professionally again and was constantly on the lookout for anyone or anything that might try.

Many of the firewood boards were cut from the outside of a tree trunk and had a substantial curve to their outside surface. Wet and slippery, full of bark, irregular in length, they did not make for very neat piling when loaded onto the saw and were quite tricky to cut. The saw blade itself was about two feet in diameter, equipped with half-inch teeth, and spun naked and threatening, powered by a five-horsepower engine. Despite the obvious hazards of such an arrangement, Craig worked blithely away, dropping haphazard piles of rough boards on the saw's table, setting his weight against them, and with all his might shoving the boards through the blade with all his might. With every pass, the blade gave a bloodcurdling shriek of protest. When a pile of boards had been substantialy shortened, Craig had to stand with arms on either side of the blade as he did this, so that as he gave his vicious little shove, his head took a frightening bow directly toward the blade. It did not take much imagination to realize with how little protest this same blade would take off one of his arms, or mutilate his face.

I once made the mistake of trying to assist Craig at this task, foolishly thinking that I could help to reduce the hazards to which his forced pace exposed him. I carried over planks for him to cut and piled them neatly on the saw's sliding table, hoping that this would allow him time to safely concentrate on cutting them. But Craig considered this an imposition and took it as an invitation to compete. No matter how fast I carried planks to him, he had to cut them faster. He seemed to relish staring at me with impatient annoyance while he waited for me to load up his saw. I finally gave up. "Don't let me get in your way Craig," I said caustically and walked away. If anything, my assistance was causing him to work even more recklessly than before.

As it turned out, this was just a summer job for Craig, who would be heading off to college in the fall. He informed us of this fact at lunch one day, with no little pride, and with just a touch of sneer at us fools who remained to suffer under Parsons' regime. Not one to let a mere kid try and take advantage of me, I informed him in the most casual of tones that I was already a college graduate, implying by my manner that it obviously hadn't done me much good.

Naturally Craig was a little taken aback.

"Was it hard?" he asked earnestly. His tough and competent work-ingman's facade was rapidly deteriorating, and I was only too happy to amuse myself at his expense.

"No, not very," I replied diffidently, and gave him as imperious a look as I could manage, all the while smiling inside, knowing how little comfort Craig could take from this form of reassurance. In any case, "hard" was not an adjective I would have chosen to apply to college life. "Difficult," or even "tricky" might have been more appropriate ways in which to describe the minor alteration in one's consciousness that higher education required. But overall, if you could keep your spirits up, and stay away from courses like organic chemistry and the kind of hard-spirited students they attracted, it was difficult to fail.

Certainly I had known my share of dropouts in my time, but they bore no resemblance to Craig. They were the kind of people who were fiercely critical of their surroundings and who had learned enough by the time they were nineteen years old to seriously question the wisdom of their elders. Craig was much too deferential to Parsons' authority for me ever to think that he could be among them. It was his habit when being instructed by Parsons, no matter how trivial the matter, to look straight ahead in a pose that suggested he was having visions of a glorious future. Old Parsons, smiling, red faced, looking altogether too much like the devil, spoke into his ear with the same forced and deliberate style that he applied to everything. When instruction was complete, Craig would nod his head briskly, and with eyebrows fur-rowed, stride resolutely off like a man who knew his job, and knew his future.

Slumber

6

Craig was leaving in a week, and Parsons had hired another man to take his place. We had absolutely no warning of this fellow's imminent arrival, so when he and Parsons appeared together one Monday morning, climbing the back stairs from the cellar, talking and joking with one another like old chums, it came as a complete surprise. His name was Frank, and at a good six feet four, two hundred and thirty pounds, his presence was huge and intimidating. Parsons did not bother to introduce us. As their good-natured chumminess, punctuated with hearty laughter, showed no sign of abating, we began to wonder just who or what this fellow was. The suddenness of his appearance from the cellar, and his obvious attachment to Parsons, made me wonder if he wasn't some sort of monster Parsons had been keeping dormant down there, and had only now decided to activate.

Whether he had originated from downcellar or not, that was where Frank was to remain and labor. He operated the mill's enormous eight-foot-high bandsaw, which until then had been operated exclusively by Parsons himself. The bandsaw was used mainly to cut very thick and long boards lengthwise into very thin and long strips. The final products measured fifty-four inches long, by two-and-a-half inches wide, by approximately three thirty-seconds of an inch thick. It was my job to collect them in a cart and take them upstairs for counting and inspection. I was to look for faults such as imperfect grain, discoloration, or incorrect thickness, tie them into bundles of fifty, and then load them into a cart to be trundled out to the mill's drying shed. After the pure drudgery of trimming dowel, this proved to be a fairly leisurely and pleasant duty, and I took to it immediately, though it was a good two or three hours before I thought it proper to ask Parsons exactly what these strips were used for.

"Tennis racket strips," he replied matter-of-factly, and strode off.

"Oh." I nodded my head as if the matter were now entirely clear.

24

Later I asked Charlie if he wouldn't mind telling me what on earth a tennis racket strip was. He nodded toward an unstrung tennis racket hanging on the wall next to Parsons' office, and explained that the strips were laminated into tennis rackets.

"You see, the people he sells 'em to, take 'em and steam 'em. Then they bend 'em one by one around a form, and glue 'em somehow or other."

"Unh huh. But why are the strips two-and-a-half inches wide? I've never seen a tennis racket that thick."

"Make 'em two at a time, slice the thing in half somehow." He paused to fix his gaze on that undefined area of mental concentration, and continued. "Used to be the main part of the mill's business, but no longer. Nobody buys wooden tennis rackets anymore, they're almost all metal now." There was a certain wistfulness about Charlie as he said this, and he appeared as if he were a man sadly disappointed with a world that could have such foolish preferences.

For the rest of that week, I alternated between trimming more dowels and sorting tennis racket strips. Parsons continued to work out blanks and have them turned into dowels for me to trim, but the pace was quite slow, and I had grown so immune to the work that it no longer bothered me anyway. I had my thoughts to myself and the chance to look around the mill and observe its ways without the self-consciousness and anger that had earlier clouded my view of the place. In some ways, I had become a machine, and oddly, in those ways I was at peace. A machine did not have any reason to worry. It just ran and did not ask itself why.

The mill itself appeared to be a machine as I looked around at it, and the more I saw, the more intricate and wonderful a machine it began to seem. Charlie had informed me that until the late spring, there had been seven men working in the mill, but that except for him they had all been fired or had quit. So what I saw now as I worked was but the merest glimpse of the mill's totality; separate parts operated one at a time, as if being primed and tested for the day when they would all work simultaneously and harmoniously together, and that whole machine would once again awaken from its summer slumber.

The big machine that I'd so carefully examined on my first day, the "headsaw" as they called it, had been almost totally silent since my arrival at the mill. Occasionally its massive electric motor would be switched on, its log-carrying carriage rolled back and forth, and oil applied to its large bearings and gears, but virtually nothing was produced on it. The piles of logs that sat in neat rows out in the yard remained undisturbed, and except for the occasional adjustment of the water sprinklers playing across them, they simply lay in wait.

Our work was a mere catching up with what the headsaw had already produced. Carts of boards that had been lined up in the cellar were moved upstairs one by one, the wood ripped down, turned into dowels, or run through the bandsaw to make tennis racket strips or something mysteriously referred to as "chairbows." Gradually the cellar was emptied of its contents, and there were fewer and fewer boards to be turned into anything at all.

Craig was gone, having left just as it seemed we were finally running out of work. One afternoon both Charlie and I finished our assigned tasks and could find nothing else to do. We waited around, straightening up a little and pushing sawdust around with brooms, hoping that Parsons would give us something more substantial to do. But he steadfastly refused to look at us and even appeared to be growing annoyed at our presence. He was not a man who sanctioned idleness, and though it was hardly our fault, it was clear that in some way he was holding us responsible for the fact that he had nothing for us to do. Finally Charlie just walked out and went home, and I was left to stand there, awkwardly shifting my weight from foot to foot, trying to look busy.

"My father knows a fella who's a pretty good friend a' Parsons," said Charlie the next day, "and he says that if the right person came along, well . . . old Parsons might be ready to sell."

"Sell? You mean the mill?" I asked stupidly.

"Well, like I say, I've heard the mill's been up for sale for quite a while."

"You think we'd get the axe?"

"I don't know. Could be he'd like to get somebody here who knew what was going on before he tried to sell. You know, as a kind of transition." I nodded, unsure of exactly what he was getting at.

"Used to have this young fella here, ran the headsaw for him. Smart fella, pretty good sawyer too. Could be that's what he's got in mind for you."

"What, to be head sawyer?"

Charlie nodded. "It'd be a good skill to have in your back pocket."

I felt a bit giddy, not quite believing that such a thing was possible. It struck me as an odd expression, to have a skill in one's back pocket. I had a vision of it bulging there, like a wallet. In any case, my future was not a subject on which I wished to linger.

"What'd he leave for?" I asked.

"Oh, I don't know." He thought for a moment and smiled. "Guess he got fed up with us. Said he was heading to Oregon to become a fisherman."

"Oh." I felt in a way that I had been put in my place. There was something about Charlie's tone that made me feel as if he were really saying he'd seen my kind before: smart, educated, ambitious, getting fed up with other people, and running off to bigger and better things. Charlie was considerably more friendly and talkative than when I'd first encountered him, but at that moment I was made to feel conscious of the wide gulf in our age and experience. But worse was the feeling of jealousy that I had for this "young fella," whom I didn't even know. His existence in my imagination made me feel as if perhaps I was not so original a character as I thought. What I was doing had been done by someone else, and that someone had already moved on.

"Tough life, fishing." I commented.

"Yeahup. I hear that if you fall overboard in wintertime, you're a goner once you hit the water." Charlie stubbed out his cigarette and prepared to go back to work.

7

A Niggling Fraction

Frank was beginning to get restless. He'd been at work at the mill for two full weeks and hadn't been allowed to budge from his cold, dark, damp spot in the cellar behind the bandsaw. We hardly ever saw him, because between his isolation in the cellar and his habit of taking breaks in the privacy of his car with the radio turned up, our paths almost never crossed. A resourceful Charlie had somehow managed to learn that he was married, had a couple of young children, had been laid off from his previous job, and had done a stretch in the Navy, where he apparently acquired the need for the hearing aid that he always wore. But aside from these gleanings, Frank remained an enigmatic figure, just some poor bastard that Parsons had chosen to stick in a hole and leave there.

Thus my early fears of Frank as a physical presence diminished substantially. He was a giant, but had turned out to be a fairly affable one as far as Charlie and I were concerned. On the other hand, the air of easy familiarity that he had been trying to cultivate with Parsons had failed dismally and was replaced with a sullen silence, even an occasional sarcastic remark thrust at the old man's turned back. His difficulty stemmed from the fact that his work was not quite up to Parsons' stringent standards. The tennis racket strips that he produced were supposed to be cut to within tolerances measured in sixty-fourths of an inch. When compared to the cumbersome logs out in the yard, this was a niggling fraction for sure. But to Parsons, precision in these matters was a question of life or death. Economy was everything when you refined raw material, and the racket strips produced for sale were to be of the finest material that Parsons could wrest from a log. Free of faults, without discoloration, and of the straightest grain, they were the mill's signal products, and Parsons' reputation depended upon them.

In my position as packer and inspector of Frank's work, I could see

28

that he was cutting the strips just a bit too thick. The little metal gauge with which I was equipped confirmed this observation. Parsons noticed also, though he didn't need a gauge for confirmation, since his eye was as sharp as an eagle's in these matters. As I was working, I happened to notice Parsons looking over my shoulder, and as my eye had become quite sharp in determining the old man's whereabouts and mood, I realized that he was quite annoyed at the improper thickness of the strips I was inspecting. For my own good, I decided it would be best if I pretended to be unaware that he had noticed the improper quality of Frank's work, and feigning the part of the good and faithful employee, pointed it out to him.

"Yea-ahs," he muttered sharply, sounding like a man who not only already knew what he was being told, but also that I knew that he knew. Feeling foolish, I put on my most servile tone. "Do you want me to pull these thick ones out?"

"No, it doesn't matter to them if they're too thick."

But it certainly mattered to him. Given that the strips were only meant to be three thirty-seconds of an inch thick, for every sixty strips that Frank cut a sixty-fourth too thick, he should have been able to produce sixty-five or seventy strips of the correct thickness from the same amount of wood. This was the kind of gross inefficiency that a man of Parsons' business acumen simply could not tolerate.

Parsons disappeared down the freight elevator in order to have a "little chat"—as he liked to put it—with the erring Frank. Five minutes later he returned looking a little grim, but apparently successful, because soon afterwards the strips began to take on a more proper dimension. This was but the briefest of hiatuses though; soon the strips began to seem too thin. Once again my gauge went into action in order to confirm what my eye had already hypothesized. Unfortunately, strips that came out too thin could only be discarded, and after an alarming number of these had begun to pile up on the floor, Parsons came over to see me about it.

"You've discarded too many!" he accused.

"Well," I said doubtfully, "I'm pretty sure they're all too thin. Do you want me to check 'em again?"

"No." He threw up his hands resignedly, and went downcellar to have another "chat" with Frank. It was not, I was made to feel, that Parsons was questioning my judgment. He was simply stating fact; I was throwing out too many. But for some reason I still felt at fault. Perhaps it was merely the curse of being the bearer of bad news.

Soon thereafter, the strips were too thick again, and an exasperated Parsons had to confer once more with Frank. By now I knew that Frank was in serious trouble. Parsons was growing redder and redder about the face and was darting to and fro like a crazed yellow jacket. For my part, I took no little pleasure in the situation, feeling at last that I had some grasp on the cyclical nature of the boss's mood, and confident in my ability to stay well clear of the storm. As for Frank, well, he'd live through it. This was just the standard initiation for every inductee into Parsons' mill.

The matter soon came to a crisis, and despite my self-confidence I became fully involved. The strips were coming out thin again, which was by far the worst of the two sins that Frank had learned to commit on the bandsaw, and I was fearful of the consequences. I was also mindful of the fact that by doing my job the way I was supposed to I would once again be the bearer of unfortunate tidings, and this time it could only be worse. Though I was convinced that Frank was in danger of getting canned, I had absolutely no interest in helping to bring it about. Frank was an affable giant, but a giant nonetheless, and I felt that the only thing worse than incurring the wrath of Parsons might be to incur the wrath of Frank. As a result, I did the only thing a coward could and packed Frank's shoddy work for shipment.

This proved to be a costly mistake. I was just returning upstairs from a leisurely tour of the toilet, when to my horrified surprise I spied Parsons fussily sorting through the bundles I had already finished. He waved me over with a distracted air.

"I've just counted thirty out of the fifty that are supposed to be in this bundle, and I swear I haven't seen one of the right thickness yet." My heart sank. I felt suddenly like a shame-faced little boy going before the principal.

"How many bundles have you put out in the shed?" he snapped.

"I-I, I don't know." His eyes hardened. "I didn't know you wanted me to keep count," I protested whiningly. But Parsons had no interest in my excuses.

"Let's take a look out there."

We rode the elevator to its intermediate stop between the cellar and the main floor, and lifting open an overhead door, stepped out at ground level onto a walkway that led directly to the shed. This was the route by which carts of material were moved between the shed and the main building. The shed itself was a large, open, hangar-like building. It was divided into a variety of rooms and bays filled partially or wholly with various mill products in the process of being dried out or readied for shipment.

The tennis racket strips occupied a large room to themselves, where they were propped up on their ends along two long walls that stood at right angle to each other. It was a disorderly and inconvenient arrangement because one bundle leaned up against its neighbor in such a way as to make it difficult to see where one ended and the next began. It was a hazardous venture at best to try and extract a single bundle from this mass without causing serious dislocations. Nonetheless, Parsons went right at them and with righteous vengeance began angrily grabbing at bundle after bundle.

"Here!" he exclaimed. "This one's too thin . . . and this one's too thin, and . . . here's one that's too thick!" The temperature had turned cold that day, and Parsons had given me no time to dress for an excursion outside. I stood there shifting my weight, hands clasped in a kind of downward prayer in an attempt to keep warm, watching while Parsons, by now practically drooling with excitement, spelled out the evidence of my guilt.

"This one's only got forty-eight in it!"

Finally, after pawing through about thirty bundles, breaking them open, and spilling them across the floor he pronounced sentence with an uncharacteristic clarity, emphasizing the space between every word: "I — want — you — to — go — through — each — and — every — bundle — that — you — have — brought — out — here, pick — out — the — thin — strips, and — make — sure — that — there — are — fifty — good — strips — in — each — one."

The effect of menace in his voice was so distinct that I did not have the heart to explain to him that it was going to be impossible for me to distinguish between the hundred or so bundles that I had put out there and the four hundred or so that I had not. In fact I was pretty sure that at least some of the bundles that he had so ruthlessly extracted as evidence against me had been put there well before either Frank's or my time. But it was a sure bet that Parsons was going to return for a second tour of inspection, at which time I would be held responsible for each and every fault that he could find, no matter who was responsible.

By now I was practically freezing to death and was faced with the prospect of several hours' worth of labor during which it seemed unlikely that the temperature would rise. I wanted to go back inside and grab a jacket before I got started, but was so intimidated by Parsons' manner that I dared not. The old man was clearly teetering on the brink of rage, and it would take but the slightest whisper to send him plummeting into an abyss, hapless employee in tow. I could only imagine what he would think if I had been so audacious as to follow him back into the mill for a purpose so trivial as personal comfort, especially in light of the serious crimes that I had just committed.

So for the next four hours I foolishly allowed myself to shiver as I sorted through each and every bundle, tearing some apart, putting them back together, and trying desperately to keep track of what I was doing. The fact of the matter was that nearly every bundle I examined had one or two faulty strips in it. Parsons was unaware of the extent of this blight, and had it in mind that I had only a hundred of these bundles to sort through when actually there were closer to five hundred. It was therefore inevitable that sooner or later the old man was going to start wondering what was taking me so long and come back out, demanding explanations which he had no intention of hearing. This was, I was coming to realize, just another of Parsons' many peculiarities; he would come prepared to listen to you only when he knew that you had absolutely nothing to say.

It was considered proper technique at the mill to bind the fifty strips that constituted a bundle with a single piece of twine at one end. This made for a particularly cumbersome package because the strips themselves were so thin, and quite flexible. They were grouped into stacks of twenty-five apiece, which were then laid alongside one another and tied together. But no matter how tight one tied them, it was inevitable that the string would work itself loose as the wood dried and shrank, and it was not uncommon for a carelessly handled bundle to come apart completely. I had begun my career as a tennis racket strip bundler by employing two pieces of twine instead of one, thinking myself clever and creative for doing so. Parsons quickly put a damper on my enthusiasm by explaining that this was simply not how it was done. He muttered some half-comprehensible justification for this rule, which I later reconstructed as meaning that the extra piece of twine produced a discoloration that his customers did not like. As an explanation, it certainly had an air of plausibility about it, which from the point of view of a boss trying to maintain his authority was all that was required. But I kept my doubts.

Knowing Parsons' ruthless instinct for efficiency, I could not help feeling that it really came down to the simple and absurd fact that he didn't want to waste any more twine than he had to. Twine was a major point of supply in the mill, as nearly everything got tied up with it. It was purchased in great bushel-sized bales that unwound into cables of forty or fifty single pieces. But this twine was not to be dispensed casually. On the wall over the bale, there was an entire set of measuring sticks, each one related to a particular product, or size of product, giving the exact measure necessary to bundle that product. The difference in the minimum calculated length of twine required to tie a thirteen-sixteenths inch dowel bundle and a fifteen-sixteenths dowel bundle was a matter of an inch. But woe to the worker who confused them. So the tennis racket strip bundles remained hopelessly clumsy objects with which to work, and all the more so because of the way in which they were propped on their untied ends and leaned against a wall to dry. Five or ten bundles stored in this manner presented no great problem, but I was faced with two walls, each one supporting something like two hundred fifty bundles, or more than twelve thousand flexible wooden strips leaning precariously against one another for support. The system was, in my opinion, asinine. Insofar as it posessed that particular quality, it was constructed, and refined to the point of perfection. Whoever had arranged the five hundred bundles on those walls had done so with the consistent principle in mind that they would be flexible along the wall instead of against it. The effect of this "system" was to make the already probable cataclysm of falling and bursting bundles a statistical certainty.

Once again my misplaced creativity came to the fore, as I tried to restore some semblance of order amongst the drying tennis racket strips. My method was simply to alternate pairs of bundles so that one pair would employ its flexible movement against the wall, while the next pair would be flexible along it. The resulting structure not only represented sound engineering, it was neater and more satisfactory to look at. Now if Parsons felt compelled to pick out substandard bundles, he could do so without threat of causing the entire agglomeration to collapse. Naturally I was quite pleased with my handiwork, and was hoping that it might redeem me with my boss. After all, he was already predisposed against me, and my laggardly pace was sure to make things worse. Perhaps, I thought, the genius with which I had rearranged the racket strips would restore me to grace.

Parsons came strutting out just as I was finishing, and as predicted, wanted to know what was taking me so long.

"I had to go through them all."

"Yea-ahs," came the familiar dry and all-knowing reply that never made clear exactly what Parsons knew or believed. "What've you done with those bundles?" He screwed up his face in dismay.

"I rotated 'em so they wouldn't all be leaning against one another." Doubt was beginning to crowd my voice. "It looked like it all might collapse."

"Well that's not the way we do it," he said, and added as if in kindness, "best turn them back again." And in that now all-too-familiar motion, he spun on his heels and made a beeline back to the mill.

The next day, when I had returned to sorting through Frank's work before it was moved out to the shed, I did so with a deliberately meticulous attention to detail. I had absolutely no interest in repeating my previous day's experience in the shed and was now perfectly willing to shift the burden for shoddy work firmly onto Frank's shoulders. As the faulty strips began to pile up on the floor, I even managed to adopt some of Parsons' cruel particularity, taking great pleasure in singling out the offending strips and casting them to the floor with contempt. Once again, as inevitability worked its will, Parsons noted the growing pile of useless strips lying on the floor. But he did so without questioning my judgment, as he and I were now straight on the matter, I having paid my debt in the solitary confinement of the shed. Frank was the one on trial for his life now, and Parsons was waiting patiently for the evidence to mount before swooping in for the kill.

In the meantime Charlie had been out to the shed and reported to me that I had better go out and take a look at "the mess out there." It was immediately apparent what he was referring to, and I tiptoed out there with the caution of an acrophobic approaching the edge of a cliff. Approaching the area where the tennis racket strips were stored, I was at first happily convinced that the situation did not look all that bad. But the closer I got, the worse things looked, until when I was at last amongst them, the matter had taken on the proportions of a disaster. One entire wall of bundles, at right angle to the other, had come crashing and sliding along until the two had collided. The result was something like a giant game of pick-up sticks, in which the sticks had not only swollen in size, but had multiplied in number by a factor of a thousand.

When I had finally gotten the mess straightened out, I returned to the mill convinced that everyone was thinking me a fool, fully prepared to present an icy glare to anyone audacious enough to look in my direction. But my mishaps paled in comparison to the scene that had just taken place between Frank and the boss, of which I caught only the tail end.

"Well thanks for tellin' me!" I heard Frank yell sneeringly. Then a red-faced Parsons came up the cellar stairs and went stomping across the mill and into his office, slamming the door behind him. The high-pitched buzzing of the bandsaw was heard anew; it seemed as if Frank had not been fired. After all, I thought, Frank is a family man, he has responsibilities, he can't afford to get himself fired. However, responsibilities or not, the next day found Frank conspicuously absent. An advertisement in that morning's paper calling for a hand at Parsons' mill confirmed the matter. Frank had been fired.

Sabotage!

We had hardly seen or heard from Frank, but somehow his absence was felt. Neither Charlie nor I knew how to operate the bandsaw, so we had no idea what Frank's problem had been. Obviously his work had been coming out all wrong, but it was unclear whether he was truly to blame. It was just as probable Parsons had refused to acknowledge some peculiarity of the machine and was blaming it on Frank instead. He had seemed a nice enough fellow, and I suppose that Charlie and I had our individual regrets over not having gotten to know him better. It was almost as if someone had died, a unique creature gone extinct before it had been seen fully alive.

For his part, Parsons was all coldness and scowls. He took to walking in a hunch around the perimeter of the mill, barely communicating with us. For two days he kept to himself, closeted in his office, or hidden behind the bandsaw in the cellar, or managing to disappear altogether. If we tried to address him, he would only look at us from the corners of his eyes and mumble vague monosyllabic replies, slinking and holding his hands cupped to his chest as if protecting some small and delicate creature in them.

On the third morning, a particularly cold and dreary one, which found Charlie and me dazedly waiting for work to begin, Parsons surprised us by coming over and sitting with us. The effect was that of immediate intimacy, because this was our turf, and he rarely violated it unless he intended friendship. Drawing himself up close and looking at us with a quizzical smile that looked a little dangerous, he whispered conspiratorially, "Now when I hire people to work for me I expect that they are working for me, and me alone, not for anyone else." He leaned back for perspective on our reactions. Charlie and I looked in unison, first at Parsons, then at each other, and then back at Parsons. Both of us were mystified. Parsons' expression remained unchanged, and he watched us intently. "Now I have certain evidence," he measured his

36

words carefully, "that certain people working in this mill have been working for someone else, and I'm afraid that I cannot tolerate it." His voice had a harsh, accusatory air. Confused, I looked over at Charlie for guidance, but all I saw was a slack jaw and eyes wide in astonishment. For the moment, that was all Parsons had to say, and he quickly set us to work and turned his attention elsewhere, giving Charlie the chance to whisper, "I'll talk to you about this later."

An hour or so passed before he had his opportunity, sliding up to where I was working while Parsons was engaged on the phone.

"What the hell was that about?" I whispered excitedly.

"I dunno, he has these little spells now and then, gets kinda' paranoid."

"About what?"

"Well there was this fella working here a while back who admitted to taking five hundred dollars to sabotage one of the saws."

"Wait a minute! Sabotage? Here? What for? He's crazy!"

"Well, I don't know. It did look a little suspicious the way this fellow managed to break the saw."

"Oh. So you think he isn't crazy, and the guy really did it."

"I don't know. But like I say, ever since then Parsons has had these spells . . . ." Just then Parsons emerged from his office, and Charlie slipped by me as if he'd never stopped to talk to me. A broad smile began to creep uncontrollably across my face, and I felt a little giddy. This was going to be exciting: true intrigue and all in the confines of Parsons' little mill. At break time, Parsons again sat with us. His peculiar expression had eased some, and I had hope that he was going to say something to let us know that he was normal again.

"Well? You've had time to think about it. What do you say?"

We didn't know what to say.

"A man can only serve one master," he pronounced imperiously, "and I want you to swear that you are working for me, for me alone, and for no one else." Charlie had returned to his earlier slack-jawed and wide-eyed look and appeared to be saying, "Am I still on earth, or have I passed to the nether world?" After a moment of deadly silence, he regained his composure. "Well, uuh, I did talk to you some time ago about only workin' part time. Is that what you mean?"

Parsons smiled and shook his head. "Nope, nope." He shook his head for a few seconds more, and then suddenly stopped. The smile dropped from his face, and he fixed us with stern eyes. "No, I have certain evidence that people working in this mill have been paid to

37

work against me." He paused for dramatic emphasis, though it was unclear whether he was speaking in the present or past tense, so it was difficult to tell if this was a direct accusation or not. "Now," he continued, "I want you to swear that you are working for me and me alone." Feebly, almost showing an instinct to raise his hand like a bad schoolboy asking permission to go to the toilet, Charlie ventured a protest.

"I kinda resent the implication, Henry. I've always done good work for you . . . ." But Parsons cut him off with a wave of the hand.

"Charlie!" he said sharply. "Do you swear?" Charlie deflated almost immediately and cast his glance back to its accustomed focus on the floor. After the briefest of considerations he mumbled, "Yes, I swear."

Having dispatched with Charlie, Parsons turned his attention to me. "Do you swear?"

The question shook me from a stupor. Up to that point I had been under the comfortable misapprehension that I was a mere observer of absurd events, not a participant in them. But by now Parsons had me fixed in his gaze, and Charlie was sitting there as if to bear witness. I was forced to compose myself and accept my role in this peculiar farce.

"Yes," I said. "Sure, I swear." Anything to please the boss.

At first, the absurdity of Parsons' demands provided me with a lasting source of amusement. I began to entertain myself by considering the implications of what had just occurred. Was there not a contradiction, I mused, between swearing an exclusive oath of allegiance to Parsons when I had already done so for the benefit of my country? After all, Parsons had made it clear that "a man cannot serve two masters." But then, as I considered the matter, I realized that there was a way in which the problem could be easily circumvented. If Parsons had sworn an allegiance to the country, and I an allegiance to Parsons, then perhaps it could be argued that I was serving my country by proxy. It was a rather feudal notion, but by that token not altogether inappropriate to the circumstances.

"Well, I know that I can take the words of you both," Parsons continued, seeming relieved at having obtained our sworn oaths, "because you both come from good families."

I could not speak for Charlie's family, because I did not know them yet. As for mine, I supposed that the appellation was appropriate, because whatever else they might be, my family was certainly "good."

"Charlie," Parsons pronounced confidently, "I've known your family for many years." He then paused as if to reflect upon them. "As for you," he practically pounced on me, "you've got thirty-six acres riding on it."

This last and final statement on the subject took me aback. Thirty-six acres was the approximate size of the parcel of land that my father had tried to buy from Parsons several years before. Did he think that this was the secret aim behind my seemingly bizarre desire to work in a sawmill when I had a perfectly respectable college education behind me? It had never occurred to me, nor, I was sure, to my father. In any case, the entire bargain seemed more like a figment of Parsons' antique imagination than any modern-day reality with which I was familiar.

In those heady days when New England was the true cradle of the industrial revolution, when the phrase "Yankee ingenuity" was something more than mere fodder for the nostalgia of American antique buffs, a man or a woman might indenture themselves to a master craftsman in America in exchange for the price of passage from Europe. At the time of the revolution, a full three-quarters of the population in some colonies either had been, or were then living as indentured servants. Conditions were unusually severe. Though not sharing the unhappy fate of the black slave, the indentured servant remained in legal bondage for a period of years during which he or she had to suffer the merest whim of the master, or risk fines, imprisonment, or worse, until fulfillment of the legal obligation. Despite a theoretical obligation on the master to provide his servant with a skill, the weight of the judicial establishment rested firmly with the propertied class, and the servant had little redress if—as often happened—the master failed in his part of the bargain. I was beginning to question how much things had actually changed.

Parsons and I shared a distaste for the dislocations of our own dubious century, but we differed sharply in our responses to it. His views on life were, at best, conservative, and I imagine that he was more than a little in sympathy with the local apostle of "liberty or death," William Loeb. For my part, it had come as a shock when I finally came to examine a copy of Mr. Loeb's scurrilous daily journal, the *Manchester Union Leader* and encountered a headline reading, "Blacks Better Watch Out!" It would be unfair of me to claim that Parsons was absolutely in sympathy with the paranoiac right-wing outburst that followed, describing affirmative action legislation as a conspiracy of blacks and communists aimed at destruction of American values, but the aura was right. Twenty years back, Parsons himself had given up the sawmill business in order to take a crack at the editorship of the *Haddam Courant*, a paper whose current editorial policy often puts it to the left of the *New York Times–Washington Post*–CBS News "Jewish media conspiracy." He had originally owned a sawmill elsewhere in Vermont, but had sold out in order to buy into the *Courant*, hoping perhaps to settle into the kind of genteel occupation proper to an older man who has given his life to productive and profitable manufacture, the holiest of American pragmatic causes. But as he informed Charlie: "There was a conspiracy to buy me out." By now the paper was in the thoroughly pinkened hands of a minor Massachusetts conglomerate that published such organs of flaming radicalism as the *Essex Journal* and the *Whitinsville Free Press*.

Parsons returned to what he knew best and purchased Mr. Pitman's ash mill. The mill had recently suffered extensive damage in a fire, and Parsons concentrated his energies into getting it back into shape. Above all else, no matter what happens, a man must make himself useful. Other men of his age and position might seek the easy path to retirement, but Parsons labored mightily in his mill from seven to four-thirty, establishing accounts, hiring and firing workers, finding suppliers, and always keeping a personal hand in the production of what were reputed to be first-quality ash wood products.

Parsons was a man who forced himself to live by principle: work, work, and more work. That was what a person was put on this earth to do, and any man who could not make himself useful was a parasite. Retirement, he believed, would have meant senility and death, so he dug in his heels before a world gone soft, and continually looked askance at its fads and trivialities. Others might laze around, allowing themselves to go slowly to hell, but he was making himself useful in his old age by producing goods, providing employment, and giving business to others. These things he did by sheer force of will, and it was his right, therefore, to look at the world with that peculiarly pinched expression of skepticism that formed his mask.

I, of course, was not of this particular school of thought. Having been raised in the best coddling tradition of Benjamin Spock, the "baby doctor," I was soft from day one: always looking for the injustices of the work ethic, always worrying about life's losers. Somehow I simply could not get beyond the view that a person rarely received just compensation for his work and that few of us were ever given the opportunity to feel useful. More often we felt used. I had the idea that if someone was to feel useful, then he must believe that the powers he served had some higher moral purpose, and this disqualified most of the employers I knew anything about.

Both Parsons and I inhabited the rarified atmosphere of the naive. We sat staring at one another from opposite banks of an uncrossable mainstream flowing on into the future. I supposed that part of the reason I had come to the mill was to look for something from the past worth preserving. The first thing I found there was an old man scrutinizing the future for something worth accepting. We were both disenfranchised romantics. But he was a mill owner and a boss, while I was merely a worker; he had the power of money, while I had only my wits and my youth.

The mill was to close down the last week in September, the one week out of the year that Parsons' mill was allowed to rest. There were other holidays of course, Thanksgiving, Christmas, the Fourth of July. But these were days of duty to family, church, and country. The annual vacation was another matter. It was pure concession to a man's laziness, his desire to sleep until the decadent hour of six-thirty or seven, to enjoy a full breakfast, to linger over his coffee. Then, and only then, he might begin on a week-long orgy of wood splitting, putting up storm windows, and tuning up the car, all in preparation for Winter. Having exhausted all of these pleasurable pastimes, he might then get to work of a serious nature and go fishing.

I, however, was to be spared the ordeal of such a vacation. I had only been in attendance at the mill for a little over a month and did not merit such consideration. I was to remain there by myself, and labor mightily. It struck me as odd that a man who had so little faith in me that he'd required an oath of allegiance before allowing me to continue to work under his supervision would subsequently allow me to spend five days in his mill without any supervision at all. Surely, the opportunities to commit various dastardly acts of sabotage would be unlimited. Perhaps it was a test. Or even stranger, perhaps Parsons really believed in sworn statements made under oath. Then again, there was something rather odd about Parsons' entire view of security. Despite an abundance of accessible openings into the mill—doors, windows, and hatches—there was absolutely no provision for locking them. Anyone with the inclination could walk right into the mill and create havoc at will.

It had even been Parsons' habit to leave the key in the ignition of the mill's truck while it rested overnight in the cellar. But then one rowdy night some misguided youths decided that it would be interesting to appropriate it for a purpose, or purposes as yet undetermined.

Of course Haddam is a small town, and by that I mean that it is small enough so that probably one out of five of its inhabitants knew Henry Parsons' truck when they saw it. It was not long before the young rascals were apprehended and the truck returned to its rightful place in the cellar. Parsons felt compelled to take some sort of remedial action, but did not wish to overreact by pocketing the key every night, so he simply stored it in his desk drawer upstairs, its location known to virtually anyone even remotely connected with the mill, including a number of disgruntled former employees. Asked if it might be a good idea to install a few locks, or even something as exotic as a burglar alarm, given several instances of alleged sabotage, Parsons would simply wave his hands and shake his head, saying that such steps were "not necessary."

In certain matters, Charlie had a way of being particularly persistent, or, from another point of view, annoying. For several days after Parsons' little lecture on the nature of loyalty, he would raise the issue of the mill's lack of security wherever and whenever the opportunity arose. In the mornings when we had arrived and were waiting to go to work, at break, at lunch, and again at the end of the day, he would offer vociferous comment on the ease with which the mill could be made secure.

"It wouldn't be too hard to mount a few locks on these windows," he'd observe. Or, "I hear they got this new kind of burglar alarm that goes off if you even think of breaking in."

Mostly these comments were addressed to me, though always in a volume and tone calculated to reach Parsons' well-tuned ears. When that evoked no response, Charlie took his case directly to the old man. After shaking his head and smiling sadly in the way of the all-knowing, Parsons pronounced his favorite phrase for the week: "Not necessary."

Charlie had a mule-like quality about him and he persisted. I began to worry that if this kept up Parsons' patience would at last be broken and we would both be made to pay. But far from causing annoyance, Charlie's persistance seemed to provide Parsons with an endless source of amusement. In fact, from the high paranoia of a few days before, Parsons' mood improved steadily until he seemed to have reached a state of positive mirth. He knew what Charlie was after. It was clear to all of us that the bedraggled millhand wanted an explanation. He felt that it was his due after countless humiliations like the loyalty oath, and he wanted it now! Parsons was damned if he was going to give Charlie what he wanted until he absolutely had to, and was just as determined to squeeze every last ounce of pleasure he could from Charlie's frustration. The imminent explosion I had feared before now looked as if it would come from the opposite quarter.

Finally, Parsons saw that Charlie had had enough, and in the familiar way that he had approached us on the day of the loyalty oath, sat with us at the end of lunch one day in order to tell us this tale: "Had this neighbor once, decided to install one of those fancy new electronic burglar alarms. Well they installed it all right—cost him a bundle too. They got it all hooked up, and switched it on at night when he and his wife went to bed. Three hours later the alarm went off and woke them up. Turned out nobody'd broken in, and what's worse, the alarm was supposed to notify the local police, but they never showed up. Well, he calls them up and says. 'Didn't you get my alarm?' 'No,' they say, 'it never signalled us.'

"The next day, the alarm company comes by and fixes the alarm. That night they go to bed and wake up three hours later because someone is banging on the front door, blue lights are flashing every which way outside their windows, two-way radios are blaring, and someone yells, 'Open up, it's the police!'

"Seems they received the alarm all right, but it must have been some kind of delayed reaction from the previous night, because there was no burglar, and no alarm had rung in the house. So the company comes back to fix the thing again, and by god if they didn't nearly get it right this time. That night the alarm went off, and the police showed up. Only problem was there was still no burglar.

"The company came by to fix it again, but it still wouldn't work right. So finally the president of the company himself shows up, walks in the front door with a refund check, and disconnects the alarm."

Parsons smiled complacently to show that he'd finished. Charlie looked up from the floor with a smile and said, "And I bet they haven't had any trouble since." Parsons nodded, as if to say, "now you've got the idea."

It was certainly an adequate explanation of Parsons' feelings about burglar alarms and seemed to pacify Charlie. Still, I couldn't see what harm a few extra locks would have done.

Dusting the Mill

10

My assignments for the duration of the mill's vacation were quite specific, designed to assure that I would not lack for work. I was to wash every windowpane in the main building—of which there were hundreds—and to do so on both inside and outside surfaces. Apparently, this was somewhat of a traditional task for anyone unfortunate enough to be in my position, because Charlie was able to offer a few words of advice. He explained that the local hornets—or yellow jackets as they are called by some—found the eaves of the mill's flat roof quite hospitable to their domestic needs and that one had to look out for them when working outside from window to window. He illustrated his point by giving me vivid descriptions of the crazed war dance into which these vindictive insects had driven him by their merciless attacks. I countered quite calmly that the hornets would be "no problem for me," as I had never yet been stung, and was confident in my ability to come to an accommodation with an insect whose cooperative instinct was legend in entomological circles. Charlie's only response was a sidewise look of pity and annoyance for someone who didn't know sound advice when he heard it. But he was quite adept at minding his own business, and so returned to that practice, which at the moment involved thorough enjoyment of one of his mentholated cigarettes.

The second task Parsons decided to assign me presented me with considerably more dread than the first. "I would like you to dust the mill," he said matter-of-factly. I hesitated for a moment, unsure of what I had just heard, trying to catch some kind of mental echo.

"Dust?"

"Yea-ahs," came the familiar dry reply. "Of course you'll need to use a stepladder to get up high, and we've got a long-handled feather duster here. . . . "

Parsons was miles ahead of me.

"Dust?" I created my own echo, while Parsons stopped in order to indulge my obvious incomprehension. "Uuuh . . . where do you want me to dust?" Possibly he just meant that I should sweep up a little.

But Parsons was a man who said what he meant, and meant what he said. Fixing me with a look of mild amusement, he switched to the measured tones that could leave no doubt as to his meaning: "I — want — you — to — dust — every — surface — on — which — dust — might — light."

I was horrified. It was reasonable enough to wash windows in a building that needed every lumen nature could spare, but to *dust a sawmill*? Aside from pieces of wood of various shapes and sizes, the principal product of a sawmill was dust—tons of it—and Parsons' directive was equivalent in my mind to the removal of the Sahara desert one grain at a time. My work was beginning to take on the sickly smell of a horribly cruel joke.

Of course, the mill was equipped with a dust collection system of its own. It consisted of an elaborate series of ducts running from every machine in the mill, through an enormous blower in the cellar, and outside to a house-sized building, the sole function of which was to act as a repository. But while the system did a reasonable job of removing the heavier, visible dust that the mill produced in such abundance, it did nothing but stir up and redistribute its microscopic cousins, those tiny pieces of matter that put the lie to our notions of clean air when the late afternoon sun streams through our windows. As any good housekeeper knows, such tiny pieces of dust have an insidious ability to get where nothing else can, especially dust mops and rags. As time passes, what were once invisible particles become a visible agglomeration, the removal of which becomes a serious physical and mental challenge. The size of the mill, and the complexity of the objects within, made the challenge into a nightmare.

Nonetheless, when Parsons had at last made clear the true nature of my tasks, I knew much better than to ask why it was necessary. Mine was to do or die, my oath of allegiance having sealed the unwritten contract that now appeared to exist between us. I was his apprentice, and would recognize the fact that his forty years' worth of experience as mill owner and Sawyer made him master of his trade.

Silence

11

It was an odd feeling to come to work all alone. I left home with the same expectations as those of any other Monday morning, but the dulled dread with which I usually faced a work week took on a different form when I actually entered the mill. I knew that I was to labor here by myself, but somehow I was surprised by the place's emptiness, its darkness and its silence, and felt like an intruder. Where was everybody? For a moment I panicked, thinking that somehow I had been fooled, or had forgotten something, and that the rest of the world was privy to some special knowledge from which I'd been purposely excluded. I felt like a little boy who'd been ditched by companions he'd considered to be his very best friends. Then I remembered.

I fumbled around until I found the circuit breaker that switched on the lights and was surprised by their blinking fluorescence as they struggled and buzzed their way to illumination. Before me lay the main floor, its machinery stretching back into far and mysterious corners that beckoned me to come and explore their hidden secrets. I had been working here for over a month, but it had never looked like this to me before. The place that I had tried to imagine on those days when I used to drive by had remained hidden to me these past few weeks, and only now did I feel it coming into focus. The stillness remained unbroken for several long moments until I caught a slight movement out of the corner of my eye, which made me switch my gaze in fear. But it was only the placid progress of the second hand sweeping the big clock over the door to Parsons' office, reminding me that I had work to do. Suddenly the mystery of the mill and its ways began to fade into the drudgery of the stupid and endless-seeming tasks with which Parsons had cursed me. The sense that I was the victim of some vast conspiratorial joke rose stronger and stronger, and I began to picture a grinning Parsons nodding toward the sign that said "Exit."

And as my only options were to carry out the work I'd been assigned, or to walk through that door and never come back, it was now a simple matter of choosing between two humiliations: that of working, or the far worse one of being unemployed.

The most odious and endless-seeming tasks are best approached systematically. I began to dust by working the perimeter of the mill, dragging a large and cumbersome stepladder behind me, starting at the top of a section of wall, working my way down, moving the ladder a little, and working another section. I planned thereafter to work toward the mill's center, cleaning off the steel I-beams that supported the roof, the blower ducts, plumbing and heating pipes, and the light fixtures. Then I would work the machinery itself, brushing in and out amongst its mechanisms, uncovering the structures that made it go. Finally, in what I envisioned as a kind of pleasurable epilogue, I would sweep the floor of its accumulated cover, leaving the entire mill exposed like some sort of archaeological site, pristine and museum-like.

Despite the fact that I was getting covered from head to toe in a fine white powder that made me look as old as father time, and despite the fact that my nasal passages had become thoroughly clogged, and that an annoyingly large portion of the dust I dislodged returned to the same surfaces, I actually found the work quite relaxed and pleasant. Aside from Parsons' absence, there was the wholesome serenity of peace and quiet in the wake of extreme levels of noise.

When I'd first arrived at the mill, Parsons had shown me a supply of sanitary cotton ear plugs that he kept in his desk drawer.

"You'll see a need for these before long," he quipped. "We do make quite a bit of noise around here."

That first day I spent a great deal of time fussing with those annoying little pieces of cotton, trying to keep them adjusted so they would stay in my ear, shut out the noise, but not be too painfully compacted. Properly adjusted, the cotton reduced the high roar of the mill's machinery to a low and tolerable rumble. But after a day of adjusting and readjusting the things only to have them fall on the floor and get covered in sawdust, I decided to adopt the more modern style of hearing protection, a pair of OSHA-approved headphones. Naturally, Parsons did not approve of headphones, just as he looked askance upon most modern contrivances, but to his credit he did supply them. Cotton was good enough for him, and it was a great deal more protection than I had seen used by many of the old millhands in the area. It never failed to sadden me when visiting other sawmills nearby to find men pushing sixty who'd probably never known any other kind of work and who had little to show for it, aside from the hearing aids they displayed like badges of courage.

But for this week, I would need neither cotton nor headphones. I could listen to the smaller sounds about the mill: the cars on the road outside, the trees with their rattling fall leaves, airplanes droning across blue skies, the creak of the mill's doors in the wind, and even the sound of my own footsteps across the mill floor. None of these things could be heard while the mill was running, and their sound now gave the place a placid, ghostly air that seemed full of promise.

The second morning of my solitude, I arrived to discover that the mill was home to more than its workers. A large black cat was surprised in her sleep by my arrival, and dashed what was clearly a practiced route out one of the windows kept permanently open. That evening, as I was preparing to leave, I looked up to see that same cat poking its head through the same window through which it had earlier escaped. She cased the joint, as cats are apt to do, and then fixed her marvelous yellow and green eyes upon me. Her look was a question, to which I responded by gently clicking my tongue. And for the remainder of the week we passed each other thus, morning and evening, like watchmen on opposite shifts.

A Wonderful Axe **12**

By the third morning of that week, I had nearly completed my dusting. Over the course of the previous two days, I had laid my hands on practically every object and surface in the mill: every wall, window sill, light fixture, circuit breaker box, steam valve, steam pipe, water pipe, electrical conduit pipe. I had dusted a door with a door knob, a door with an old-fashioned latch, three overhead doors, two sliding doors, a clock, a radio, a roll-top desk, four work benches, two grinders, two power-fed ripsaws, two hand-fed ripsaws, two crosscut saws, a dowel-trimming saw, a dowel-making machine, a Lane number 00 headsaw equipped with a fifty-two-inch circular saw blade, a chain-deck saw, a hydraulic, hand-actuated forklift, a banding machine, several tool cabinets and racks, an elevator, a sink, two drinking fountains. There were more items, of course, but for every marginal addition to that list, I can come no closer to what was the essence of the mill. It may be that I found such an essence underneath or within these machines, as I explored their workings and tried to clean out the accumulated dust and shavings of twenty, thirty, sixty, or eighty years. Through as much as a foot of ground-up wood, all derived from the trunks of thousands and thousands of *Fraxinus americana*, the white ash, I unearthed the past like an archaeologist removing the volcanic effluvia from the last moments of Pompeii.

But here I was more like a geologist than an archaeologist, because the wood itself provided as much interest as what it covered. On the top layers I would find the common stuff that I helped to produce every day, little square bits measured in sixteenths of an inch, white, wet, smelling fresh, and with a heft to it that signified "green wood." To descend through that coarse dust was to travel backward through the history of the mill itself, down to a dark, dry, and well-seasoned past produced on a day when, perhaps, Hitler had declared his Thousand-Year Reich, or Roosevelt his New Deal, or the day on which Calvin Coolidge, that dry and ruthlessly practical native son, had proclaimed "the business of America is business."

Under certain machines, in areas that had remained absolutely undisturbed through the years, I found a thin black layer about two or three inches down. This was evidence of the fire that had nearly destroyed the place twenty years before. It had begun in one corner of the main building, spread diagonally across the ceiling to an opposite corner, and then on to both outlying buildings. By some miracle of physics, or divine intervention, if you choose, the main building was left relatively unscathed, while the two outlying buildings were completely destroyed. This was the time in the mill's history when Henry Parsons had taken over.

Up until then, the place had been known as Pitman's Mill. Mr. Pitman, like Parsons, had taken a personal hand in running the mill but was getting old, and what with the fire and all the changes then coming to the sawmill business, it was time to make way for a younger man. Such matters were not simple. Just as now, when Parsons was "looking for the right fella to come along," as Charlie had put it, so Pitman was not about to sell to just anyone. The mill that bore his name was not simply an abstract corporate entity for which he could so easily limit his liabilty. It was a local institution that provided jobs, taxable wealth, and the pride of a reputation for quality.

Parsons, then looking for a way out of his misadventures in the newspaper business, was a perfect candidate for the succession: he had money, he knew how to run a mill, and he was a skilled Sawyer. Most importantly, he was a local whose reputation was understood. The only area of doubt in Pitman's mind seemed to center on the question of the mill's hands. The mill had made Pitman a wealthy man, and he had built one of the more imposing of the town's few mansions as testimony to that fact. But he was also a genial man, known locally for his fair treatment of the workers, several of whom had been with him for twenty years or more. Thus the single stipulation of the sale to Parsons was that any worker who wished would be kept on. Parsons quickly accepted these terms and set about the reconstruction of what was now to be known as the Henry A. Parsons Mill. Of course nothing in the sale agreement said anything about Parsons being genial, and Mr. Pitman's hands had all long since drifted away.

There is an ancient joke in New England concerning an old man and his favorite axe: "Wonderful axe I got here," he says. "I've had five new handles, and two new axe heads put on her, but she still works jus' fine!"

And so it is with many an old building in New England. If a New Englander needs to replace a building, he very often does so by building an exact duplicate of the original. The casual tourist, imagining himself to be looking at a very fine example of a colonial meeting house, is often surprised to learn that it is—despite all appearances—a replica, and probably a second- or third-generation replica at that.

So it was with the buildings that Parsons had reconstructed at the mill. The sawdust bin and the drying shed both had to be completely rebuilt. From the road, it would have been impossible for the uninformed passerby to guess that the new buildings were any newer than the main building. In a sense, they were not. They posessed newer material and straighter, less settled lines, but aesthetically they were the same old buildings and remained in perfect keeping with their setting.

A similar principle had been applied to the mill's machinery. Of the eleven major machines on the main floor, seven looked as if they were of the same vintage as the mill itself. These were a ragged-looking lot, and appeared to have been constructed right on the spot out of locally available technology, specifically tailored to the requirements of the mill. They ranged in size and complexity from a simple hand-fed ripsaw, three or four feet in length, to a complicated self-feeding ripsaw measuring a good fifteen feet in length, and equipped with all sorts of levers, pulleys, gears, and counterweights. But all of these older machines had been constructed from the same eclectic and interchangeable assortment of four-by-fours, plywood, aluminum stock, standard industrial bearings, electric motors, rubber belts, copper tubing, and miscellaneous nuts and bolts. Heaps of this material could be found populating odd corners of the mill, and there was more than enough of it still around to completely reconstruct several of these old machines. Timeworn and dirty, carved with odd marks and symbols according to the arcane requirements of past production, the machines shared that decayed obsolescence most common to abandoned farm machinery. They seemed to go with a time long since past, looking as if they could only function in the abstract distance of another era. It was their particular miracle that they too worked "jus' fine."

Most master craftsmen go through their professional lives making do with the inadequacies of one particular mass-produced tool after another, until finally constructing tools of their own. It is an inherent shortcoming of mass production that the tool being produced represents a general consensus on its operation. This consensus eventually comes into conflict with the individual nature of craft. That is why old tools, like old musical instruments, have come to be valued so highly. They represent a refinement in construction that is so individual as to be completely at odds with the values of mass production. In this sense, the old machines at Parsons' mill represented a contradiction: they were a craftsman's accommodation to an industrial world, tailored to his needs but constructed from the material of mass production, for the purposes of mass production.

The Two Fountains

13

For reasons I did not understand, the mill had two drinking fountains in immediate proximity to each other. One was an attachment to the old porcelain sink just outside Parsons' door; the other was a modern institutional water cooling machine, located directly inside Parsons' office. The old-fashioned device rotated at its point of attachment so that it could be swung out over the sink when in use and pushed back when the sink was needed for some other purpose. Its water flow was controlled by applying pressure to a little porcelain button that at one time had been marked with the word "press"; now the worn instruction could only be deciphered by a logic so obvious as to make one wonder why the word had been printed there in the first place. When pressed, that hard little button elicited an impressive six-inch arc of water and took some getting used to before one could determine the exact amount of pressure required for a safe and steady flow.

The newer machine—the institutional water bubbler inside Parsons' office—was contained in a drab gray metal box, which offered the supplicant sipper a choice of hand and foot actuated controls. This variety of control must have been by way of compensation for the fact that regardless of the pressure applied to the controls, the machine would only emit the most minimal and controlled arc of water, forcing its operator to bring his lips dangerously close to the spout. Of course in summer the institutional water-drinking machine had the advantage that it provided a consistently cooler drink than its old-fashioned counterpart. But otherwise there was no obvious reason why two machines of this type should be in such close proximity.

At first the matter brought to mind the Jim Crow practices of the South, where "separate-but-equal" drinking fountains were the theory, while "separate" was the more distinct practice. Yet in this part of Vermont there were very few blacks, and to my knowledge none of

54

them had ever labored in Parsons' mill. There was certainly a distinction between worker and boss, but it had not been formalized into one of rights to specific drinking fountains. At Parsons' mill the boss and his workers had equal access to the drinking fountain of their choice.

However, there could be no doubt that Parsons showed a particular proclivity toward drinking from the older machine, while the rest of us preferred its modern counterpart. In fact it made for a very interesting study in contrasts. Parsons might be busy in his office with lunch but would go to the trouble of stepping outside for a drink from his favorite drinking fountain, while we had to go to the trouble of stepping into his office to get a drink from our favorite machine. These differences in preference were not always clear-cut. Sometimes Parsons could be seen bending stiffly over the water-drinking machine, slurping water with the same peculiar precision with which he did everything, while we would sometimes indulge in the tepid effluvia from the old sink. Still, the divisions were clear: Parsons had no need of these modern contrivances and their artificially modified product. Tepid water was good enough for him, and it was a point of moral triumph over us that we were so soft as to require cool water. For our part, there was no little triumph in being able to traipse into the boss's office whenever we felt like it and partake of the waters there.

The issue became of particular interest to me that week when I'd been left alone, because I had the run of the place and no one to demonstrate my loyalties to. I tested both fountains, enjoyed their individual characters, and considered the aesthetics of drinking tepid water from an unreliable stream, when water was available in a perfectly cooled and modulated flow. I had just finished with a round of fountain sampling, and was leaning on a large push broom in contemplation that Wednesday morning when a knock came on the door leading from the office to the outside stairs. As I opened it, I was greeted by the slightly apprehensive, partially distrustful, and wholly unshaven countenance of an older man in red suspenders.

"Is Mr. Pahsuns here?"

"Uuh, no. The mill is closed for vacation."

His look remained suspicious, and I felt compelled to account for my presence. "I'm cleaning up this week."

"Oh . . . I'm Mr. Jorgenson, I live across the way, in that house thaya." He took some seconds of maneuvering to point the exact house out to me.

"Yea-ahs?" I said, unintentionally mimicking his accent.

"Well, I keep an eye on the place for Mr. Pahsuns, and I seen it dark in here, and then the lights come on, so I figure I'll take a look."

"Oh . . . well," I said mustering a smile, "he's got me cleaning out the whole place."

"Oh my." He looked about. "Never seen it this clean. Bad sign when a sawmill's this clean."

"Oh?" My voice dropped.

"Lots of sawdust means good business." He still looked around distractedly.

"Well there was lots of sawdust before, and I expect we'll produce some more pretty soon."

"Oh!" He brightened, and turned his attention back to me. "So you work for Mr. Pahsuns then." I nodded uncertainly. Who did he think I worked for?

"I seen lots a' hands come and go. He can't hold 'em long." He paused to scratch his unshaven face. "He pays me to cut grass in summer, watch the sprinklers when he's not here, and I stoke the boiler for him in winter. You know, I just keep an eye on the place for him."

"Tough guy to work for!" I said, trying to sound cheerful about it.

"Oh yes. He once asked me: 'Why don't you come work for me?' 'No,' I says, 'I want no part of that.' You know, I keep busy. Take care of my house, shovelin' the walks, cuttin' the grass, rakin', trimmin' bushes. I'm fixin' storm doors right now.

"My daughter . . . she works up at the hospital. She's got three little girls. Two of 'em goes off to school early with their mother. But the little one, she goes later. I fix her breakfast, and see she gets to school."

Having summed up his existence so simply, and seeming so content with it, I felt at that moment that it might almost be worth trading off the thirty-five years which separated us in order to exchange places. But I was still thinking about those water fountains, and since he'd been watching the sprinklers every day for so long, I asked him if the mill had ever run out of water during a dry summer.

"Oh no. He's got two water systems here. A few years back they put 'im on town water, but he don't like town water. Me neither. No, we got a spring here." He paused to twist around and point up out the window. "You see that mountain thaya? Well we got a spring up thaya that's been piped right down here for years. Comes right off the mountain . . . right into the mill here. Clearest, sweetest water you ever see. Beautiful water." His eyes seemed to light up at the mere mention of it.

I knew that if I didn't get back to work, this old codger would be talking to me all day, and despite feeling rude, started to push my broom around. "Well," he said looking a little hurt, "I'll be seein' you around I expect," and again pointing out his house added, "I live right over thaya." He turned to go, but before slipping out, he edged over to the old-fashioned drinking fountain and took a good long slurp at it, furtively eyeing me from the side to see if I minded or not.

Ray   14

I think it may have been the drinking fountains that gave me my first clue as to the true nature of the new man Parsons hired. Vacation had ended, I had successfully dusted "wherever dust might light," and had washed every windowpane I could locate, all without turning asthmatic or being attacked by enraged yellow jackets. I felt at last that I had passed the test of admission to the mill's inner sanctum, and nothing that Parsons could cook up would be any worse than that which I had already survived. I was home, and believed that I was well on the way to becoming an unassailable fixture of that mill. In fact, I was so smug that I decided to adopt a cap, an engineer's striped special that my wife had bought for me on a trip to Maine, but which I rarely had the nerve to wear in public. It was always with a measure of envy that I had observed those rugged country workingmen with their tough little caps of blue, green, or red. Charlie had one—a golfer's Irish tweed that he kept rakishly low over his eyes. Until that moment at the mill, I would never have presumed to imitate the fashion, since I'd never felt part of that fraternity. But now I thought, let people snicker at me for wearing it. I had a *right* to wear that cap!

However, cap or no cap, new trials awaited me, and they now came in the form of Henry Parsons' latest recruit.

Even the bare bones minimum at which the mill was then running required somebody to drive the truck, and so Ray O'Brien, a short and stocky man in his mid-thirties with a penchant for farmer's overalls fitted too tightly over an ever-expanding paunch, was hired as the mill's official truck and forklift driver. From the start, this stranger feigned total indifference toward Charlie and me. But he lost no time at all in establishing himself with Parsons as the friendly, voluble type, who loved laughter and local gossip. In this respect he was somewhat reminiscent of Frank, the late-lamented Navy man, but far outdid him in the extent to which he was willing do or say anything that he figured would make him popular with the boss. He did not look to us for his behavioral cues, but from the man who handed out paychecks on Thursday afternoons, and I think it finally hit me that we were in for some rough weather when I observed that Ray was making a point of publicly demonstrating his preference for Parsons' tepid drinking fountain.

Break time would come, Charlie and I would have settled on our bench, smoking, eating, or staring blearily at our world and here came Parsons upstairs from the cellar, his tracks dogged by Ray, the two of them chuckling merrily over some private joke or other. Parsons would stop for an accustomed drink at the old fountain before heading into his office, and there standing right behind him was Ray, waiting his turn, slyly glancing up at us before dipping into that hated drink. A couple of times Ray even had the nerve to follow Parsons into the office, where he would continue to work at amusing the old man. But here Parsons would fall cold and silent, making it clear to his new recruit that he had just stepped over that uncertain line of propriety, and Ray would have to slink over to where we ordinary folks sat waiting patiently and silently.

Ray displayed considerably less enthusiasm toward us. In his eyes we were insignificant. He maintained an attitude of studied neutrality towards Charlie, addressing him in the crisply inquisitive tones of a leader of men obtaining such information as he might find useful in his quest for greater glory at Parsons' mill. For me, he had no words at all and treated me with a contempt that left me completely bewildered. Perhaps he felt Charlie deserved a measure of respect that I did not. True, Charlie was older, and had several years' tenure at the mill. But what could he possibly have against me?

I decided to remain aloof and thought myself magnanimous in crediting Ray's behavior to the natural anxieties that accompany any new job. He would calm down. It was his job he wished to conquer, not me. Besides, I knew in my heart of hearts that it could only be a matter of time before that great equalizer—the wrath of Parsons—came crashing down upon us all and properly readjusted all natural alliances.

Unfortunately, as time passed I found that Ray's hostility toward me grew stronger and stronger, while he seemed on ever-more-friendly terms with Parsons, who in turn seemed more and more pleased with his latest acquisition. With his large, and partially bald head inclined downwards, his focus on the floor before him, Ray began to strut around the mill as quickly and importantly as his stiff little legs would allow.

The considerable belly, which protested so vigorously against the confines of his overalls, presented a highly visible point of momentum from which the rest of his figure seemed to take its cue. With crab-like arms swinging uselessly from round meaty shoulders, he gave the impression of the unstoppable object that physics dictates must move in straight lines, and heaven help me if one of those lines happened to intersect my minor point in the cosmos. In short, he was a bull, and he was constantly on the charge. When not roaring around in the mill's truck, or madly maneuvering its forklift, he could be seen charging from point to point across the mill floor, rarely removing his gaze from his intended course, always presenting the image of a man with a mission in life.

Having lived with these constant projections of hostility for an entire week, I was beginning to get alarmed. Ray's attitude toward Charlie seemed to be softening a bit, and the two of them were beginning to participate in friendly conversations from which I seemed excluded. My earlier notion about the formation of "natural alliances" was beginning to look a little off the mark.

But there was something a little odd about the situation. Not only had Ray's hostility seemed to have sprung from nowhere, but his relations with Parsons seemed a lot closer than I ever imagined Parsons would condone in a mere employee. I began to get the feeling that it was really Parsons who lay behind Ray's hostility towards me. It was as if, after my initial run-ins with the old man, I had settled in just a little too comfortably for his liking, and in Ray he had found the perfect tool with which to shake me up. I had to admit that my week alone in the mill had given me a certain air of possession. My hat, which was now being drawn ever further down across my eyes, must have been some sort of signal to the old man; *that* one is getting just a little too comfortable, time to light a fire under his butt. In my evening hours I began to fret, imagining a whole variety of lurid lies with which Parsons might be filling Ray's head. In my dreams, I began to encounter a red-faced Parsons with a pixyish glint in his eyes manipulating Ray's puppet strings and working him into an ever more frenzied and violent state. I was beginning to lose sleep, and the premonition was strong that something terrible and violent was about to happen to me.

I took to keeping a wary eye on our new truck driver whenever he was around and was alarmed to observe just how strong he was. When I was working to pull boards off the headsaw, I had to throw my entire body into motion in order to heave the weight around. But in his powerfully compact way, Ray, with his little hands held close to his paunch, could twist these same heavy, wet boards around as if they were the merest twigs of balsa. He looked like some sort of monstrous drum majorette manipulating a lethal baton, and it put the fear of God in me to imagine what havoc those little hands might wreak upon me.

My fears came to a head by the middle of Ray's second week, when out of the blue, Parsons decided that it was necessary to assign the two of us to work alone together stacking wood out in the shed.

Alone? With Ray in the shed? The idea reminded me of my vulnerability. The shed was not the place to spend time with someone you believed meant you harm. As large as the mill itself, it was an open, barn-like space that had been designed with the circulation of air in mind. Along one wall ran a series of bins the size of horse stalls in which hundreds of bundles of ladder dowels were loosely stacked to dry before further processing. Carts loaded to various degrees with the entire variety of wooden objects produced at the mill were scattered randomly about and often had to be shifted and shoved around before any work could be carried out amongst them. Tennis racket strips leaned in precarious attitudes along the walls. Over by the loading dock, stacked, strapped, and palleted dowels stood in a maze of eight-foot-high blocks awaiting shipment. In short, the place had a warehouse atmosphere, and called to mind all the grimly theatrical fights staged by Hollywood in just such a setting. In my cinema-stuffed consciousness, I began to picture myself as the plain-but-honest working man about to be thrashed within an inch of his life by the corrupt-and-monstrous dock boss, whose job it was to do the awful bidding of some mysterious and sinister figure from on high.

Of course, away from Parsons there didn't seem to be any reason for our mutual hostility. As Ray and I began stacking lumber, an automatic and mute cooperation sprang up between us. We began to develop a mutual rhythm in our work, and as we alternated our roles in lifting, swinging, carrying, stacking and re-stacking, the ebb and flow of work seemed to carry our antagonism away.

After a while we paused to rest for a moment, and I decided to try and strike up some semblance of conversation. Between Ray's and Craig's tenures as truck driver, there had been a gap of more than a week. Since Parsons was apparently afraid to drive the thing himself, I had offered to move it around the mill grounds as required. I had even made a couple of firewood deliveries, and thus felt familiar enough with Ray's major occupation at the mill to venture a question.

61

"How do ya like that truck?"

"Aah, it's all right." He didn't sound enthusiastic.

"Taken it out a few times myself, and it seemed like a pretty nice rig." The word "rig" stuck in my throat, as I felt a bit out of my depth in the matter of trucks.

"Gearing's all wrong for a light truck. You want to take that thing over forty-five, the engine's running so fast it feels like the whole thing wants to shake apart." This was said with an air of professional dismissal, as if neither the truck, nor I were worthy of serious consideration. He probably thought that he had me stumped with this talk of gearing and addressed me with a certain impatience, as if simply to confirm that I could not understand this kind of shop talk.

"Well, of course," I countered, "I'm kinda used to those high RPMs with that little Japanese pickup I got. But I suppose that Chevy's supposed to run slower." He seemed uninterested in pursuing this line of conversation and seemed to regard me as if I were getting just a bit too big for my britches. So, I took the opposite tack and down-graded my abilities in the matter. "Course, I had a hell of a time maneuvering that thing. Took it to the dump with a load of garbage once, and the damn tailgate jammed up on me as I was dumping. Took me about an hour to get out of there."

"Yeahup," he replied, as if not in the least impressed with my experience at the dump.

We worked along in grim silence for a while, and it became increasingly obvious that the burden for maintaining any semblance of fluent conversation rested with me.

"So, uh, where'd you learn to drive a truck?" I asked, sounding as if I was just awestruck at his skill and wanted to know what genius had instructed him.

"In the fucking army."

"Oh. You were in the army? How long?"

"Too long."

"Ha ha." I laughed unconvincingly. "Well, I mean, were you in for a two-year hitch?" Sharply pained annoyance creased Ray's face.

"Four years?" I ventured meekly.

"Twelve years," he grumbled disgustedly.

"Jesus Christ! Twelve years?" I was astonished.

"Yeahup," he sighed, "I was a career Army man." Even by the standards of the military, I knew that twelve years did not make a career. But I was a little reluctant to seek further details. After all, maybe the guy was dishonorably discharged or something. It did not seem prudent to stir up unpleasant memories, so I worked along in silence for a couple of minutes. Stacking wood is not the most interesting of pastimes, however, and despite my best efforts to mediate the struggle, prudence and curiosity began a fierce battle for possession of my tongue. Curiosity won, and I asked Ray what happened.

"Damn army. No damn good anymore. Discipline doesn't mean shit these days."

Discipline? Discipline? I couldn't imagine what difference that would make, unless . . . "What was your rank?"

"Sergeant." He announced with a defensive pride, and stood up to his full height.

"Really? Say, that's pretty good." I was truly impressed. My grandfather had worked his way up to chief petty officer in the Navy, and I knew that this was nothing to be sneered at. There really weren't all that many routes up and out if you were poor, and if the military provided the only alternative, so be it. Of course this did not change the fact that I had a personal dislike for the military establishment and had even harbored seditious sentiments against them for their handiwork in Southeast Asia. As a result, Ray and I were stepping onto sensitive ground.

"So you were a sergeant, huh? That's pretty good."

"Yeah! Damn right! Got busted down too."

"To what?"

"To private, that's what! And two times too."

"Really? Twice? How come?"

"For fightin'."

"Both times?"

"Yeah. This one time, this black dude—real baad, you know what I mean?—he comes right up to my bunk where I'm sound asleep, and punches me in the face. Just like that."

I looked at him a little dubiously.

"Yeah," he continued, "the man was a Golden Gloves too."

"Boxer?"

"You're damn right. A Golden Gloves Boxer."

He was obviously more impressed with his story than I was, but I decided it was generally healthier to play along. So, fighting hard to avoid any obvious expression of the sarcasm that was consuming me whole, I played the straight man.

"So, what'd you do about it?"

"I cut 'im."

"With *what*?" This was getting to be too much.

"With a knife. I don't take shit from anyone."

Neither do I, I felt like saying. I didn't believe a word of his story. It had the ring of the kind of drunken bragging commonly overheard in bars and challenged only by those in the mood for a fight.

"Been in a few fights myself," I said slyly. Ray hesitated in what he was doing and for the first time during his tenure at the mill looked me directly in the eye. "Lost 'em all too," I added quickly.

"Yeah, well, I don't lose fights!" He blustered and puffed himself up, but I could see a hurt in his eyes. I had his number all right; he *did* lose fights, and I'd turned a trick on him, though of course he could have pulverized me.

I was anxious to avoid this possibility and began to babble on about the fights I had lost: a schoolmate had splashed a cup of cold water in my eyes and I had gone wild, only to be knocked out cold; some drugged-up goon had smashed into my car at a stoplight, causing me to curse him out, and him to sucker punch me, sending my glasses skittering across the pavement, forcing me to eat fish and soup for a week while I regained use of my dislocated jaw. Yes, I seemed to be saying, I'd run into a few bullies in my time, Ray was no different. What did he plan to do to me?

But for the time being, Ray appeared to be satisfied that his display of pompous hostility had assured me of his manhood, and we worked on in silence for a while.

"So really," I finally broke the silence by sounding sympathetic, "how come you quit the army?"

"Like I said, no discipline anymore. You take these damn P.R.s, for example. You'd try to get them to straighten out their bunks or something . . . they'd just go, 'aah maanh.' And then I'd say," Ray pointed to his shirtsleeve, "you see these stripes? I'm a sergeant." And then pointing to a spot above his breast, "See that? It says 'Sergeant O'Brien.' I got a name, and it ain't 'man.' But these P.R.s'd just say, 'aah maanh,' and do whatever they wanted. Discipline don't mean shit in the army anymore."

As he stood there pointing to those symbolic spots of lost authority, he looked as pitiful to me as he must have looked to those soldiers. I was beginning to like the guy, but his unrepentant racism remained a sore point, and I figured I'd better let him know it.

"I remember this time when I was still living in Chicago," I said.

64

"Our neighborhood had slums on three sides of it. One day, I was on my way home from school, and this group of black kids coming the other way surrounded me. There were about six of 'em, all younger and smaller than me. The biggest one in the group, the leader, came right up to me and said, 'Boy! You wanna fight me?' I looked him over for a second, and even though he was smaller than me, he looked like he could kick my ass in a second. I mean this kid was *tough*. 'No,' I said, 'I don't want to fight you.' And then all of sudden, all six of 'em started cracking up, like it was the funniest thing they ever heard. Then the kid that challenged me, reached out and slapped me on the back and said, 'Boy! You all right!' And then they moved off, laughing and joking."

The story did not appear to produce much of an effect upon Ray. If anything, he seemed a bit annoyed at my presumption for holding forth so long on any subject. But at least I felt that the two of us had backed into neutral corners with little likelihood that either of us would come out swinging. About this time, Parsons came swaggering out to the shed on some pretext or other but mostly just to see what Ray and I were up to. I was busily chattering away about how I had been to college, had tried teaching, was married, and other essential data that might fix in Ray's mind just exactly who I was. Ray seemed to be listening quietly, if a bit impatiently, because the more I talked, the less I worked. For his part, Parsons seemed a bit astonished that Ray and I were being civil toward one another. But he quickly covered his surprise by cross-examining us on our work, and, as was his custom, explaining to us how we might have done it differently.

15

U pon occasion, when she came to town in order to shop, or for some other significant purpose, Parsons' wife would stop in to take lunch with her husband. Her plain but immaculately maintained Chevy would roll into the gravel lot, and she'd emerge slowly, almost decorously, the first thing seen being a polished pocket book, held stiffly before her. Her clothes had that distinctive crispness and shine of well-made and rarely worn apparel. And though simple and tasteful, her dress exuded a kind of Palm Beach extravagance, which clearly distinguished her from the utilitarian fashion of the town.

Posessing none of her husband's reserve, Mrs. Parsons was sprightly and amused, having retained the full self-possession of a woman who had once been beautiful and still knew how to project the attitudes of beauty. She enjoyed greeting "the men," as she called the millhands, with a pleasant and direct smile. If she knew them, she would ask after their families, as befitted a woman in her position of wealth and social responsibility.

For his part, Parsons was always a little embarrassed by her presence. If he was engaged in some task, he would pretend not to notice her arrival, or chance an awkward little boy's wave and continue with what he was doing until he had finished. On one such occasion, he was demonstrating the intricacies of the doweling machine to me with the idea in mind that I would eventually become its principal operator. Later, when he had turned his back for a moment, she smiled at me and said pleasantly, "I see he's got you working on his *favorite* machine." It was obvious that she adored him.

One morning late in the summer, it became obvious that something out of the ordinary was up. Parsons was acting very strangely, and we feared that his paranoia had struck again because he seemed to be taking every precaution imaginable to keep himself out of sight. When he did emerge from some hidden corner, it was for the briefest possible moment, darting here and there, casting anxious glances about him, and peering out the window. Finally something sent him scurrying down the cellar stairs with such dispatch that I looked around for a man with a gun.

No such person was in evidence. What I saw was a smiling procession of highly respectable, middle-class, middle-aged men and women, led by Mrs. Parsons.

"Have you seen my husband?" she asked Charlie, whose family she knew well.

"Well he was here a minute ago. . . ." Charlie scratched his head and looked around. "You want me to go look for him?"

"Oh no, that won't be necessary," she said with her pleasant smile. "We'll just wait." And with patience bred of certain knowledge of her husband's habits, Mrs. Parsons turned to her companions. They made an incongruous picture, looking very much like a cross section of a small-town chamber of commerce making polite conversation amid our cacophonous racket of a work song.

Finally, slowly, sheepishly, red-faced with embarrassment, Parsons crept up the cellar stairs, managing a little smile, and the entire group disappeared into his office. A short while later, the delegation filed back out of Parsons' office and left the premises, while Parsons returned to work.

Lunch break came, and I was shutting down my machine, removing my headphones, and dusting myself off when Parsons came darting up to me, a quiet smile on his lips and a bulging manila envelope in his hands. "Here," he said, handing me the envelope, "I think I can rely on you to take care of this." He turned on his heel and scooted away, leaving me open-mouthed with surprise.

As I sat down to lunch, I opened the envelope. Inside was a kit of materials for solicitation of United Way funds: pledge cards for employees, booklets to encourage them, gruesome little plastic pins in the shape of a blood drop to reward them, and an account sheet with which I, the United Way "volunteer" at Parsons' mill, was to keep track of our progress.

Obviously Parsons figured that he had my number. I was just another one of these "do-gooders," always in search of a cause. Here was my chance. For my part, I was horrified. It wasn't that I had anything against charity, but the United Way had an unsavory reputation for getting employers to twist people's arms in a way that completely distorted the concept of charity. It was my idea that if money was needed for cerebral palsy, or cancer, or disaster relief, it was up to the government to supply it. After all, a worker making two hundred fifty dollars a week was already "contributing" fifty dollars a week in taxes.

But what was really annoying about the situation was that I had to waste precious minutes of my lunch hour making a fool of myself, trying to get money out of people who felt pretty much the same way I did. At Parsons' mill, the slim half hour set aside for lunch was sacred, and even Parsons would tolerate no interruption.

As all three hands of the big institutional clock were grazing past twelve, Parsons would pass under it into his office, sit at his big, dusty, rolltop desk, and warm up the ancient tube radio in order to catch the noon news. Carefully spreading the lunch prepared by his wife, he ate deliberately but contentedly. And if any person had the unmitigated gall to call on the telephone while Parsons was particularly absorbed in some item of news, he would simply hold the receiver up to the radio with one hand, continuing to eat with the other. Eventually the astounded caller would ring off, probably wondering what number he had accidentally dialed.

For all of us, lunch was a literal break in routine. It was as if an amnesty were declared in the midst of the war of work, and both sides respected it. Even if Parsons was mad at you, trying to drive you crazy during working hours, he seemed to suspend his animosity for that half hour, only to pick it up again once lunch was over.

So it was with extreme reluctance that I began my "volunteer" work for a charity I did not believe in. It seemed best to get the matter over as quickly as possible. I moved from employee to employee, distributing pledge cards, and making it clear that I'd been suckered into doing it, and I was sorry, but I was not to be held responsible for the annoyance. To each one of them, it seemed like a cause for more merriment than the last, and as my humiliation deepened it came to me that this was probably how Parsons had hoped it would be.

There could be no possible revenge for this kind of trickery, although later on I was able to slip unnoticed into Parsons' office and place the special pledge card marked "Employer" squarely on his desk. This was a larger and more elaborate affair than the employee pledge cards and obviously bespoke the larger responsibilities that rested with the employer in the matter of charity. But Parsons showed an uncharacteristic egalitarianism when it came to making his contribution. Like everyone else at the mill, he contributed nary a cent.

68

With the coming of fall, the clarity of the sky, and the tinges of color shading the hillsides, the pace began to quicken at Parsons' mill. Logging trucks began to pull into the yard and dispose of their enormous loads with increasing frequency, and Parsons hired a "new man," as he liked to put it.

Jerry was a young, quiet-seeming sort, who kept to himself at breaks, and was kept further isolated by his work. He spent the entire nine-hour day, garden hose in hand, carefully washing down each and every one of the hundreds of logs out in the yard. This was a necessary step in preparing them to be "split" into boards on the headsaw, since as the loggers harvested their crop, they dragged them through the woods, and they accumulated a great deal of mud.

Mud was anathema at the mill. Despite the rather ragged and messy appearance of the mill's interior, and despite the fact that the sawdust that I had so laboriously removed had since returned with a vengeance, Parsons simply would not tolerate the presence of mud in his mill and would throw scathing remarks at us for tracking even the smallest amount of the stuff in on our boots. The problem was that it dulled saw blades in a hurry, and if allowed to get into the headsaw's bearings might prove fatal to them.

But in all probability, the matter went a little deeper than that with Parsons. He was scrupulously neat about his person, vigorously washing his hands before lunch, meticulously brushing his removed dentures afterwards, carefully dusting himself off at the end of the day with a brush he kept especially for the purpose, and finally, carefully pulling a comb slowly through his his thick mane of silver hair, an asset of which he appeared particularly proud.

In this scheme, soil could play no part. If a machine needed heavy greasing, he saw to it that someone else performed the task. Yes, he could be seen giving a discreet squirt of light oil to the headsaw now and again, gently squeezing an oil can with the touch of the maestro leading his orchestra through a quiet and difficult passage, but the viscous substance was never allowed to touch him. He might end his day covered in sawdust, but that woodworker's mess was of a particularly clean sort and could be brushed easily away, while Parsons' beautiful pink skin would always remain as testimony to his genteel aspirations.

Normally it was Charlie who washed logs. He would wash four or five, and then in his position as Log Chopper cut the logs to various manageable lengths before rolling them into the mill to be fed into the headsaw and cut into boards. But for obvious reasons of climate, it was not practical to wash logs in the dead of winter, and so a supply of clean "winter logs" was Jerry's burden.

The imminent onslaught of winter was the prime reason for the increase in truck travel, since their task would soon be impossible also. Great racks on wheels, they carried incredible loads of the forest harvest. In proportion to these rigs, the men who drove them seemed of incredible size also. They had come into manhood hefting large and lethal chainsaws and wrestling with logs twenty times their weight. Their physical strength was of a magnitude unmatched by that produced in any other trade. I've seen a pair of them actually pick up a small car and carry it sideways because it was in their way. And yet to see them operate the clawed crane with which logs were loaded on and off their rigs was to watch a miraculous demonstration of dexterity and grace. By means of a group of hydraulic levers, these cranes were like extensions of the operator's arm itself. Grasping logs, shaking them, rolling, nudging, almost seeming to feel them as if they were pick-up sticks, it was a ballet of Bunyanesque proportions.

In one instance, I have seen a logger in a hurry offload a full truck of thirty or so full-sized logs in less than ten minutes. But this was when Parsons wasn't around to supervise the operation. Usually the log truck would arrive and wait until Parsons could get out there and personally oversee the deposition of each log on the small mountain that was being constructed in the yard. Clipboard in one hand, yardstick in another, the old man would scramble up on the log pile itself and, standing a full fifteen or twenty feet above the ground, carefully measure each log, make a notation, and direct its placement on the pile, all the while seeming totally oblivious to the deadly weights that the logger was gingerly maneuvering around him. On these occasions Parsons wore a white safety helmet, but this was a purely symbolic act, an OSHA-approved fetish to keep the evil spirits away. In the event of a mishap, that little white piece of plastic would have been utterly useless. Of course Parsons must have been aware of this fact, but seemed to take pleasure in the garb anyway, as if he were playing a little joke on the world. But the thing that used to strike me as most remarkable about this particular act was how he could have so little faith in his own employees, while routinely, almost casually, placing his life in the hands of those loggers.

There were now five men laboring at the mill on a full-time basis. This meant that from the low ebb of vacation week, when I worked alone, the mill's pace had risen to a point where the equivalent of my entire week's suffering was being reproduced every single day. We were no longer performing "chores," or running out of work altogether and standing around trying to figure out what to do next. Instead we were all kept constantly busy, and as a result the mill itself seemed to be rising from a dormant state into life.

Jerry continued washing logs and keeping to himself. His was not a forced pace, but rather a patient and meticulous one. He could be seen out in the yard, dressed in his slickered apron and rubber boots, golfing cap drawn down across his glasses, cigarette perched in his mouth, slowly rolling a log to and fro and hosing it off. At lunch, he would sit in his car reading paperbacks and listening to classical music on the radio. Here was a young man who clearly chose to ride above the fray. Of course the rest of us felt a little sorry for him, thinking that he must be awfully bored. Parsons had hired him on a temporary basis, and it was understood that once the winter logs were washed he would be gone. At least that was what Ray told us.

Ray had by now carefully cultivated what he supposed was his position as an "insider." It was therefore natural that he could speak to us with authority on the matter of Jerry's future at the mill. For our parts, Charlie and I were quite willing to cede Ray any position he now wished to claim. Strangely enough, now that Ray and I had come to some sort of accommodation, neither Charlie nor I were taking the former sergeant very seriously. His violent demeanor had proven to be so much bluster, and besides, we could see signs that the honeymoon between Ray and the boss was beginning to lose its romance.

Ray's main task for the moment was that of shifting logs around the yard. With the aid of the mill's forklift, he would take logs from the small hill left by the loggers and carry them over to Jerry, for washing. He then took the logs that Jerry had finished and either carried them to a second, growing hill, or gave them to Charlie, who would ponder how to cut them to length. This task was easy enough for Ray to master, and he was soon riding high, putting around with the mill's decrepit lift, feeling secure in a position that he saw as making him irreplaceable.

Of course Ray had other reasons to feel especially privileged. As the mill's truck driver, he was allowed to leave the premises and roam at his own pace, without the sense that a red-faced Parsons might be spying on him from any corner, demanding to know what was taking him so long. If he dawdled a little too long while making a delivery, he always had the excuse that traffic was backed up somewhere, or that he had had trouble finding a place. In any case, it had to be admitted that when he was leaving to make a delivery, the rest of us watched him drive from the yard with a pang of envy, and thought that any man who could escape Parsons' influence—even for half an hour—was indeed a man of privilege.

But as cold weather came closer and closer, the phone at Parsons' mill began to ring with increasing frequency, as caller after caller wanted know why the load of firewood ordered in the spring had not yet been delivered. The fact of the matter was that the list of people wanting a cord-and-a-half of highly prized ash kindling at forty dollars a load was almost infinitely long. And when country people, especially older women who may not be equipped to cut their own fuel, start to smell the onset of winter, a severe anxiety bordering on mild panic begins to set in. This panic began to make itself known to those of us who had to answer the phone at the mill, and we, at last freed of truck driver envy, were happy to put the man on the line so that he might put the distressed caller's mind at ease.

Delivering firewood to local households was not supposed to form a major part of the mill's business. The idea was that the mill had scrap to dispose of, and people were happy to take it off our hands. Parsons had calculated a price for delivery that saw him deriving no profit whatsoever, viewing the operation as a kind of community service. But, it had taken on an importance way out of proportion to its actual role in the business. There was a strict protocol involved. And so when the widow of a particularly important man-about-town, one who had owned banks and founded colleges, called and asked me if she might be moved up a few places on the list of eager customers, a quick consultation with the boss revealed that the answer was a firm "no."

"We do not grant special privileges here," Parsons pronounced imperiously. "We follow the list, and it is strictly on a first-come-first-serve basis." He said this so as to leave no doubt in my mind about it and was obviously very proud of his ability to be so very egalitarian in the matter. "Of course," he added, "if a local business were to call and tell us they needed the wood, we would make an exception." Here he smiled cunningly, for he had made it clear that at least in the matter of firewood, he was a man who stuck firmly to Republican principles.

By now Ray was becoming a little frantic. It was one thing to be able to leave the mill's premises, but Ray was no longer able to enjoy it. Both Charlie and Jerry were depending upon him to keep them supplied with logs, and as the pace at the mill began to pick up that became a more and more frequent demand. As the number of Ray's firewood deliveries was also increasing, he sometimes allowed Charlie and Jerry to run out of work. In Parsons' eyes, this was a mortal sin.

For his part, Parsons had not attained his station in life by missing an opportunity when it came along. He had learned long ago that as the boss it was critical to maintain firm authority over his employees, and he was now afforded an excellent opportunity to teach the hapless sergeant a lesson in humility. So, seeing that Ray felt a little pressured by his responsibilities, Parsons followed the logic of the situation and gave him additional duties. Quite suddenly, it had become necessary to prepare finished dowels for shipment. Ray was duly dispatched to the shed to carefully stack and strap the numerous pallets. It was not as if another of us could not have been spared to carry out this task, but Parsons wanted *Ray* to do it.

For poor Ray it was beginning to mean a lot more running around than he had counted on. As he worked, he became increasingly grim, running ever faster from place to place on his stubby little legs, while at lunch he complained bitterly to us of the way he was being treated. For our part, Charlie and I had to work valiantly not to show our pleasure at his predicament.

The Log Chopper **18**

▲▼▲▼▲▼▲▼▲▼▲▼▲▼▲▼▲▼▲▼▲▼▲▼▲▼▲▼▲▼▲▼▲▼▲▼▲

Charlie was the mill's log chopper. It was his privilege to take logs from the yard and reduce them to more manageable size. On any given day, no matter if it was clear or rainy, scorching or freezing, he could be found working outside the mill's big wooden sliding doors, heaving those behemoths around with a force and authority that gave even his shabby figure heroic proportions. Logs are products of nature, and as such do not lend themselves easily to the simplified geometric order man seeks vainly to impose upon his universe. They come with all sorts of bumps, curves, twists, and other irregularities that raise hell with anyone trying to roll them across a flat surface such as the deck on which Charlie worked. Thus Charlie's nature was that of the lion tamer, who needs always assert his authority over the ferocious beasts in his command.

Aside from looking for the insidious traces of mud that Jerry might have missed, Charlie's object was to send each log's thousands of pounds of irregularly distributed bulk flying across the deck, over a set of wobbly planks, and banging onto a kind of railroad cart meant to hold logs in place while they were being cut up. This required an otherwise gentle Charlie to administer a very rough justice to the late-lamented tree trunk. This he did by applying his full strength to a device that resembled an oversized baseball bat with a spike at one end and a hinged hook along its side quite near to the spike. This was a tool basic to the trade, known variously as a "peavey," a "cant-dog," or simply—according to Parsons' puritanical utilitarianism—a "logger's hook."

To behold the flourish with which a skilled and reasonably strong person like Charlie could hook a log with his peavey, tug on the long handle to get the log rolling, and then prod the thing along so as to maintain its mad momentum was a thing of dramatic beauty. It inspired in me all kinds of envious longings, and so when invited by practical necessity to lend a hand, I grabbed a hook and leapt upon the deck with an expectant glee. Here I was taking a rather childish and (some would probably argue) obscene pleasure in standing tall, hook in hand, ready to battle the elements. I felt the same kind of delicious expectancy that a baseball player feels on deck, endlessly swinging his bat while looking to the audience for that particularly fair lady whom he is certain to impress. I myself was looking toward the road that ran by the mill, hoping that providence would send some beauty sailing slowly by in her top-down convertible. But in this case, providence proved the wiser. I was so startled out of my reverie by an incredulous look from Charlie that I gave an ill-timed and over-enthusiastic jab with my hook, missed the log altogether, and went clattering wildly across the deck.

Needless to say, I then proceeded with considerably more caution, and much less romantic fantasy, and was duly rewarded with a steady progression of insights into the variety of pulls, pushes, prods, and pries by which even the most modestly muscled person can work his will over an object that outweighs him by twenty times. Archimedes may have had a lever that he claimed could move the earth, but only a god could have provided him with a fulcrum and platform to carry out his boast. The logger has all of these things, and with them he can move a log that weighs but the tiniest fraction of the earth. Yet by just that tiny fraction, he feels like a god. And Archimedes? Maybe he rolled logs too.

Having convinced a log to rest comfortably on the cart, Charlie would then proceed to measure and mark it for cutting. The loggers supplied the mill with logs ranging somewhere between ten and fifteen feet in length, and Charlie was to chop them into some combination of the five or six lengths standard to the mill. These shortened logs would then be sent to the headsaw to be split into boards. It would appear that Charlie's task was a simple matter of choosing a set of standard lengths that would result in the least amount of wasted log. But each of those standard lengths corresponded to a particular final product or group of products, and, as already indicated, different kinds of products required different qualities of grain. Thus Charlie's task was not that of a simple arithmetic division but a division based upon his judgment of the log's internal qualities.

This represented the true art of Charlie's task; how does one know what a log's grain is going to look like without splitting it open to have a look? By looking at a log's surface, noting its curve, the color of its endgrain, its bumps and other irregularities of bark, and by guessing what part of the tree it had come from, Charlie could "see" into its interior and estimate the qualities of grain therein. The simple appearance of what he did and the slow, deliberate pace at which he did it masked the seriousness of his meditation. In its own way, the pace at which he worked was as forced as anyone else's because any misjudgment on his part could result in a great deal of wasted material.

Once a log had been marked for cutting, the cart on which it rested could be rolled back and forth along a pair of rails so as to position the log under the suspended cut-off saw. This was merely a modified chainsaw about five feet long, hinged at one end, and coupled to a large, powerful, but mercifully quiet electric motor. Unlike its hand-held, gasoline-powered counterparts that simultaneously poison, deafen, and vibrate you into paralysis, it was a pure joy to operate. With one hand, almost anyone could pull its blade down through a three-foot-thick hardwood log in a matter of seconds. Of course the usual chain-sawing hazards were still applicable, though sometimes in rather unexpected ways. If the log had been positioned incorrectly on the cart, the saw was quite capable of getting so thoroughly jammed up half-way through that it could take a good five or ten minutes of pushing, pulling, levering, and other forms of calculated brutality before the unfortunate log chopper was able to free the thing undamaged. This was always a humiliating experience but was dangerous only to the extent that the boss noticed what had happened, and unleashed his wrath as a result.

On the other hand, a chainsaw's tendency to kick back is of a considerably more serious nature. In the case of a hand-held chainsaw, the blade grabs onto the wood instead of cutting through it and without warning comes flying back at your face. Of course the mill's cut-off saw was fixed at one end so that it was impossible for it to fly back in your direction. So instead the log would volunteer. The near-silent operation of that electric motor was hideously deceptive, and the same power that could slice through a large log in a matter of seconds could also take a three-hundred-pound chunk of it and send it spinning and flying back in your direction before you'd even had time to think of an appropriate obscenity with which to greet it.

The Headsaw **19**

The headsaw, as its name implies, is the center and very soul of a sawmill. Here logs are made into boards, and every process that precedes it in the line of production can be said to be a mere preparation, while everything that comes after a mere refinement. There are hundreds of constructions throughout the hills of New England that appear to be little more than tin-roofed shacks, but have the right to call themselves sawmills, merely because they house this one machine. Though elaborate-looking at first glance, Parsons' headsaw was a fairly simple device. The log sat upon an eight-foot-long, steel-framed carriage called a log beam, held there by a series of vertical, spiked clamps called dogs. This entire construction rode on a narrow-gauge railroad track parallel to a fifty-two-inch circular saw blade and carried the log through the saw. Further refinements gave the sawyer precise control over the thickness of the board being cut and determined the angle at which the log would enter the saw blade. Power was supplied by an enormous fifty-horsepower electric motor, which sat waist high on the floor, and was coupled directly to the saw blade and indirectly through a clutched lever to the carriage.

A log would be rolled onto the log beam and held there—usually by an assistant—while Parsons, in his capacity as head sawyer, looked it over to see how he imagined the grain ran and where its hidden imperfections might lie. As with Charlie's earlier judgment, this was an educated guessing game at best but one that was ruled by the logic of geometry. Grain is a three-dimensional affair, representing a map of the tree's growth. Where the tree curves and twists, so does its grain. Where the sides of the tree are parallel to one another, so are the lines of its grain; and where there are bumps, dips, or other perturbations in the tree's surface, so may you expect to find them mirrored by the grain in the tree's interior. It is the head sawyer's job to find a plane through each log that best follows what he supposes is the

78

direction of the grain. The strongest board is the one that is not cut across the grain.

It is not by accident that the head sawyer's job is called "splitting" a log. As anyone who has split wood with an axe can tell you, it is the grain that is being split, and where that grain curves so does the split. The most primitive kind of sawyering is the sort that was performed by such notables as Abraham Lincoln with sledgehammer and wedge. The resulting boards were fairly rough because their surfaces followed the undulations of the tree's grain. Modern woodworking requires flat surfaces for its purposes and has constructed machinery to produce them. As a result, the abstract geometric dictates of the two dimensional plane have been imposed upon a complicated three-dimensional organism of nature, and it is the sawyer's job to mediate between the two.

High school geometry teaches us that a plane is the product of two vectors of motion. The head sawyer, therefore, has two dimensions in which he must adjust a log before cutting it in order to achieve the most acceptable plane. With the help of an assistant, Parsons would grab the log with a small peavey and start to rotate it in place upon the log beam, his eyes darting from end to end, looking for its curve. He would turn the log, hold it, and try to rock it in place. Then he might turn it some more and glance from end to end again, all with a restless urgency tempered by the soft precision of careful adjustment. Here he was looking for the predominant curve of the log, to place its concave face downward. In so doing, he aligned one dimension of the log's curve with the plane of the saw blade. After he was satisfied with these rotated adjustments, he would again line his eye up along the length of the log. With the adjustment of levers attached to the dogs, he pulled one end of the log out to adjust the angle at which it would enter the saw blade and thereby determined the second dimension of the plane. Finally satisfied, Parsons nodded to his assistant, who would slam the spiked arm of the rear dog in place, while he himself slammed down the arm of the front dog. And so with a *kerchunk-kerchunk*, the log was dogged firmly to the carriage, ready to be split. Parsons would stand at the ready, facing the carriage, which was to move from right to left in front of him. He felt to his left for a four-foot lever that stuck out of the floor, resembling a brakeman's switch, with which he would control the carriage's movement. Meanwhile his assistant had scurried around the waist-high plywood box housing the giant, clock-like mechanism that transferred power from the motor to the carriage and saw blade. This box was the heart of the saw itself: within it essential belts and pulleys whirred; on top of it, buried in sawdust, lay the odd assortment of hand tools that the years had seen useful in this operation; around it leaned the men who worked the saw. To one side, stood the sawyer, ready at the feed, while on the other side, at the receiving end, the one or two assistants waited in crouched expectancy, eyes concentrating on the enormous saw blade that spun naked directly in front of them.

The electric motor sat there, its fifty horses placidly humming, while its lethal adjunct sliced and swished the air, commanding respect from all who worked close enough to feel the odd little breezes it made as it spun. Gingerly, Parsons would pull on the big clutch lever, tensing himself as if to prepare for the impact. The big carriage with its passenger log would start to rumble and creak slowly along its tracks, moving toward that awful force: fifty horses flinging twenty-five sharpened chisels around a fifty-two-inch arc with a quiet centrifugal violence expressed in a steady *shhhh*. Parsons would ease up on the lever and allow the weighted momentum of the cart to just drift into the blade. The *shhhh* of sliced air then harmonized with a gentle *brrrr*, like the soft shuffle of cards. Parsons pulled his weight on the lever, feeling the resistance of log against blade right through the machine's mechanism. The *shhhh* and *brrrr* were suddenly transformed into the enormous angry drone of thousands and thousands of bees held in a collective groan; one—two—three—four, and stop. The sawmill's cry was heard plainly up and down the road outside. Then there was a moment of hesitation as again the soft *shhhh* of the blade could be heard, but now mixed with the slight ringing with which a metal blade declares its triumph over wood. The newly created board perched precariously on edge, before deciding to fall from the blade and onto its side with a *plop*. The rumble and creak of the carriage resumed as it returned to Parsons' end of the saw. Within four or five seconds, Parsons made his adjustments for the second pass, and again the rumble of the carriage, the *shhhh*, the *brrrr*, and the angry drone of bees began.

The assistants now went to work. They were runners, gingerly but quickly grabbing wet, heavy boards just off the treacherous blade, running to pile them on the right cart out of the seven or eight lined up on the floor, and then running back to retrieve the next new board as it fell off the saw. After Parsons had worked his way through a log— rotating and readjusting it so as to capture its best grain—he might need help to roll another one onto the carriage. It was up to an assistant to run around the plywood housing of the saw's central mechanism and give him a hand.

Certain boards had to be cut to shorter lengths as soon as they came off the saw. The single assistant working alone with Parsons came to dread these. Now, in amongst all his running, he also had to perform as a sawyer, judging grain, figuring divisions, and forcing boards through a hazardous crosscut saw, before running back to his station at the headsaw. Thus he ran from spinning blade to spinning blade, and to avoid falling into one of them he could not afford to take his eyes off his feet. It was necessary to recognize the progression of Parsons' movements from their sounds; the *kerchunk* of dogs, the ringing of the ratcheted lever that controlled a cut's thickness, the rumble and creak of the rolling carriage, the pitch of the saw blade's cry as it approached the end of its cut, all told him where he would have to move next.

The only moment when the head sawyer's assistant could afford to look up was during those few precious seconds when he had fought his way ahead of the sawyer's pace and had time to stand at the headsaw as the log was feeding through. Then he had no choice but to fix his gaze upon that awful fifty-two-inch blade, which spun as if to mesmerize and warn like an industrial deity, *"Keep yourself under control, I am death."* It was all the wisdom a person needed, to learn and remember, to ritualize his movements in and around that saw. It taught his hands to pick boards off the saw with complete delicacy and how his body should heave and hoist them onto their respective carts. Between these movements, it taught every physical reality of the space he inhabited: the number of steps, arm lengths, and seconds between machine, machine, and cart, where the floor boards stuck up along his path, how he must lean his body at the headsaw and at the crosscut saw, where he must take little steps and where big ones, where he could move quickly, and where he must slow down.

For the assistant, pace was dictated by the head sawyer, and he did his best to accommodate himself to it. Parsons was an older man, not given to jumping too violently upon his tasks. His was a more gradual, building kind of approach to the matter at hand. He preferred to start out with one assistant and measured himself by slowly piling up more and more work until the poor assistant was ready to beg for mercy. But mercy did not come from Parsons. Instead it was just another millhand—usually Charlie—who from his corner of the mill could hear the headsaw's all-consuming pace and would drop his own work in order to rush to his fellow's aid. Parsons had no objection to this improvised reordering of priorities because it was a mark of his strength and because he wanted nothing to distract from his pace once he'd found it.

A sawmill's machinery invokes a gruesome index of accidental death and mutilation. A machine that with blasé violence can split a magnificent tree to its heart in seconds can also create unspeakable carnage when brought into contact with human flesh. For a person who works around these things, it is an ever present reality, a knowledge to be stuffed into the nether reaches of consciousness but *never, never* to be forgotten. Nervous little stories abound. The very same crosscut saws around which I have worked so closely are efficient killers if they please. Metal blades form slight little cracks that—if unnoticed—widen until a critical moment when the blade shatters and flies off its arbor with such force that you might look up to find your workmate of a minute ago without a head attached to his body. Such things are reported to have happened in the past and are laughed off with the knowledge that they could happen again at any moment.

Charlie once witnessed the headsaw unleash its fury in a most unexpected way. A "young fella" was working the headsaw and had just fed a log through the blade, when for some peculiar reason the board that normally should have fallen sideways off the big blade, fell back into it, got picked up by one of the saw's teeth, and was catapulted back toward the sawyer, missing his head by inches before demolishing a substantially constructed workbench across the mill. According to Charlie, who recalled the incident with a little chuckle, "The fella was as white as a sheet." Had that fifty- or sixty-pound hardwood slab struck him, it would have been his head that was demolished and not the unfortunate workbench.

These were freak accidents, of course. But by the very fact of their unpredictable nature, they froze us into the kind of rigid discipline practiced the world over by people who might be boozers, womanizers, and gamblers but who understand probability with a scientific precison.

The year before my arrival, Parsons himself had been involved in a fairly serious accident, but it was no freak. Sometimes a small scrap of wood got lodged between the saw blade and the wooden platform that ran alongside it. Usually it was a simple matter of poking at it with a stick until the object was dislodged, fell into the blower system, and was whisked away. But sometimes the object would be too large, and allowing it to be taken away by the blower's suction could result in serious damage to the system itself. In fact, this was one aspect of the mill's operation that seemed to seriously unhinge Parsons, and it gave me secret pleasure to see his absolute panic in the face of such events. If a large piece of wood happened to fall into the blower system he would shout, "Oh my god!" and at a clip that was astounding for someone of his age go tearing all the way across the mill and practically throw himself at the big lever that turned the blower off.

It was in fearful anticipation of such a circumstance that one day Parsons did the rather foolish thing of reaching down with his hand to dislodge a large scrap of wood and got his hand caught between the side of the spinning blade and the platform running alongside it. As a result, the skin across the entire back of his hand was peeled off and remained hinged there as a flap, exposing muscle, bone, and cartilage to plain sight. The pain was so intense that the old man told his millhands to lay him on the floor, lest he faint, and really do himself in. It was Charlie who wrapped the wound, and he and another man took Parsons to the hospital.

The next day, everyone showed up for work at seven o'clock sharp, not knowing what to expect. At ten minutes after seven, when Parsons had not yet shown up, they were like kids at school, hearts soaring at the possibility of a day's relief from their ruthless taskmaster. At a quarter after, they were positively gleeful, openly smiling at one another. But at eighteen minutes after seven, Parsons showed up sporting a bandage that made his hand look like a bear's paw. He was goddamned if he was going to let a little accident keep him from working. Wasn't it bad enough that the damn bandage had made it near impossible to get dressed? He'd never been late before in his life!

For all their fearsome nature, the mill's machines had the calm soul of a monster tamed. Imagine a mythical beast with the strength of fifty horses tamed under the ministrations of a sorcerer and his assistants, and you have an appreciation of the calm power to be felt by a person working in safety around a machine so potentially destructive. When the pace was right, when Charlie had provided good logs, when Parsons' assistants could provide a controlled counterpoint to his beat on the headsaw, when it was "going right" for the head sawyer, the mill was humming, the mill was alive, biology and machinery were as one, our exertions were effortless and perfect, we made them in harmony, and fear did not touch us.

When Parsons' pace was not right, sometimes ours was, and we could get him going. Or perhaps our pace was off, and he could get us going. But on some days, things just were not going to work, and that was that. A log would be fed into the big blade, the drone of bees would build and then break off suddenly into a tortured whirring sound that meant the log was jammed onto the saw and would move no further. The fifty horses would be snapped off in a panic by a slightly rattled Parsons, and the rest of us would gather slowly from the four corners of the mill, crow bars and hefty planks in hand, ready to start heaving and pushing until the log was disengaged from the blade.

The entire mill would have come to a halt now, and all eyes were focused on Parsons. He would switch the headsaw back on, and as we watched intently, slowly edge over to the spinning blade and put the palm of his hand against its face, carefully feeling it from its center to its outer edge. Shaking his head, he would shuffle over to an odd corner to retrieve a dented, rusted, old bucket and a sorry-looking broom with its bristles half rotted away, both of which I had been sorely tempted to throw away when I was cleaning up the week of vacation. Filling the bucket with water, he would drag it over to the blade, water dripping across the floor from its innumerable holes, and proceed to apply the old broom to the side of the blade. Those of us who found this activity interesting were rewarded for our curiosity with a face full of spray and had to step back sharply. Again he would lay his hand on the surface of the blade and run it along with the mystical precision of a shaman performing his magic, before reapplying the ancient water-soaked broom.

When a saw blade jams inside a piece of wood, it usually continues to spin in place, and the resulting friction produces a blade-warping heat. And since a warped blade will continue to create a great deal of friction and warp even more, something must be done to straighten the blade. By feeling the blade's surface with his hand, Parsons was seeking out its hot spots, and by applying water he was cooling them, thereby tempering and straightening the blade. Thus Parsons performed his ritual cure for the saw blade's ills, alternating applications of water with more laying on of the hands, until, at last satisfied, he would put bucket and broom aside and return to the business of splitting logs.

The Carts

20

The big wooden carts onto which we loaded the headsaw's products were filled to capacity and then rolled onto the freight elevator and carried downstairs for storage in the cellar. There they remained until they were again needed. Resembling old railway station carts, they had five-foot beds of solid oak with removable stakes at each corner. They rolled about on two big cast-iron wheels fixed at the cart's middle, and the cart tipped back and forth upon two smaller wheels, one at either end. These smaller wheels wobbled and spun around like the front wheels of a shopping cart and gave the loaded carts a maneuverabilty that was quite surprising, considering the weight involved.

There was an art to handling these things when loaded, which had a lot to do with one's appreciation of momentum. It seemed remarkable at times, but a single thin man of one hundred and fifty pounds or so could get a several-thousand-pound load to roll if he put his mind to it. It took an almost absolute concentration of physical and mental powers to overcome inertia, and then an absolute refusal to stop once moving, but it could be done. Sometimes a good half-minute of grunting and puffing was required before the right combination of leg and back muscles was discovered and the cart consented to move an inch or two. A slight difference in body English made all the difference between success and failure. But once that inch was yielded, there could be no turning back or reconsideration of proper courses. Consistent brute force was the only way to prevent another such monumental struggle, and one simply kept moving, careening dangerously through narrow spaces between machines, people, and other carts, making a sharp turn into the elevator, giving a monumental push to get it over the little space between elevator and floor, and then pulling back for all you were worth, like a jet pilot reversing his engines as he hits the runway, in order to avoid crashing into the elevator's rear wall.

The elevator was completely open on the two sides from which it could be loaded and was barely large enough for a fully loaded cart. As a consequence, you had to be particularly careful to make sure that something wasn't sticking a little too far off the cart after loading it on the elevator. Otherwise it was quite possible that it would catch the wall as the elevator moved. The resulting effect might not only destroy the elevator but also tip several thousand pounds of wood into your lap as you rode along with it, a mess you would never have the opportunity to clean up.

As Parsons had earlier indicated with his customary understatement, the lanyard with which the elevator was stopped and started did indeed take "some getting used to." The distance between stop and start on the cable was very small, and you could be traveling downward toward the cellar floor, give a little tug on the lanyard with the idea of stopping there, but find that the tug was interpreted by the elevator as an order to go back upstairs without bothering to stop at all. Whereupon you might reply by giving a little tug in the opposite direction to get the machine to head back down, but it would decide that you meant it to stop right there between floors.

Meanwhile, the entire contraption would be heaving, bouncing, and shaking from the strain of indecision, and causing you to cast anxious glances upward at the steel cables that were being made to absorb this punishment, and by which the elevator and—literally—your life were now suspended. In such circumstances, it was easy to forget which way you wanted to pull on the lanyard, and as often as not you started back upstairs to the point from which your odyssey had begun. As your eyes cleared the floorboards, and the main floor came into view, you would be greeted by the simultaneously mystified stares of those laboring there, trying to figure out what you hoped to prove by this display of imbecility. Eventually, I got "used" to the elevator by getting it to ride down by itself, while I used the stairs. It was no surprise to me that "there aren't too many of this type of lift around anymore."

The mill's cellar held the enormous band saw to which Ross had been chained, a very old and substantial planing machine, the mill's steam boiler, a variety of electric motors and other odd machinery no longer in use, the toilet, a space for the mill's truck, and a large, open area reserved for the mill's carts. In all, the mill owned about forty carts. Some were stored out in the shed, some were scattered about the main floor, but the greatest number were to be found in the cellar.

The proportion of full to empty carts constantly changed, and by this proportion it was possible to get an accurate idea of the mill's inventory of products.

Except for the clipboard on which he recorded the stock of logs lying in the mill's yard, Parsons' office revealed absolutely no record of inventory. Such matters seemed to be carried in the old man's head, aided only by a little notepad that he kept in his shirt pocket and upon which he occasionally made the briefest of notations. Considering the large number of different items involved, such business practices astounded and mystified me, until I realized that the carts themselves provided him with the means for conducting his inventory. Long ago he had worked out how much of a given product at a given stage of production was required to make up a full cart. Thus he could tell you that a cart fully loaded with fifty-four-inch boards fresh off the headsaw would convert into approximately half-a-cart of finished cane dowels, which when bundled should make thirty bundles of fifty, or fifteen hundred dowels. Parsons could make a similar series of conversions for every product at every stage in its production.

When he needed to know details of his inventory, Parsons simply had to count carts and make the appropriate conversion. This was the key to his strategy for figuring out how much of what the mill would produce, as well as when it would produce it, in order to meet orders efficiently. The mill's carts functioned together as a kind of giant abacus, on which the continuous equation of production was constantly being balanced and rebalanced.

The Ripsaw

21

The mill's ripsaw was a very small and primitive machine, hardly worth the effort of a glance. But aside from the few products turned out on the band saw, every one of the thousands and thousands of items that the mill produced was fed through this single machine. Here boards of all lengths and thickness were ripped into the smaller pieces that would be further reduced into dowels or left as they were. This was a kind of final sawyering and involved the same sorts of judgments as did that of the log chopper or head sawyer. Yet the relative scale of things was dramatically different because a single board was now to be reduced many times, and the pace of work at this machine had to be very fast.

The machine itself looked to have been knocked together almost entirely from spare parts, more a product of evolution than of conscious design. About waist high and three feet long, it was a very narrow little machine that resembled a kind of half-scale ironing board made up from the oddest assortment of junkyard refuse. Of course as an ironing board it would have been a dismal failure because no proper housekeeper would have such an abomination in the house. But as a ripsaw, it functioned like a miracle of the highest technology. Its essential feature lay in the coupling of a very large and powerful electric motor to a tiny six-inch saw blade, so arranged to spin very, very, fast. The result was an innocent-looking thing capable of neatly ripping through a thick piece of white ash as if it were nothing more substantial than a cake of soap.

Though by no means as deadly as many of the mill's other machines, operating the ripsaw demanded a special kind of discipline. Boards were fed through rapidly and continuously, and the operator had to stay very alert. A minor lapse in concentration could cost a finger with little more than a quiet *zzzzip* in return.

This was probably the reason behind Parsons' reluctance to allow anyone besides himself to operate it. Young Craig had actually campaigned for the position, and at one point in his foolish enthusiasm he even offered to stay after work in order to learn how to operate the thing. But there could be no doubt that Parsons had made as much note of Craig's careless work habits as I had and probably did not treasure responsibility for the maiming of such a nice, clean-cut young man.

Unfortunately, Parsons' monopolization of this machine tended to slow the entire mill's pace to a crawl. Obviously he could not operate the headsaw and the ripsaw at the same time, and this meant that the mill's pace could only operate in fits and starts as he switched from one machine to another. But arrival of the winter logs and hiring the new men made it clear that he intended to pick up the pace, and this meant that someone else had to operate the ripsaw.

According to Charlie, the character who had operated the ripsaw in years past was somewhat of a local legend. A born-again Christian who didn't smoke, drink, swear, or indulge in birth control but who could work like the devil himself. He was a "talk-it-right-up kinda fella," as Charlie put it. Always cheerful, never seeming to suffer under Parsons' barbs, he'd been in Parsons' employ for seven years, and, Charlie continued, "There wasn't anything Howard didn't know about the mill. Knew some things even Parsons didn't know."

Parsons once scolded me for turning the blower system off for the ten minutes of morning break. "We don't do that," he had pronounced with his customary imperiousness. The reason was that apparently good old Howard had calculated the current draw on every machine in the mill. It takes more juice to start a machine than to run one, and Howard had figured the amount of time a given machine would have to be shut down before it became worthwhile from an economic point of view. In the case of the blower, it took longer than the ten minutes of break. Such a calculation had never occurred to me, and I acted as would the average employee, thinking that our ten minutes off would be a lot more pleasant without the substantial noise of the blower as a background. It had probably never occurred to the fastidious Parsons that economic gain could be had by sitting through this maelstrom. But it occurred to Howard, and he had followed the logical consequences of his faith to their proper conclusion. It would have been "dishonest" to knowingly allow the boss to follow such wasteful practices, and so it became Howard's "moral" duty to apprise him of the situation.

Naturally, Howard was Parsons' dream come true: hardworking, cheerful, subservient when necessary, and apparently a mechanical genius. His ability on the ripsaw was legendary, and his workaholism had earned him a permanent place in that most exclusive of districts, Parsons' heart. When it came time for Howard to buy a house, Parsons put up the down payment. This was not sentimental largesse on the old man's part, for here he had captured a rare bird indeed, and he aimed to keep him. Good workers were a scarce commodity, what with all these uppity unions and such, and it was just about impossible to find anybody willing to stay in a job like this for more than a year or two.

The outlook on Howard looked good. But after six-and-a-half years of pushing boards through the ripsaw, the muscles around Howard's heart became inflamed, and the doctors told him that if he wanted to live he'd better rest up a while. Word of his condition spread, and with his reputation for hard work and mechanical genius he was offered what Charlie called a "honey of a job" installing dairy equipment for the local agricultural supply cooperative. Naturally everyone said that Howard deserved his good fortune, and nobody dared be jealous. For working so hard and being so completely honest, he had been justly rewarded with work that paid well and befitted his talents.

Fortunately for Howard, his medical condition had not required extensive hospitalization. If it had, and he'd relied on Parsons' health insurance, he would have been bankrupted. The Parsons plan of medical benefits came in the form of a decaying poster on the office door. It displayed pictures of the four food groups and read: "The Best Health Insurance Is A Balanced Diet."

To be fair, Parsons was concerned about safety in the mill, and if he observed any practice that appeared to be particularly foolish or dangerous he took immediate action. But mostly, he viewed health and safety in the same way that he viewed personal success; it was a matter of personal will. After all, he was seventy years old and had never been sick a day in his life. Howard's condition had shaken his confidence a bit. Poor diet and questionable practices at work were not Howard's weaknesses, and it was inescapable that the ripsaw was responsible for Howard's ill health.

Thus the born-again Christian's martyrdom became the impetus for Parsons to take a tentative step into the twentieth century. He allowed himself a tax write-off and bought a fully automated, self-feeding, Japanese-made ripsaw. A big block of cast steel, painted with a slick green enamel, equipped with sterile-looking buttons and jeweled indicator lights, it arrived out of the blue one day, along with a boisterous crew of riggers to install it.

The rigger's art, which no doubt found its origin in the construction of the pyramids, does not seem to have changed all that much over the years. Always a labor-intensive occupation, in its more modern manifestation it seems to involve the use of approximately five times the number of men actually required to perform a given job. They casually stand around scratching their heads and pass witticisms back and forth, as they carefully determine the most effective combination of rollers, jacks, wedges, and ropes to move an immovable object. It seemed the ideal occupation to me, since it looked like hard work was considered absolutely unnecessary. Except for the absence of refreshment, the atmosphere could easily have been mistaken for that of the corner bar.

Parsons seemed both annoyed and amused at this spectacle of collective inertia. "Useless bastards," he mumbled at one point, a smile playing upon his lip. Their work habits were not of special concern to him though; they belonged to a local construction firm, and a fixed fee was to be paid for their service, no matter what their efficiency. But after a while, the old man decided that enough was enough and that perhaps these men were too much of a disruptive influence on his own employees. He started clucking around them like an old mother hen, worrying every move they made. They responded in a good-natured sort of way but essentially told him to mind his own damn business and started to make irreverent little cracks about him when his back was turned. These generally consisted of two-word constructions, usually beginning with 'old' and ending with variations such as 'geezer,' 'coot,' 'fart,' 'skinflint,' and 'poop,' all of which came drifting over to where I was hard at work. Nevertheless, these pranksters did seem to know what they were doing. No sooner did they decide they'd had enough socializing and that all systems were go than that solid steel casting of a machine glided into place as though it had been preordained and prophesied in some ancient book of scripture.

In the meantime, I had been assigned to trim a phenomenal number of dowels, and was racing like a madman to get through them and onto something a little more leisurely. This is how I am, finding myself best off when I can get through unpleasantness as soon as possible. But when Parsons had slipped downstairs for a few minutes, one of the boisterous crew, who looked to be a dead ringer for Glenn Ford, asked me in a brotherly sort of way if I was getting paid piece rate. When I said "no," he went into momentary shock before turning to his buddies with the unmistakable expression of one who has just seen the picture-perfect illustration of a fool at work. Soon thereafter, their wisecracks were directed at me.

"What the hell do they know?" I thought to myself. It wasn't as if I spent all my time doing this kind of work. I just wanted to get through it. And as if to prove my point, I actually pressed my pace faster and finished in record time. After all, a person had to take some pride in his work, no matter how degrading it might seem to others. But obviously, this was a rather foolish notion with which these types had long ago parted company. Jesus, I thought, anyone who looks that much like Glenn Ford ought to have more pride than that. And oddly enough, for the briefest moment, I felt a certain loyalty to my boss. Who were these guys to come in here and make fools of us all?

As Parsons experimented with his latest acquisition, it was obvious that he did so with utmost distaste. The old ripsaw had required a careful and controlled feed, which the old man achieved by laying his palms flat on the board and walking them hand over hand in a ritual movement that was both an efficient and a safe way to push a board through the blade. But the self-feeding feature of the new machine caused it to snatch the boards away with a force that caused Parsons to lift his hands in surprise, dismayed as the saw worked its own efficient will.

A solid steel box five feet in height, the new machine consisted of a small belt traveling across a flat table. An overhead arm contained a set of spring-loaded rollers that forced the boards down onto the belt, and also held the murderously spinning blade. The overall effect was that of an oversized and solidly indestructible sewing machine. Its very structure said a firm "no" to any notion of personal modification, and so, when not looking dismayed, Parsons would fuss and fudge over its few adjustable features to get it to perform as he thought it should.

But this new machine was representative of its age and as such was not designed for easy customization. It had definitely not evolved as had the old ripsaw but was carefully engineered to perform a large variety of functions, of which the operations at Parsons' mill were just a part. Small woodshop production is going much the way that small farming is going, and for much the same reason. Increased efficiency requires a reduction in the labor component in favor of more advanced, efficient, and expensive machines. Only the largest operations can afford customized machinery under these conditions, so it is inevitable that old men like Parsons are going to be wistful when a machine starts to take their prerogatives away. They know that such machines may be more productive, but they also know that they will never do the job to the same standard of quality.

In a sense, Parsons' mill was twenty-five years behind the times. Other profitable mills in the area had begun out of the same simple machinery and processes as had Parsons'. But they had capitalized and modernized, greatly increasing the volume of the work they performed. Their headsaws were fully automated, and their head sawyers sat in wire mesh cages pushing buttons that ran a machine at twice the rate of Parsons'. Obviously a man like Parsons could not compete with such operations, and had made a conscious decision not to. If Parsons had survived, it was because he desperately held on to that small corner of the market in which quality could still fetch a higher price. That corner was getting smaller and smaller these days, and just to hold on to his share of it Parsons was beginning to resort to the capitalized efficiencies of his mainstream competitors. As others cornered the market, the market cornered Parsons.

So Parsons gave up on the ripsaw and stuck to the headsaw, whose processes remained unchanged. He had found someone to run that new saw anyway: a smart young fella who seemed to like hard work. And though he was a bit wild and rebellious, that was a burden worth bearing. After all, what millhand lived that old Parsons couldn't break if he put his mind to it? So he gave the saw to me. It was a new responsibility, and I knew it. Now my work was going to control a whole level of quality at the mill, and I was going to be a Sawyer. Beyond that, a whole series of techniques associated with working a new machine were going to be left up to me to devise. The "right" to run this machine was also going to elevate me to a unique status amongst Parsons' employees, for I was going to require an assistant.

Denny   22

Denny arrived in midweek. One morning as we trudged rag-
gedly into the mill, there he sat on an upturned box, blond
and rosy-cheeked and sporting a blue farmer's cap. As usual, Parsons was not in the mood for introductions, so we were simply put
to work while he took our newest member in hand. As the farmboy stood up to work, it became apparent that we had a true muscle man in our presence. A formidable anatomic challenge to Ray's
rather comic dominance, this specimen was solid beef from head to
toe and looked as if he might have been raised on the same regi-
men as his family's livestock.

Dour to the extreme, Denny stared fixedly ahead with a soft but
penetrating odor of American-Gothic about him that made me feel
instantly sinful. Given this staunchly conservative air, I did not see
how he could ever come to approve of the rest of us: I with my beard
and glasses, Charlie with his living embodiment of a hangover, Ray
with his incessant and meandering chatter, and Jerry, so distant and
separate from everyone else as to hardly figure into matters at all.
Indeed, for several days Denny remained aloof and had me convinced
that he must be fervently occupying his mind with memorized passages
from the good book.

At our customary nine o'clock break, while the rest of us were busy
picking out something to eat from our lunches, Denny did not eat. He
just sat there on an upturned box immediately outside the door to
Parsons' office, impassive as a eunuch. By the third day of this routine,
Parsons began to take a sort of slight, imperial interest in him. He had
noticed that Denny never ate at break, and this intrigued him. Parsons
himself never stopped for break, and Denny's abstinence looked promising. "Never eat in the fields, do you?" He inquired rhetorically.
Denny shook his head in the negative. This seemed to please Parsons

even more. It didn't look like he'd be getting much back talk from this one. "Well," Parsons continued, "you work hard, save your money, and buy the things you want." Parsons sounded as if he'd just pronounced the Holy Trinity, and Denny nodded solidly in the affirmative, while a broad, satisfied smile spread across the old man's face. By my lights, that smile was a sinister one, but there could be no denying the almost holy seriousness of purpose that seemed to surround this powerful young man.

I had made several attempts to communicate with Denny, but having failed to elicit much more than a nod or two, I settled for mere observation. As a specimen, he was unmatched by almost anything I'd seen before. From a distance he appeared short, but this was mere illusion wrought by the thickness of his trunk and legs. There was not an ounce of fat upon him, but I could make out nothing that resembled a neck or a waist, as the sheer bulk of his musculature eliminated these features. His hair was straight, blond, and longish and his eyes had a kind of crystal-clear blueness that gave them a slightly startling quality of penetration. His skin was hairless, and a pure ivory color that was offset by bright, rosy cheeks. All of which added to the effect of his middle-American godlike stature and which inevitably led me to a depressing self-appraisal of my obvious genetic deficiencies.

But after a time, Denny's demeanor began to soften a bit, and his features seemed a little less imposing. When addressed, he began to nod with increasing frequency, and every so often a slight tremor could be seen playing about his lips, as somewhere the epicenter of a smile quaked within him. It was difficult, after all, to spend much time in Parsons' mill without finding at least some humor in the proceedings there. Now that Ray had some physical competition, his antics took on a new tenor, as he began to regale us with stories meant to convey the impression that he was a man of the world whose sexual appetites knew no bounds. Taken together with Charlie's comic inexactitude as to time and place on a Monday morning and my own overearnest efforts to meet the increasingly eccentric demands of Parsons, the place often produced a fine theater of the absurd.

It was not long after Denny's arrival that I found myself at bureaucratic cross-purposes with the Vermont Department of Motor Vehicles. It seems that they had sent me a pair of license plates with one set of numbers on them and a registration certificate with quite a different set of numbers. This would not do, since policemen are not particularly known for their understanding when it comes to discrepancies of this sort, and I set about to rectify the problem immediately.

Like many governmental agencies, the Motor Vehicle Department maintained hours at its own convenience, which meant that most of its customers had to call from work. I did precisely this and got a very nice young woman on the other end of the line who explained that I was not to worry. If I didn't hear from her within the next fifteen minutes, I was to assume that all was well and my corrected registration was in the mail. The allotted fifteen minutes passed without incident, and so I assumed all was well and went outside to help Charlie with some particularly cumbersome logs.

An hour or so later, I was accosted by Parsons, who said with a very peculiar smile, "Your friend *Becky* is on the phone."

"Becky?" I was mystified. But Parsons' smile merely widened.

"*You* know," he said, "your friend *Becky*." I was a little perturbed now, trying to remember if I knew anybody named Becky. I did know a 'Becca once, but the state of our relations made it highly unlikely that she would be calling me at work.

"Honestly Henry, I don't know anybody named Becky!" Parsons' smile was by now positively lascivious as he gave me a kind of knowing look, as if to say, sure you don't!

"Well," he clucked like a nosy old gossip, "she *says* she's from the Motor Vehicle Department."

"Oh! Oh! Yeah, my registration."

Parsons continued to smile knowingly as I stepped past him into the office in order to pick up the waiting phone.

"Hello?"

"Hello. Is this Tim?"

"Yes."

"Was that your boss I just talked to?"

"Well yeah, I think so."

"Well he just gave me the most incredible talking-to!"

"Yeah, that sounds like my boss. What'd he say?"

"He said that I ought to be ashamed of myself calling you at work like this, and didn't I know that 'Tim is a married man,' and if I didn't stop messing around with you he'd tell your wife about me!"

"He did?"

"Yeah!"

"Oh god! I'm sorry. You have to understand, my boss is a little eccentric."

"Well, I expect so." she replied.

Three days later, my registration arrived intact, though at clear cost to my reputation. Still, I had to admit that Parsons was onto something there because she did have an awfully sweet voice.

A Third Sawyer   23

A s much as I hated to ascribe rationality to Parsons' motivations, it now became clear to me that the man operated with considerably more foresight than I had first given him credit for. When in my first week he had assigned me all those tens of thousands of dowels to trim and sort, it had not merely served as a form of initiation in order to see whether or not I could "take it" but also as a form of apprenticeship to the ripsaw. Do anything ten thousand times, and you are bound to get pretty adept at it; stare at the grain of enough dowel rod, and you are bound to get an idea of what it's supposed to look like. This was the essential prerequisite for the ripsawyer's job. He had to know what kind of grain was needed for the product at hand and how to produce it in thousands and thousands of pieces. Essentially he was the mill's third sawyer, and like Charlie the log chopper and Parsons the head sawyer he too had the sawyer's problem of maximizing the yield from a quantity of wood while maintaining a consistent standard of quality.

The difference between the skills required of the mill's three sawyers was a relative matter. When Charlie made a crosscut, he did so on the basis of a judgment that could waste a great deal of wood if incorrect. But he had the fewest cuts to make and therefore the most time to consider them. Parsons was in the middle and had to make five to ten times as many cuts. But if he decided that he'd made a mistake after the first pass on a particular length of log, he could easily adopt a new cutting strategy to suit what he saw in the log, and his initial error would not prove particularly costly. In my case, it was easiest of all to see the grain of the wood I was cutting. Unlike Charlie and Parsons, I had it right there in front of me on the boards I received, and there was little guesswork involved. But by the same token, I was making between five and ten times the number of cuts as Parsons and somewhere between twenty-five and a hundred times the number of cuts as Charlie was making. To keep up I had to work faster by that same proportion.

The imperturbable Denny was to be my assistant, and this filled me with nearly as much apprehension as did the fact that I was going to have to conquer the machine itself. The prospect of working directly opposite and under the stolid gaze of this impenetrable young Hercules was enough to make the hands of a surgeon shake. But as usual in these matters, it turned out that my imagination had gotten the better of me. If anything, Denny proved to be the ideal assistant. His job was simply to stand at the receiving end of the saw, along with two empty carts on either side of him. He would load one cart with usable blanks, later to be turned into dowels, while loading the second cart with scrap to be sold as firewood.

The ripsaw was now entirely our machine, and while the results of our work were going to be held up to Parsons' merciless scrutiny, our methods for producing that work were to be entirely our own. Here was a place in the mill where Parsons couldn't tell us what was right or wrong, because he didn't know. He had ceded the machine to us, and that was some personal advancement in itself. The saw's self-feeding feature meant that I wasn't going to have to endanger my hands by pushing each board all the way through the blade. It was simply a matter of setting a board on at the right angle, giving it a little shove, and letting the machine pull it straight through. No matter how you set the thing, once you let it go it would give you a perfectly straight cut.

This meant that I could start a board through, and by the time Denny had got hold of it at the other end, I would have started a second board through. In this way, the two of us worked out a kind of simple juggling act in which he'd be throwing a board back at me as I was feeding one toward him. And by this innovation, we were able to at least double the rate of production over the old ripsaw, which used to see a single board passed methodically back and forth until it had been entirely sliced up before moving on to the next board.

In a matter of a day or two, Denny and I had managed to establish an efficient rhythm. The high-pitched *zzzzip* of the ripsaw working its will and the flat smack of the board that Denny tossed back at me formed a kind of violent counterpoint whose pace could be raised and lowered to suit the mood. It had a lot of the feel of a good solid game of catch using hardballs and mitts; the rhythm's the thing, but the main love is throwing something dangerous at your partner's head and protecting yourself from the return. For Denny there was a constant juggling act: blanks to be neatly stacked, scrap to be separated, boards to be thrown back my way. For me there was the constant fixed stare at the grain that each board presented me.

Here I'd set the board moving through the blade at the angle that best fit the curve of the grain; the machine grabbed the board and it took possession of it, and the cut was set. Next board: different curve, different angle. First board back: did I get it right? If yes, just feed it straight through again. Second board is thrown back at me: did I get it right? No: readjust the angle of feed. First board is back: feed it straight through. Another couple of cuts and I can see that I will have to readjust its angle again because the grain changes completely in the board's middle. Second board is back again. . . . This is how it would go, hour after hour, until judgments became automatic, and I too lived as any sawyer does, within the trees we were cutting.

In keeping with their function as the measuring cups of the mill's production, Parsons had figured there ought to be an equilibrium between the two carts Denny and I loaded up. So there had to be one cart of scrap for every cart of usable wood. If you think about it, this meant that nearly half the volume of the wood that came to me was being thrown off the production line, which for the mainstream of the lumber business would be wholly unacceptable. But Parsons' was a quality shop, and the old man watched the ratio between those two carts like a hawk. Anytime Denny and I produced more scrap than product, Parsons began to get the idea that I was throwing out good wood and trying to ruin his profitability. But anytime we worked the ratio in favor of the product cart, he would get the notion that we were producing inferior goods and trying to ruin his reputation. Naturally this put a person between a rock and a hard place, which is exactly where Parsons liked to have you. It wasn't exactly his way to elucidate what you might be doing wrong. He preferred to keep you hovering somewhere in midair with a constant sense of queasy uncertainty. If he wasn't positively ranting over some trivial error or other, then you could be pretty sure that your crimes, whatever they might be, were of a minor nature.

But the old man's mood swings were so rapid and unpredictable that it was often difficult to tell exactly where you stood. Sometimes you would be working merrily along, when Parsons would come storming

100

out from some hidden ambush and start furiously pawing through your cart of finished work. You would try to continue calmly as this was happening, but this could only be a sorry front, since a cascade of fire and brimstone seemed imminent. Like the hornet that flies directly at you, circles your head a few times, and then takes off, Parsons usually left you alone, wondering what had led to so aggressive an examination. Apparently the man believed in the fear principle, and his thinking probably centered around the phrase, "Keep 'em on their toes."

But by and large, Parsons seemed quite pleased with our progress. Of course he himself did not give us any indication of this fact. Instead we learned of our progress from Charlie, who was spending a lot of time outside helping Jerry wash logs in those days. "You fellas must be doing something right in there. Why when Henry comes out to talk to us, why . . . he's downright polite!"

Naturally it was nice to feel that the boss was pleased with you because it meant that maybe he'd stay off your back for a while. But with Parsons there was no resting on your laurels. We'd proved our worth to him, but that didn't mean we deserved any special privileges. Why yes, he'd given me a dollar raise spread out over the course of the last couple of months, but don't be getting any special ideas. Sure you'd figured out how to run that new saw, but you didn't have any ownership over that thing; it belonged to Parsons' mill now. The old man was still going to make his beelines at your work, and while he might be restraining his worst instincts, he could still be heard to mumble, "Well I guess these two need a tune-up." And by that it was clear that an ass-kicking was in order.

Maybe Parsons thought I was getting cocky, or maybe he thought I wasn't giving Denny enough credit, or maybe for no reason whatever, but one day out of the blue he decided to take Denny and make him his assistant and gave me Charlie in his stead. It was at this point that I discovered something essential about this soon-to-be-aging millhand. His easy-going nature was not a product of laziness. His nature was willful, and he stubbornly refused to adapt to my pace. He didn't return boards to me with the crisp snap that Denny seemed to enjoy but instead brought his naturally contemplative air to bear upon every board passed through his hands. He was just passing his hours there, it seemed, and there was no need to rush. I was intimidated by Charlie's seniority and didn't really feel that I had the right to force my pace upon this good man. So our pace slowed to about half of what it had been with Denny and stayed that way for an hour or so. It was one of

101

the longest and most torturous hours of my life. I was getting bored to death with this pace, and now with more time to consider the grain in each board, they actually seemed to be coming out worse.

I tried to increase the pace slowly, thinking that it might improve my mood a bit. But Charlie stubbornly resisted any alteration and made it clear that we were going to work at his pace, not mine. This got me mad, and as much as I hate to admit it, I did exactly what Parsons would have done, and victimized him. Out of nowhere I started to feed board after board through the saw as rapidly as I could manage, and poor Charlie started to drown. He dropped boards, scrap, blanks, and they started clattering across the floor so that the entire mill could hear it. The tactic worked, as Charlie momentarily picked the pace back up. But he was a wily devil and seemed determined to teach me a thing or two by taking any opportunity he could find to slow me down. And so the pace constantly seesawed back and forth, me trying to speed things up to my crazed rate, Charlie working to keep me down to his. He wasn't in a hurry to get anywhere; just where the hell did I think I was rushing off to?

In the meantime, Denny was not working out well as Parsons' assistant. He was too slow on his feet. Like a baseball slugger, his ability came from massive upper body strength, rooted in place. Parsons began to get extremely angry with him and started to insult him. I couldn't hear what the old man was saying, but could well imagine because Denny was obviously on the verge of tears. His size made you forget that he was still very young, a boy in a man's body, and it took me aback to see him in such a state. The next day, I got Denny back, but the ever-present blue cap with the feed company logo was gone. It was replaced with a red cap which advertised an entity known as the Winn Corporation, and stated: "I am a Winn-er." As they say, he was a good kid.

The Doweler

24

The doweling machine, which Mrs. Parsons had so cheerfully characterized as her husband's favorite, as if it were some infinitely charming offspring, came after the ripsaw in the mill's line of production. Its particular miracle was that you could feed a square blank of hardwood in at one end, and within a second or two a perfectly formed dowel popped out at the other end. Unlike the preceding saws, the doweler required virtually no judgment to operate. It was simply a matter of standing before it with a pile of blanks on the left and placing one blank after another between a pair of steadily rotating rollers. The rollers grabbed them and forced them without mercy through a set of cutting knives in the machine's interior.

It demanded some basic coordination, since the operator was supposed to feed blanks in rapid succession, butting one up against another. With shorter dowels the feed became quite rapid, and keeping up meant staying alert. The things could be fed in right or wrong, but there was no in-between. If you had done it right, the blanks fed through smoothly, satisfyingly, making a comical, calliope-like whistle as they exited the machine. If you had fed the thing wrong, jamming a blank in at some grossly acute angle, the machine would demonstrate a savage power to demolish the leading half of the blank before it became entirely jammed. Then it had to be carefully disassembled in order to extricate the remains.

Thus the real skill was not in running the machine but in setting it up. Any machine that takes an element of skill away from its operator has got to compensate through some subtlety in its interior. The doweler's intestines were a solid mass of cast gears, bearings, and weighted cutting knives. The thing was virtually indestructible. But for all their compact massiveness, the machine's workings were precise and adjustable and called for some artful tuning if they were to run just as they should. It was probably this contradictory aspect of the thing that

103

so endeared it to Parsons. Like the old man himself, the machine was seasoned, tough, and full of peculiarities.

Outside of defects in the grain, every fault in a dowel was traceable to some subtle maladjustment of the doweler. Sometimes a dowel would come out of the machine with a slight roughness to it, and Parsons, holding it up to the light, or rubbing his fingers along its surface, would say, "Got your rollers adjusted wrong." A couple turns on a handle would produce the needed cure. Thinking myself acquainted with the machine's peculiarities, I would then make the same adjustment the next time I believed I espied the same fault. But this time my "adjustment" would only serve to make matters worse, and I had to appeal to the mill's highest court. "No, no!" he'd say. "It's your cutting knives that need adjustment." The knives would be duly adjusted by Parsons, and the fault disappeared.

Soon enough some third fault, which seemed intimately related to the first two, would make its appearance. But this time the master would declare "It's your rate of feed that's in need of adjustment now." Shortly thereafter, the original fault would reappear, and convince me that it was something new and original due to its obvious similarity to all the other faults which the machine produced. Of course this only made the old man mad, and he'd say, "I already showed you how to adjust for that one!" "Oh yeah. Right," I'd respond sheepishly, all the while wondering exactly which of the three he meant.

Inevitably some fourth maladjustment would make its presence known. Only this time, being quite confident that I had learned my lesson, I would recklessly identify it as something I'd already been shown and aimlessly adjust the machine in order to compensate for it. Wrong as usual. I would be informed, "Your knives are dull, better take them out and replace them with some sharp ones." This I would do, but in the meantime I was in a nervous state over how I was going to compensate for all the adjustments I had made under the false impression that I had known what I was doing. Such is the nature of an amateur tune-up; it is an irrational maze that only the very lucky, or highly talented, negotiates with success.

The rollers feeding blanks through the cutting knives were four in number. Every time you altered the diameter of the dowels, you had also to remove those four rollers from the machine and replace them with a different set. There were ten such sets, each corresponding to a particular dowel dimension. On one occasion Parsons asked me to "change the doweler over to thirteen-sixteenths."

"How do I do that?"

Look of annoyance. "You'll find the rollers marked for fifteen-sixteenths over in the cabinet there."

I immediately headed over to the cabinet that contained the forty or so rollers, but a sudden thought stopped me dead in my tracks. Why would he want me to install rollers marked for fifteen-sixteenths, when I was supposed to be making thirteen-sixteenths inch dowels? But by this time I had learned enough about Parsons to know that as a man of few words he usually meant exactly what he said. I did as I was told. Unfortunately, as I pulled roller after roller from the cabinet in question, straining to make out the obscure hieroglyphs stamped upon them, nothing appeared that resembled either fifteen-sixteenths or thirteen-sixteenths. Again over to Parsons I went and informed him of the difficulty. His face took on an all too familiar, pained, deity-imploring expression by which it was understood that he had suffered many such fools before and expected many more to come his way in the future. He paced over to the cabinet and almost instantly, without reference to the numbers stamped on them, picked out a set of rollers, handed them to me with a look of disdain, and stalked off. I greedily searched for the markings that I had somehow managed to miss.

"Hey wait a minute!" I said aloud to myself. "I saw these, they say seven-eighths!" Was he sure? But by now, he was busy at the headsaw, and I knew much better than to disturb him again. If they were wrong, then it would be his fault.

Of course the rollers he had handed me were just the right ones and worked perfectly. It turned out that in certain cases you could substitute one size roller for another, although you couldn't always do so. Despite the presence of numbers on the rollers, you could not rely on them to help you identify the correct set. You knew the roller by sight or you didn't, but in either case the identifying numbers were practically irrelevant.

This characteristic had been applied elsewhere on this machine as well. Proper adjustment of the cutting blades required a set of tiny little blocks that were temporarily and strategically inserted into the machine as a means of calibration. As with the rollers, there was a different block for each diameter of dowel. Some were made of brass, some of aluminum, and some of wood. All were kept in a decrepit old tool box filled to the brim with an odd assortment of wrenches, screwdrivers, nuts, bolts, and several years' accumulation of sawdust. Finding the right block was just another in a long list of exercises that made up Parsons' particular brand of psychological terror.

"They're all marked," he informed me, as if the matter were simplicity itself. Strictly speaking, the old man's assertion was quite correct. They *were* all marked. But just like the rollers, not all the measurements were represented. Even worse was the fact that the same identifying number could be found on blocks of wildly different dimension. In some instances I could find no block with which to calibrate the machine, and in other instances I could find three. In the end, with Parsons' kindly assistance, I realized that there was absolutely no relation whatsoever between the numbers inscribed on the blocks and the size of dowel for which they were supposed to calibrate the machine.

Sometimes I would get lucky and was able to figure out which block I was supposed to use. As most people know, a block has six sides to it, but these ones weren't exactly even all around, so the proper orientation for adjustment wasn't always clear. So once again, I had to risk the damnation of my soul by asking for advice. And then, having ascertained the exact orientation of the exact block for the exact diameter of dowel, the thing still wouldn't run right, and Parsons still had to come back and demonstrate the procedure. You see even if Parsons had made it easy by clearly and unmistakably identifying which roller and which calibrating block went with which diameter dowel, tuning the doweler also demanded the right "touch."

Thus, while the techniques for adjusting the machine appeared to have been organized along simple and rational lines, this was merely a perverse illusion. The doweler was in fact wholly irrational in its behavior: tough and precisely consistent when working well; ornery, eccentric, and almost impossible to understand when not, the doweler was the perfect reflection of its owner. And that's probably why it was his favorite machine.

Ray's Fall

25

The warmer days of fall began to wane. Foliage was at its height, and tourists filled up the valleys with their vans and campers. We began to make a point of eating our lunches outside as much as possible. Good weather would soon be in short supply, and we were less and less choosy about what we found acceptable as a "fine" day. In late summer days, when the average temperature was consistently in the seventies, a drop into the sixties would send us all scurrying inside with fits of shivering. But now that a temperature of forty or forty-five degrees was to be expected in the early morning, a climb into the fifties and the promise of a warm sun saw us all lounging about outside like revelers in a tropical paradise.

Man of habit that he was, Parsons took no notice of the weather at all and always remained in his dusty office with his ear to the radio, garnering the local station's approximation of the news. Jerry continued to sit by himself in his car reading books. Denny disappeared homeward in his sporty hopped-up jeep, which roared and rumbled like a Sherman tank and displayed the improbable message on its bumper: "Beer drinkers get more head." Our farmboy was not so innocent, nor as morally imperturbable, as it had first appeared.

The three "elders," Ray, Charlie, and I, sat upon a log on the deck, spread our lunches around, and held forth on subjects as varied as cars, tourists, the weather, drinking, the ladies, Parsons, and the sad state of the nation's economy. It was usually Ray who dominated these discussions, his mood fed by endless cups of coffee dispensed from an enormous thermos. He was somewhat of a romantic when it came to local culture and enjoyed provincial little stabs at the flatlanders from Connecticut and New York who were then invading with their tourist dollars.

"The wages down there might be seven, eight, nine, dollars an hour, but look at how crazy they are," he said, illustrating their neurosis with a violently feigned quaking of the hand. "It's just crazy down there!" And then, without stopping to gauge his audience, he suddenly changed subjects with a shout.

"Gawd! You wouldn't believe the dog I was with last night! This ever happen to you? I'm in this bar, over in Redmond you know, one of these 'apres ski' joints and this broad sitting next to me at the bar starts rubbing her leg up against me and says. 'Hi, I'm Gloria!' Oh boy," Ray's eyes moved heavenward. "Well, it was kinda dark in there, you know, and so well, *you know*. But this morning I wake up, and I'm going 'where the hell am I?' I look across the pillow at this chick in the daylight . . . what an ugly bitch! I almost threw up!"

This story struck me as being a lot like the one he'd told us about the Golden Gloves boxer. Somehow I couldn't help feeling that I had heard it all before, though I couldn't say exactly where. I suspect that Charlie had a similar feeling, because after Ray had capped his tale, we both turned our heads away in slow disbelief. The fact of the matter was that this was really a kind of macho standard, which, like similar racist standards, was frequently spawned in mens' bars as a means of establishing one's loyalties. The difference was that whereas you could get away with the most outrageous claims about the excesses of non-whites, in the matter of women your audience might have some real knowledge of the subject, and it was necessary to create an air of plausibility. Thus Ray never presumed to convince us that he was any kind of Casanova, but it was important to make it clear that *he got his action*, no matter how sorry it was.

Once again, Ray would shift into high gear and move onto new subjects. "That lift is a piece of crap if I ever seen one, and believe you me, I've seen quite a few. You see how high them log piles are? I tell you, that lift don't want to go that high. What with all that weight up there, she just wants to tip right over. I got to get right up against that pile and just sorta push 'em up and hope they stay. I'm not dropping 'em in place like I should be." Ray paused to slurp at his coffee and look for some sign of our sympathy. The two of us in his audience dutifully stopped eating. I nodded, while Charlie looked up and squinted at the distant log pile as if he were carefully considering the problem.

Ray cleared his throat to continue, and we took this as a sign to resume eating. "It's dangerous as hell piling them up that high!" His voice was turning a bit shrill. "You know what happens when a log pile like that collapses? Well I'll tell you, the roof on that lift won't provide diddly for protection; a couple of them logs rolls back on me and it's *kussschgloomp!*" The image of Ray, squashed like a bug under a collapsed log pile, did not mix well with the digestive processes, so I gave up and put my lunch aside.

He then launched into the subject of the hornets' nests that were to be found among the log piles, and which his work forced him to disturb. This was a favorite subject of his and was so often discussed that it had begun to take on the unsightly shape of an obsession. He seemed convinced that the entire county's hornet population had been apprised of the genocidal acts into which a vindictive Parsons had forced him, and that as a consequence, he was a marked man. Ray's paranoia had so overwhelmed him that on a number of occasions he believed that he was under attack when he clearly wasn't. He'd be sitting calmly munching away at his extensive lunch, when suddenly, and for no apparent reason, he would get up and bolt, and dancing around the yard he'd yell, "Get away from me you little fuckers! Get away!" while the rest of us searched in vain for the whereabouts of the offending insects.

Ray had even gone so far as to complain to Parsons about the hornet situation. But Parsons, never a man open to complaints about working conditions at his plant, said simply: "Hornets? Yea-ahs, they live here." The implication being that Ray only *worked* at the mill and that it was a privilege that could be revoked at any time by Parsons, the hornets, or any other creature that called the place home.

Finally one day, Ray's obsession drove him into a kind of momentary hysteria. A single hornet came zooming toward us, with probable intention of stealing some sugar from one of our soft drinks. Ray started screaming and waving his hands at it. This got me mad, and I spoke the only really angry words I ever ventured against Ray, "Just leave him alone will ya! You're gonna get him really mad!"

"Ah shit!" he cried and retreated to a far corner of the deck, taking his lunch with him. But after a minute or two of sulky silence, his hyperactive nature got the better of him, and he suddenly broke into a boisterous version of the *Vietnam Rag*, Country Joe and the Fish's antiwar anthem of the late sixties. Since I knew the chorus, I joined in. Charlie had never heard the song, which surprised me. I'd played the record many times when I was fourteen or so and thought it hilarious. But of course at that age I'd had no real idea of the awful realities behind it.

"We'd be sitting in some trench," Ray explained, "people were shooting at us, and that song would come on over the radio. So we just sang along. We thought it was funny as hell." And this time, when Ray launched into the chorus, I just listened along with Charlie, who had on the saddest of expressions.

About this time Ray entered into a serious conflict with Parsons, the origin and genesis of which were never entirely clear to me. The matter seemed to have begun offstage, and when it came out in the open it had already ripened. Suffice it to say that an increasing antipathy had developed between Ray and Denny and that this was due to a certain rivalry over which of the two muscle men would remain most in favor with the old man. Clearly Denny was winning the competition, and while the farmboy was a mere "punk" in the retired Sarge's eyes, it had to be admitted that he was a very strong punk.

Ray's bullying nature—always a matter of questionable authenticity—had given way to a kind of sad, hyperactive clownishness.

"War hero!" I heard Parsons sneer behind Ray's back one day.

As his status at the mill declined, Ray's resentment of the place seemed to grow. His complaints about the condition of the forklift were increasingly frequent and bitter. "Listen to that thing, sounds like it's running on two cylinders. Damn thing is pitiful!" Such observations were not well received by Parsons, who maintained a kind of wartime-British, "chin up" attitude about adversity and saw no need to take corrective actions unless a situation seemed a matter of life or death.

Finally one of the big tractor-type tires on the lift went flat, and it cost Parsons a couple of days in lost time and four hundred dollars. As a result Parsons entered into a new phase of his personal cycle of paranoia, becoming absolutely convinced that Ray had deliberately destroyed the old tire. Ray was highly insulted by the implications of Parsons' accusations and walked out on the spot. He failed to show up for the next two days, and on the third day an advertisement appeared on the front page of the local paper calling for a truck driver and lift operator at the mill.

Apparently Ray had been suffering under the delusion that he was indispensable and was just going to take a couple of days off to punish Parsons. But when he saw his own job advertised in the paper that morning, he decided that maybe he had better get on over to the mill to put things right. He came storming into the mill in a panic, catching us by surprise.

"Do I have the job, or don't I?" he cried at Parsons. And Parsons, sounding perversely benign and grandfatherly replied, "I'm awfully sorry Ray, but I'm afraid I just can't use you anymore."

"All right then," Ray whined like a threatening child, "I'm gonna go right on down to the unemployment office." He thought this might have some effect on the old man, who would have to pick up part of the tab for Ray's compensation.

"Well!" sneered Parsons, "that's your right!"

Ray turned on his heels, and with hunched shoulders his little steps carried him quickly and angrily out the door. Charlie and I were the only witnesses to this scene, the others not having arrived yet, and we both turned our backs to it, gazing sadly, fixedly out the window in order to avoid the Sarge's humiliation.

"Certainly made a damn fool of himself, didn't he?" sighed Parsons. We said nothing. The others were arriving, and we shuffled deliberately and slowly to work.

Charlie **26**

"**Y**ou like jazz?" Charlie asked me a couple of days after Ray's final bow. "There's some great jazz gonna be down at Noah's Ark this Saturday." I did like jazz, though I was a bit surprised that this country log chopper had such urbane tastes.

Unfamiliar bars generally make me nervous, and so, probably sounding unnaturally square for someone my age, I inquired after the place's reputation.

"Oh the place is okay! It's my local!"

"Oh, well, in that case. . . . " With such an endorsement, it would have been insulting to refuse.

It was fairly obvious that both Charlie and I were suffering from a mild case of insecurity now that Ray was gone. Despite his raucous eccentricity, the Sarge was an effective foil for the old man, and we gladly suffered—even exploited—him for our own peace of mind. He had been our decoy. But now Charlie and I, having maintained a comfortable independence from one another while Ray was around, saw our interests coalesce as his broad protection slipped away, and we stood naked before the wrath and scorn of that terrible old man.

The following Saturday evening Amy and I cautiously made our way down the long flight of stairs to the cellar dive, famed locally for its hip ambience, and found it appropriately murky, smoky, and noisy. The featured attraction was a handsome black woman of enormous girth, who was belting out "Eight Days A Week" as we entered. She was accompanied by an all-white rock band consisting of five overly enthusiastic, electronically enhanced noisemakers who seemed determined to drown her out at every turn. It was not exactly my idea of jazz, but the singer had impressive power and was doing a remarkable job by simply holding her own against the deluge behind her.

The place was packed, and it took a good few minutes before we were able to spot Charlie, who emerged from a crush of bodies looking somehow shrunken and insignificant. I had been expecting some sort of rousing, cheerful carouse with a fellow worker. But in this environment, he seemed utterly overwhelmed. Draining a mug of beer and tottering unsteadily on his feet, he stared at me for a few seconds before he was struck by a lightning bolt of recognition.

"Tim!" he almost fell over backward from the spitting force of his speech. "Here! Get yourself a beer! Here! Stand here!" The bar was packed three deep, and Charlie maneuvered me roughly to the only open spot. "It's the waitress station, but it's okay, 'cause she's a friend of mine!" The sound of so much drunken good cheer served only to heighten my own sense of sobriety. I managed a weak smile and allowed myself to be pushed along.

I ordered a couple of beers, and threaded one through a tangle of bodies to get it to Amy, who—not having the anchor of the bar itself—was struggling valiantly to hold her own against the ebb and flow of the raucous crowd. Meanwhile, Charlie had disappeared and I began considering the best route of escape from this madhouse. But from my vantage point, I could see that such an effort would have called for the kind of physically aggressive insistence that requires fortification, and so for the moment I satisfied myself with several long drafts of beer. But no sooner had I resigned myself to this fate than a tall young woman in a tight-fitting dress emerged from the crowd and, neatly blocking my wife with her backside, sidled up to me and pushed her hip into mine. Unsure of her intent, I shifted sideways a bit in order to relieve the pressure, only to find it immediately and deliberately renewed. Subsequent defensive maneuvers on my part were similarly ineffective, and the two of us, this unknown woman and I, were soon out of room in which to pursue our peculiar little dance. Finally I shot this tall temptress as effective a look of disdain as I could manage under the circumstances and was relieved to spot Charlie across the room, tussling with a group of tourists over the possession of an open table. I rushed over to lend assistance, and the dual apparition of two "locals," each desperate for his own reason, was apparently sufficient to drive these flatlanders away.

The three of us sat down, and Charlie, yelling and spitting out the name of his waitress friend, ordered us a round of beers. By now the music was grinding to a halt, and Charlie began to propagandize Amy. "Why that old son of a bitch! He's got himself the smartest hand he's ever had right here." He grabbed at my arm. "He just picks and picks and picks at his brain, and what does he give in return? Nothing! That's what!" He paused to take a gulp of beer, and as if drinking in the thought itself a second wave of anger seemed to overwhelm him. "Now you listen to me! I want to tell you something! If this husband of yours ever comes home from work and says, 'I got fired,' don't you give him any grief. You hear me? 'Cause this husband of yours takes more grief from that old man than any of us!" Of course it wasn't exactly Amy's way to give me grief in these matters, and she nodded and smiled as if to reassure Charlie by saying, "Don't worry, I won't."

Flattered as I was by Charlie's concern for our domestic peace, it was causing me increasing embarrassment. Charlie's voice was no longer lost in the wilderness of rock music from which it had been launched. The band had stopped playing, but Charlie boomed on as before and now threatened to become the object of the entire bar's attention. Despite the cacophony of drunken bar talk roaring around us, heads turned in our direction as Charlie held forth, and I was quite relieved to find him temporarily distracted by the discovery that his beer mug was empty. He waved over his waitress friend, who arrived at our table fixing Charlie with the sainted smile of a nun ministering to the needy. "'Nother round!" he cried. But with motherly concern, she cast an unmistakably suspicious glance in my direction. I immediately reached for my wallet, wishing to make it clear that I was not one to take advantage of a drunk. But Charlie, suddenly in control again, put his hand up and said to her, "It's okay, I work with this guy." She nodded and smiling obligingly went off to get our beers as once again that fearful band began to clamber onto the stage.

On the way home, Amy and I rode in silence for a while. I was a little embarrassed at Charlie's behavior, which was not at all as I'd described him to her. "No," she'd replied to my doubtful question, "I liked him." She was, after all, becoming accustomed to the excesses of millhands. The students she worked with were their children by and large. Kids who had terrible problems in their families; kids who were often in trouble with the law before they were sixteen. Violence, it seemed, was never far from the surface. But often they were "sweet kids," she would say, who seemed inexplicably to have lost control over their lives, and it worried her to think what was to become of them.

Apparently Charlie's bout with drunkenness had continued unabated for the next twenty-four hours, because by noon the following Monday he had not quite sobered up. Of course Parsons was quite familiar with the weekend habits of his log chopper and considered that the best cure for all such excesses lay in the solid redemption of hard work. That morning he worked us with a fury.

"Lordy, lordy, lordy," sighed Charlie when lunch break mercifully rolled around. "Got to lay off that drinking. I just about died this morning." Then sitting down next to me and leaning over to confide, added, "I'm an alcoholic you know."

I nodded out of politeness, though it had never really occurred to me to label Charlie in this way. Yes, I suppose he was an alcoholic, but that term, once so fraught with dark and hideous meaning, seemed to have lost its significance lately. These days it seemed that practically everyone was turning out to be an alcoholic, and it was becoming quite fashionable among the rich and famous to declare oneself as such. It all seemed like just another sidetrack to the redemptive rage of born-again Christianity then sweeping the country. The papers were full of the stories of well-known "personalities" who had openly submitted themselves to the barbarities of some treatment clinic or other. A popular former first lady had made such a confession, only to have it revealed later that her definition of alcoholism consisted of two or three drinks every evening. By such a definition nearly the entire country was alcoholic, and what might have started as a constructive social movement was beginning to look suspiciously like a born-again temperance movement. It was a long way from the social indelicacies of a former first lady to the crunching weekend binges of an impoverished mill hand, and it didn't seem to me that any TV personalities were going to be able to bridge the gap.

Charlie was a local boy, at least by local standards. He had grown up in town and gone to the local high school. He was *known* locally, though what he was known as is quite a different matter. He had done the unusual, and headed straight for New York City after graduation. There he lived off the landscape, much as a city child might attempt to "get back to the land" by heading for the country. But in New York that meant running one kind of a hustle or other, working as a fly-by-night mover or delivering firewood. And it was there that he picked up that trace of jive that he allowed to drift into his speech when the company was right. "People were real kind to us. They used to invite us in for something to eat. Felt sorry for us I guess." And by "people," it somehow came across that he meant black people.

"Caught some good music while I was down there."

"Oh yeah? What'd you hear?" I was hoping for some reference to a jazz great or two.

"Oh, Chubby Checker was really big right then."

"Oh." I kind of grunted my disappointment.

"Yeah, but I tell ya, we had some good times. One time this buddy an' me went to this club up in Harlem. Man we were in that place all night. Everybody was doin' the twist, havin' a great time. We were the only white dudes in the place, nobody cared."

Here the extraordinary thing I had noticed about Charlie when I first came to work at the mill began to make sense. There was something about him, a kind of soulful sophistication that seemed out of place then but now made sense. It was simple: he loved black people. He'd been a small-town boy, growing up in a region where black culture must have seemed as remote and frightening as if it were cannibalism. But somehow, growing up among those whitewashed steeples and clapboard walls in those rolling green valleys, a longing had arisen in him, which even he had probably not understood until he'd hit that club in Harlem.

Charlie's father was not a local. He'd arrived in Vermont in the thirties when, strangely enough, he'd been on the run from the big city. He was originally from Boston, where he'd had some reputation as a professional wrestler. One afternoon, at home with his new wife, Mister McClintock heard a knock at the front door of the apartment, which when opened revealed a man pointing a gun at him.

"Mister McClintock?" inquired a surly voice. Out of fear, Charlie's father nodded in the affirmative. The stranger fired a bullet into his chest, and fled. Staggering backward and reeling around, Mister McClintock came face to face with his wife, who had come running at the sound of the shot.

"For chrissake!" she shouted, "if ya have to bleed, don't do it all over the carpet. Get in the bathroom!"

Although he survived this mysterious attack—a case of mistaken identity, according to Charlie—it was obvious that Mister McClintock's days in Boston were numbered. And so he and his wife picked up and moved to—what was then—the remote town of Haddam, and opened up a hardware store.

"Ever hear of McClintock's Hardware?" Charlie asked. The question struck me like a revelation. Until that moment, despite Charlie's tale and my knowledge of his last name, I had not made the connection. Of course I'd heard of McClintock's! It was the fabulous hardware store of my boyhood summers. It was one store I loved to visit!

"That was your father's place!"

116

McClintock's was by far the best hardware store in the region. It did not stock its space with pots and pans, toasters, egg timers, and ironing boards. It specialized in hardware: common nails, finishing nails, ring nails, double-headed nails, coated nails, wood screws, machine screws, lag bolts, stove bolts, flat washers, split washers, hinges, hooks, latches, clamps, chains, ropes, wires, turnbuckles, turnbuttons, screens, faucets, pipes, plugs, pins, tubes, tapes, hubs, pulleys, belts, bearings, and more and more and more. All of the thousands of varieties of hardware, all openly displayed in big wood or metal bins, all costing a matter of pennies apiece, and all of them like penny candy to the ambitions of the creative builder of things.

It was said that if there was a tool known to man, Mister McClintock probably had it stored on some dusty shelf or hidden in an odd corner of his cellar. And if he did not have it, he knew where to get it. His was not a simple store but a gate into the infinitely varied universe of hardware. Here the first instinct was not necessarily for profit; much unprofitable effort was expended because "this fella needed somethin' with which to do somethin' that he needed to do, and I know a fella who's probably got one he doesn't need anymore."

So went the conversation up front at the cash register, where the old-timers congregated in twos and threes, passing an hour or two on a hot Saturday afternoon in August. I would duck past this group, unnoticed, as a kid can do, and head for the other side of the store where the open bins of hardware lay. Alone there, amid the sweet smell of old wood, feeling the creak of ancient floorboards down narrow, dusty corridors, I could be blissfully lost in the search for just the right combination of nut, bolt, and washer. When at last I emerged carrying my purchase to the cash register and the old men's conversation gently deferred to my business, Mister McClintock would sell me my half-dozen lag bolts at six cents apiece, seeming pleased with me and my business and the solid quality of the merchandise I had so carefully chosen.

That was Charlie's father's store! And one of those old men had been Charlie's father! "Of course I remember your father's store, Charlie. I used to love that place!"

The only incongruity in this perfect nostalgia was that Charlie had referred to the place as "McClintock's Hardware" when I distinctly remembered it as "McClintock and McClintock's Hardware." Charlie's face darkened when I mentioned this.

It seemed that Charlie's father had a somewhat wayward brother, who had never come to much account. At a late age, Charlie's father took him into the business, making him his partner. Thus "McClintock's Hardware," was rendered "McClintock and McClintock," as I remembered it. But somehow, through the dark, legal maneuverings of this brother, and the brother's wife, Charlie's father arrived at the store one morning to find that it was no longer his and that Charlie's aunt and uncle were now in sole legal possession of the place. Mister McClintock's own brother had stolen his business! By then, on the far side of seventy, Charlie's father had no heart nor perhaps any legal grounds on which to reclaim his life's work, and he quietly retired.

But things did not go particularly well for Charlie's uncle either. Such things do not pass unnoticed in a small town. People began to avoid him, they refused to talk to him, nobody would do business with him, and even his regular barber across the street refused to cut his hair. Thinking perhaps that time would heal the wound, Charlie's uncle hung on for two years. But still he was treated as a pariah, his business was evaporating, and still he had to seek his haircuts elsewhere.

Those familiar with the town will know that there is narrow-gauged steel bridge crossing over the Connecticut River into New Hampshire from the lower end of town. Because of the narrowness of the roadway and the solidity of the steel superstructure that hems it in, crossing that bridge can be a nerve-wracking experience when traffic is passing in the opposite direction. Such a passage puts one in mind of one's fragile mortality, and it was on such a passage that Charlie's uncle discovered his. Crossing one evening in his brand new Lincoln, for which he had given much, his life was snuffed out by the full force of an oncoming tractor trailor. Subsequent inquiries by the authorities, backed by the sworn testimony of the truck driver, determined that Charlie's uncle had deliberately turned his car into the path of the oncoming truck.

So after nearly ten years' absence, Charlie returned home. When he'd left, his father was a respected businessman, a Town Selectman who lived with his wife in a beautiful house on the edge of town. When Charlie returned, his mother had passed away, the government had taken the house to make way for the interstate, and Charlie's father had been reduced to the status of part-time employee in a competitor's store.

Charlie worked around for a while, holding down a variety of jobs, until he found his place with Parsons. There he remained, despite the hardships, because, as he explained, "I have debts to pay." I never inquired into the nature of these debts, but I do know that he still gets his hair cut by the barber who used to be across the street from McClintock's Hardware.

Steam **27**

R ay's departure did not prove to be a serious inconvenience for Parsons. In fact it was beginning to look as though the old man might have deliberately provoked it. The winter logs had all been washed, so for the time being there was no pressing need for a forklift driver. Parsons was a tentative hand at operating the thing and was able to keep Charlie well supplied. Ray had simply become an annoyance that Parsons no longer needed to tolerate. What with his bitter denunciation of the forklift's condition, his loud depiction of the absurdities of modern military life, and his rather immodest claims on virility, Ray was not fitting in well with the Parsons model of appropriate employee behavior. And besides, in economically troubled times there were plenty of fish in the sea, as evidenced by the steady stream of applicants filing through the mill in response to Parsons' advertisement for a truck driver and forklift operator.

Such ruminations put me in mind of my own expendability. I had supposed that the extent to which I allowed Parsons to "pick and pick" at my brain, as Charlie put it, was the extent to which I would last. But it was becoming increasingly obvious to me that brains alone were not enough. Jerry, who'd originally been hired on a temporary basis, was being kept on permanently. Parsons had moved him inside as a kind of utility man and was introducing him to the same wide variety of tasks that he had forced me to master. It began to dawn on me that Parsons was up to his old tricks again, and that I was being provided with a little competition. These days Jerry was almost always serving as Parsons' first assistant at the headsaw, and the former log washer was showing signs of enthusiasm for the job. He would step in on Parsons as they worked closely together and immediately take to whatever task Parsons happened to leave him. By pressing his position in this way, he made it clear that if Parsons had allowed it, he would have jumped on the big feed lever itself and started splitting logs singlehandedly. The real revelation was that Parsons showed absolutely no sign of resentment, and I had to think—knowing Parsons as I did—that this really represented downright encouragement.

I suppose that the situation should have left me feeling more jealous than it did. After all, hadn't Charlie suggested that the job of head sawyer might be mine? Hadn't I—this college-educated, city slicker—taken a great deal of pleasure from the notion that I might gain mastery of this most exclusive and honorable of country trades? But no, somehow in the last few weeks that had all slipped away. It was as if my only pleasure could come from the mere approach to that exclusivity. If I were to grasp the trade itself in my hands, that exclusivity would be lost, and I would have spoiled the whole thing. It was a strangely self-defeating attitude, I suppose, but one that Parsons made hard to avoid. In any case, I liked Jerry. He was a smart and decently irreverent young man who'd had his share of knocks, and the notion that the job might go to him gave me an odd sense of relief.

A large cloud of doubt had formed in my vicinity in the weeks since Ray had been fired. I'd been languishing for too long at the ripsaw, feeling a bit too comfortable for Parsons' tastes. I kept looking at Charlie, who'd managed to last so long by languishing in *his* job, working slowly, steadily, competently, and there I saw a kind of wisdom I had not recognized before. I'd come to the mill "probably trying to prove something," as I imagined Charlie would put it. But now that Ray was gone, and I could no longer sneer at what I'd considered vulgar ambition. My own ambition seemed equally vulgar and inappropriate.

It was now growing steadily colder. We were approaching mid-November, and everyone was spending as much time indoors as possible. Arriving before dawn, the temperature around freezing, we moved to our tasks as stiff as corpses. The weather was still changeable; on the better days, with the sun out, we might warm up after an hour or two. But more and more frequently that stiffness did not leave us, and we went about the mill bundled from head to toe, blowing on our fingers and wondering: when, when, *when* is he going to turn on the heat?

The matter quickly became an obsession, and formed the focus of many a lunch-time discussion. I suppose we hoped Parsons would overhear us and be inspired to take some kind of remedial action on our behalf. But this was a rather forlorn hope, considering the fact that the old man was definitely not one for letting others make up his mind for him, especially if they were lowly millhands. His sense of economy was ruthless and complete: heat would be introduced into our midst when he was good and ready, and not a minute before. After all, there had been no hard freeze yet, and so long as the mill's plumbing was in no imminent danger, what was the point in wasting valuable fuel just so people could be warm and toasty and start drowsing on the job?

So he remained quietly ensconced in his office, seemingly absorbed in the noon news, munching fastidiously, showing absolutely no sign that he heard anything of our complaints. Of course we knew he really was listening, since a man of his paranoid tendencies could hardly do otherwise. But it was obvious that long ago he'd learned the immense value of stonewalling; it frustrated your opposition, tried their patience, and sometimes forced them into stupid acts that could be put to advantage.

In this case the stupidity was mine. During our various discussions of heat, I had been foolish enough to mention my lifelong interest in steam and in its various mechanical applications. I don't know how or why I got onto this subject, nor did my companions seemed particularly interested. But this intelligence must have caused Parsons' ears to prick up and swivel in my direction, for not three days later I was introduced to the big, wood-fired boiler, downcellar.

Naturally, since I momentarily forgot with whom I was dealing, I took this move as an indication that the old man's heart had softened. At long last we were going to get some heat. I even took it as a kind of personal triumph that I had been honored to facilitate the matter. But this whiff of vanity evaporated when it was pointed out to me that, yes indeed, we were going to fire up the boiler, but we were *not* going to be providing any heat. It seemed that the boiler had a second, more arcane function, aside from providing heat, and this second function was our exclusive concern. The old buzzard had done it again! In one stroke, he'd simultaneously flattened my ego and added crushing weight to the frustrations of everyone else.

I was thus introduced to the art of steaming wood. Under certain circumstances, a dowel blank developed so much warp that it could not be fed through the dowel machine without becoming thoroughly jammed. These were fairly rare, and there might only be two warped blanks for every hundred straight ones. But after a period of months, they could add up to quite a sizeable number. Parsons, ever the ruthless economizer, had developed a method for restraightening them with steam and had them put aside for a time when he had an employee on hand who deserved this godforsaken and thankless task. It seemed that he had found such an employee in me.

The boiler itself was a monstrosity, a crusty old asbestos-covered rhinoceros, sprouting a bewildering array of pipes, valves, and gauges, and containing innumerable doors, hatches, and dampers, connected to an elaborate system of counterweights that controlled half-a-dozen flues, fireboxes, and ash pits. I am not one to be intimidated by machines, but this one put the fear of God in me. And while Parsons merrily introduced me to the thing with his usual incomprehensibly rapid instruction, I found myself supremely grateful when he volunteered to fire the thing up this first time.

The rationalist in me tried to put the situation in perspective by recalling the foolish childhood terrors I'd felt in the presence of the oil burner in my parents' house. That thing used to send me flying up the cellar stairs at even the slightest premonition that it was going to start up. To me it had seemed like some sort of boy-eating monster with fire in its belly and tentacles reaching to every corner of the house, waiting to suck me in with a sudden whoosh! And then I would be gone, consumed by those awful flames. Of course I was a big boy now, and things like this weren't supposed to bother me. But although I had grown, the boiler I faced had grown proportionately, like some grotesque demon from the past returned to haunt me, a demon I was now expected to tame.

The main product of a boiler is steam, which happens to be a very handy substance for carrying heat where it might be needed. In our case, that steam could end up in the fan-driven radiators hanging from the ceiling upstairs. But since that was a use the old man opposed, the valves controlling the flow that way were shut tight. Instead the heat was directed to a pair of coffin-sized, water-filled troughs equipped with lids and located in the darkest and dingiest corner of the cellar behind the boiler. These were wood-steaming tanks, and the idea was to load them with the warped dowel blanks, steam the blanks until they were pliable, and bend them straight again.

Parsons was clearly very proud of this economizing inspiration. Gleefully he rolled over a cart which must have contained at least a thousand warped blanks and set me to work. He'd fired up the boiler by now, and the water in the steaming tanks—an awful, black, scummy-looking stuff—was boiling away like some noxious witches' brew. My job was to reach into these tanks wearing a pair of rubber gloves, pick out a stick or two, and then, spending a couple of minutes on each one, roll them laboriously back and forth, back and forth, between a pair of rollers until each stick was straight again. This back and forth motion was tedious enough, but every time I reached into the tank, I'd get a face full of steam, my glasses got fogged, and I'd have to grope about blindly for a stick to grab. The gloves provided minimal protection, and I had to be careful to get my hands in and out of the water within five seconds, otherwise it felt like I wasn't wearing any protection at all.

After half an hour of this particular entertainment, my right hand had become so badly scalded that it was impossible for me to reach into a tank for even the briefest moment without excruciating pain, and I was forced to rely upon an awkward left. My work boots, which I'd taken great pains to "waterproof," were soaked completely through as a result of being constantly dripped on, and my feet made an unpleasant *squish* with every step. But for all this, I'd made no noticable dent in the cart.

Making some rough calculations, I came to the unpleasant realization that it was going to take at least three full days of this torture before I'd finish, and in frustration I fell to cursing, throwing off my rubber gloves in disgust. Reaching to brush a dampened forelock from my eyes, I was struck by the most awful revelation of all. My hand smelled terrible! In fact, it didn't smell like a hand at all, but like a foot! And not only a foot, but the worst smelling foot I'd ever chanced to experience! This, after a good twenty years' worth of locker-room experience, is saying quite a bit.

In short, the situation was torture, pure and simple. Parsons had cooked this business up as punishment for who-knows-what imaginary offense. Maybe it was my new-found complacency in the face of competition from Jerry. Whatever the reason, he knew exactly what he was doing, because now that he had me exactly where he wanted me, at the lowest of miserable lows, he decided to land the final blow. At that very moment he set Jerry to work for the first time on the ripsaw upstairs. I could hear it. I knew that little *zzzzip!* sound when I heard it. And when I tiptoed up the back stairs to confirm it, there I saw it; he was working on *my* ripsaw, while I was to remain downstairs, mired in misery.

Reluctantly, resigned to my fate, I trudged back downstairs, hopelessly anticipating the slow crawl I would have to endure to escape

Parsons' doghouse. But when I got to the wood steaming tanks, I noticed that they were no longer boiling with merry abandon. In fact they were hardly boiling at all. The water had become tepid, and the sticks were no longer emerging from the tanks with any pliability. Stepping around to the front of the boiler, I found that its pressure gauge was just above zero. It was time to face the beast and start loading up the firebox.

The main trick to this boiler, or any other boiler for that matter, is to make sure that it's hot enough to keep up a steady head of steam but not so hot that it blows up on you. The earliest boilers, such as those on Mr. Fulton's steamboats, used to blow up with a frightening regularity. Mark Twain's brother died as a result of one such accident, and another accident prompted him to record this partial account, overheard in conversation: "Was anybody hurt?" "No. Killed a nigger." Such recollections put me in mind of my own status at the mill, and I angrily threw a load of wood into the firebox.

Twenty minutes later, the boiler had built no appreciable head of steam, and, in fact, the pressure gauge was now somewhere *below* zero. I chucked in another load and opened every damper I could find. Still nothing happened. So I proceeded to load the firebox to absolute capacity, cramming its every nook and cranny with pieces of every size and description and topped the entire concoction off with a couple shovelfuls of sawdust. Again I opened every damper I could locate and this time, absolutely determined to succeed, closed all the steam pressure outlet valves. Within fifteen minutes, I noted with some satisfaction that the pressure gauge was moving steadily upwards. So I opened the outlet valves and strutted bravely back to face the dreaded wood-steaming tanks. Soon the water was bubbling again, and I began to marvel at my own foolishness for ever having been intimidated by a simple boiler.

However, it was not very long before I began to notice that the water in the wood-steaming tanks was beginning to boil with a fury that I didn't quite remember from the last time around, and so I calmly strolled over to see how my old friend the boiler was doing. Despite the fact that the pressure gauge was marked with numbers as high as thirty pounds, Parsons had informed me that anything over ten pounds was probably a very bad idea, owing—I sup-posed—to the boiler's decrepit state. But much to my horror, when I did get a look at the gauge, it informed me that the boiler was running at a pressure of fifteen pounds, which was particularly disconcerting since the pressure safety valve was supposed to open all by itself at ten pounds.

Now, fifteen pounds of pressure per square inch may not seem very high to a mind used to modern engineering, with its turbines and high-stress metal alloys. But for the antique specimen of a boiler in the basement of Parsons' mill, that level of pressure provided a specter sufficient to send the developer of the hydrogen bomb into a panic. I opened the firebox door to find a roaring inferno that would have done excellent service in a crematorium and was barely able to get the thing shut again without getting burned myself. In a panic I opened every valve and shut every damper I could find on the thing, muttering, "Down! Down! Please go down!" The pressure gauge then paused and wavered a bit, as if considering the request but soon determined that it preferred going upward. In desperation I opened a valve letting cold water into the boiler, but this merely added a couple more pounds of pressure. Steam was leaking from every joint of every valve and pipe of this now-demonic monster, and I felt sure that Armageddon was imminent. But now that we had arrived at that desperate moment when God and country mean nothing, when all normal moral values seem but antique artifices from another universe, when I was ready to yell for everyone to run for their very lives, finally, mercifully, the safety valve popped, releasing a single, solid, shooshing jet of steam that rocketed to the ceiling and billowed voluminously throughout the cellar.

Parsons came running downstairs. Apparently steam from the safety valve was jetting through a hole in the floor that had been drilled for such a contingency, and poor visibility was now impeding work on the main floor. Brushing away steam, he maneuvered his way to the chimney at the back of the boiler and opened a damper I'd never even seen before. "Bypass damper. Puts cold air in the chimney. That ought to cool your fire down." After a while, the pressure came down to five pounds, where it held steady, and Parsons, smiling a little, said, "You haven't quite got it right."

For the rest of that day, and most of the week, I did not once turn my back on that pressure gauge for more than five minutes at a time. Between loading the wood-steaming tanks with sticks, straightening them, running over to the boiler to adjust a damper or to throw in some wood, I didn't stop running or worrying once. "Whew!" I exclaimed to Charlie. "Just watching that boiler is a full-time job. That

126

thing is so slow to respond, you got to be twenty minutes ahead of it, or it'll take over and start running you!"

"Well," he replied with mock irony, tilting his head back so he could peer at me through the glasses that had slipped to their accustomed perch halfway down his nose, "you said you liked steam!"

Pete

28

Among the upturned buckets upon which we millhands sat as we passed our breaks, one was particularly prized. Its distinguishing feature was a sprung and cushioned black vinyl seat that had been liberated from some now-extinct office chair, and which perched upon that bucket in precarious balance. Not only did this cushion provide a more comfortable seat, it added height to its occupant, and generally gave him a sense of heightened importance while he occupied it. In keeping with the throne-like quality of the seat, it also happened that it was placed centrally in among the others, so that not only did its occupant sit more comfortably, but was also in a position to moderate the ebb and flow of break-time conversation.

Generally we traded this seat off in the most democratic of fashions, it being understood that there were certain social responsibilities that accompanied its use. As a consequence, the first few times that I occupied the seat while in a depressed state, I was greeted with some resentment because I was supposed to be leading the conversation instead of weighing it down with my dismal moods. For a brief time Ray had asserted his dominance over the seat, but as he fell out of favor with the boss, and his clownish dominion became more and more strident, our collective hostility was directed at him. He soon got the message and quit the chair, making only occasional forays into reoccupation.

Charlie rarely occupied this privileged bucket, but on the few occasions that he did, it was with a full awareness of the responsibilities involved. Denny never presumed that he was worthy of the privilege, while Jerry's claims were on the ascendant. But it was Pete, Parsons' new lift and truck driver who came into our midst one dismal day with the aim of total usurpation.

Pete was another bull. With a heavyweight's proportions, he was taller and more powerfully built than anyone I'd seen at the mill, and since he was not yet out of his early twenties, he remained in fighting trim. Sporting a little mustache and wearing a stubbornly glazed expression, he had a murderous air that made him look like a sadistic prison guard. As usual, we suddenly found this new acquisition at the mill one morning, carrying on with Parsons in the same uproarious manner as his bull-like predecessors, Frank and Ray. It seemed that Pete and Parsons lived in the same town in New Hampshire, and dispensing with introductions, Parsons perfunctorily waved us off to work with the back of his hand, while he and Pete caught up on all the latest village gossip.

When break time came around on that first day, Pete showed absolutely no shyness about mixing in our company, and was even so presumptuous as to claim the cushioned seat as his own. From there he began, without prompting and in no uncertain terms, to tell us just how he happened to arrive in our midst. Apparently he had done service as a truck driver for a local haulage firm but was fired for managing to destroy a semitrailer full of cigarettes; they had come tumbling loose when Pete took a corner just a little too fast. His dispatcher offered him an ultimatum: come across with ten thousand dollars for the damaged merchandise, or take a walk. Of course Pete did not have ten thousand dollars, and if he had, it was unlikely that he would have handed it over.

Finding himself out of work, Pete took to blaming absolutely everyone but himself for his circumstance: The trailer'd been loaded improperly; he'd had to work twelve-hour days; the boss was a son of a bitch; the company was controlled by the Mafia. This all may have been true, but it soon became apparent that Pete's driving habits were none too careful. From the very start he handled Parsons' little dumper like he was taking it into combat. Restraint, or a concern for safety, were not factors greatly emphasized in Pete's world. You'd see him bouncing and bumping across the mill yard and out into the stone-blind curve of the street without even bothering to consider whether a car might be coming along the other way. Pete was an angry man, and it seemed as though, wrapped as he was in that bull's body and surrounded by the sheets of that truck's steel, he moved out into the street to challenge death itself.

In fact, Pete had been involved in a fatal accident. He was the passenger in a truck that had careened into a car and killed the woman driving it. The driver of the truck, a friend of Pete's, stood trial for reckless endangerment. "It was the damn road," Pete insisted. "We hit a patch of ice, and I'll tell ya, there's nothin' gonna stop a truck when that happens. I told 'em at the trial. I testified, but they didn't listen." Pete's friend ended up serving time on a manslaughter conviction.

Nobody asked Pete to tell us these stories, nor do I think any of us had known about the incidents, but it was obvious that he needed to tell them. They just spilled out in a kind of offensive barrage, the tone of which indicated that as far as he was concerned the world was populated by a bunch of asshole fools who didn't know an honest accident when they saw one. But it was obvious that behind it all lay a smouldering guilt and that he demanded absolution from us.

As the days passed, Pete showed absolutely no sign of relinquishing his monopoly over the cushioned seat. When break came he always made damn sure he got that seat. And if he had the slightest suspicion that someone else might be heading for it first, he'd be sure to quicken his pace in order to cut him off. Sometimes this maneuver got to be a little bit tricky. It was a tradition at the mill that the man nearest to the blower system switch would signal lunch break by shutting the thing off. Since few machines could be run without the blower going, this move effectively shut the entire mill down. But as the blower switch was at the opposite end of the mill from our lunch area, the man who shut the blower off was at a serious disadvantage when it came to the selection of seats. Pete was not a man to resign himself to the fates, and so, the few times that the job of shutting off the blower fell to him, he had to make sure that he got his timing just right. He'd sneak up to the blower switch when he thought nobody was looking, snap the lever to "off," and then rush madly over toward his precious cushion before anybody else had a chance to put down whatever he was doing and get there ahead of him.

I suppose that the rest of us ought to have resented such childish and rude behavior, but it seemed amazing that anybody could care so much about something so trivially symbolic as a seat cushion. After all, occupation of that seat may have indicated respect for the fellow sitting there, but there were no mystics among us, and no magic was embodied in that junked cushion to command our automatic respect. Pete had taken the seat by force, and force was something that we had no difficulty in recognizing at Parsons' mill. But it was not something that interested us very much.

Naturally Parsons was absolutely delighted with his new man. And to celebrate his arrival, he decided to keep me firmly in the doghouse.

For the time being I had graduated from the torturous business of steaming dowel blanks and was moved back upstairs. But instead of putting me back on the ripsaw where I belonged, Parsons had me back to trimming dowels and kept me there for an entire fifty-hour week, while Jerry and Pete were put to work at the ripsaw and then moved to the doweler. It was a particularly humiliating arrangement for me. Not only was I back to where I had started at the mill, but I had to watch as the two of them did an absolutely terrible job at the doweler.

Parsons had set the thing up for them, and it ran fine for a few hours. But inevitably the thing started to get out of whack, and dowels started jamming up or coming out all wrong. Since they seemed unable to get the thing to run right, I felt obliged to save them from the wrath of Parsons and showed them a couple of adjustments. But after a while this caused some small resentment, especially on Pete's part. After all, who the hell did I think I was? All Pete had ever seen me do was steam dowel blanks and trim dowels. I was not one to ruffle anyone's feathers, especially when the feathers in question belonged to such a sizeable beast. "Let them ask Parsons," I thought. "That'll give 'em an education."

Parsons was in a reasonably good mood that day, having—as I explained—found Pete to be a pleasing prospect. So the first couple of times they wandered over to the headsaw and broke the old man's concentration for advice on the doweler, he was quite obliging about it. But after a while, I could see his patience was beginning to wear thin. Jerry had a much better understanding of the limits of the situation than did Pete, so the next time things started to go awry, he decided it might be better if they turned to me for advice again. But Pete's disposition toward me had become so hostile that I merely shook my head at Jerry, and raised my hands as if to say, "Sorry, but you're on your own with this one." Under the circumstances, Jerry did the only intelligent thing he could and sent an oblivious Pete over for more advice from the old man. Parsons stopped what he was doing and came storming over. He made a few angry adjustments and delivered his stock speech about having "already showed you how to adjust for that!" It was clear that the end of the road had been reached, and even Pete began to recognize the hazard in bothering the old man any further.

However, our troubles were not yet over. Somewhere along the line Pete had gotten the idea that he was supposed to dump the culls from the doweler into the basket which held the culls from my trim saw. This was all wrong and was causing me all kinds of extra work. When

131

I pointed the error out to Pete, he merely sneered, "You ain't my boss yet! That's the way Parsons showed me how to do it!" It would have been useless to try to explain to him that I wasn't trying to be his boss but that I was simply trying to save myself from a totally unnecessary load of work. So for the time being, I grimly resigned myself to the extra work.

As I worked along I began toying with the idea that maybe Parsons actually had arranged for Pete to be making this error, and this was just another of his elaborate schemes to depress my spirit. This thought, paranoid as it was, got me madder and madder, until I finally came to a resolution. It was either Parsons or Pete who was responsible for the situation, and I intended to find out which. So, knowing that I was playing with dynamite, and that Parsons was not going to appreciate being disturbed again, I decided to complain to him.

As I approached and stood before him, waiting for him to stop and notice me, I could see that critical mass was near at hand. For two full minutes I stood there, he making it clear by ignoring me that if I was to break his concentration it had better be for a damn good reason. But I was angry also and stood my ground.

According to Charlie, in the three years he'd been working there, he'd never seen Parsons really lose control. But where others had failed in years past, I at last succeeded. Stomping across the floor to face Pete, his face a deeper shade of crimson than I would have thought possible, Parsons jumped up and down and threw his clenched fists wildly about, screaming at the top of his lungs like a child in a tantrum, "No! No! No! That's not the way I told you to do it!" He jumped and stomped some more, and screamed again, "No! No! No!" Astonished at the awful force I'd unleashed and shaking with fear, I stood on the sidelines muttering over and over like someone who has just killed in self-defense, "I told him, I told him. He didn't want to listen to me. I told him."

While I shook with fear, Parsons shook with anger, and everyone else looked on. Pete just looked a little stunned. Someone had just cracked the bull across the head with a two-by-four, and now he was paying attention. Later on Charlie started laughing at me. I'd told him that I felt like kind of a snitch, getting Pete into trouble like that. "No, no, no," he laughed, "that was cool, that was so-o cool. I never seen 'im *that* mad before!" Then he laughed, and laughed, and laughed.

A Jogger

29

It was not long after Parsons' big blowup over Pete, that Denny the dour farmboy decided he'd had just about enough of working at a sawmill. Somebody had offered him reasonably good money to work in the woods as a logger, and since this was the kind of work for which he was really built, it seemed the perfect opportunity for him to make his escape. This turn of events seemed to affect Jerry the most because the two of them had become buddies. They worked together frequently alongside Parsons at the headsaw and seemed to take a lot of pleasure in making rude comments at the old man's expense while his back was turned.

Jerry made no bones about his displeasure with Denny's decision, and with Denny himself. Jerry had done a little logging himself, driving a skidder for his brother who was in business up north, and he did not have a high opinion of the trustworthiness of the fellows wielding chainsaws for a living. Too many a tree had come crashing in his direction without warning as he perched on that skidder like a sitting duck, and he did not consider it much of a professional ambition to become limbless or lifeless.

But Denny had never really been cut out for millwork. His talent was for steady and heavy labor. The mill may have provided reasonably steady kinds of tasks, but the heaviest work was handled by Charlie, rolling those big logs around. Otherwise, for a man of Denny's strength, the work was relatively light, and it was obvious it did not provide him with enough of a physical challenge. Before Ray's departure Parsons once sent the five of us to shovel out the couple truckloads of soil that had accumulated under the log deck over the course of a year's worth of log washing. It had been one of those rare Indian Summer days when sensible people take it as easy as possible and enjoy the weather. With five of us shoveling at once, the task had become a kind of social event, and each shovelful served only as a reluctant pause in a man's conversation.

We were all taking it easy, except Denny, of course. He'd started right in and with great pleasure shoveled and shoveled like a madman from start to finish without once breaking stride or losing his breath. After about an hour, when we had finished, he had easily accounted for half the volume of soil lifted high into the truckbed but looked as fresh and pink cheeked as ever, while the rest of us had taken on the appearance of bedraggled skid row refuse.

Just as we were finishing, a youngish man with a neatly trimmed beard and a nicely matched running outfit jogged by down the middle of the street with an absurdly inefficient gait, oblivious to our incredulous stares. We wanted nothing more at this point than to collapse in an exhausted heap, and the sight of this fellow tripping by seemed like some kind of an insult against the natural order of the universe. Denny continued blithely shoveling at his mad pace while following the jogger with his eyes. "Waste of time," he intoned. "Probably living off of unemployment."

To me, however, the jogger looked a little too prosperous for your average welfare cheat. He could have been an accountant, or even a social worker. "Maybe he works behind a desk, and needs the exercise," I said, coming to his defense.

"Yeah," sneered Denny, his tone making it clear that as far as he was concerned it was all pretty much the same thing.

A New Man

30

"I think old Henry's got his new man," Charlie informed me. Parsons had been advertising in the paper for Denny's replacement, but I was doing my best to ignore the proceedings, believing that it was inevitable that Parsons would hire someone else to give us grief.

"He does?" I didn't see anyone.

"Yeah. There's a guy in Henry's office now, filling out an application. I'll wager that he gets the job. Looks like the type he likes to hire." Curious as to what this "type" looked like, I strolled past the office door. Inside an older fellow—somewhere in his fifties—with a full, gray beard and heavily framed glasses looked up from the rolltop desk where he was laboring and shot me a mischievous grin.

His name was Hank, and as Charlie had prophesied, he came to work a couple of days later. He had the look of an old cowboy, favoring a checked shirt and faded jeans, ambling about on bowed legs and carrying about him the air of a man who has seen it all in his day.

At lunchtime, or "chow," as Parsons had lately taken to calling out at about forty-five seconds after noon, Charlie and Pete both slipped out the door and headed for the grocery up the block. This left me to sort through my lunch, while Jerry—in a daily ritual that was obviously the source of much pleasure—carefully tapped and unsealed a fresh pack of cigarettes. Hank had disappeared downcellar to the toilet and could be heard returning up the narrow, creaking stairs at the back of the mill. Parsons sat in his office as the radio broadcasted the day's news: it seemed that although the President's top security men had erred in predicting an assasination attempt by a mob of crazed Middle Eastern "hit-men," the mistake could be traced to the shady dealings of certain Eastern European "disinformation experts." As I mulled over the evil associations that the word "east" seemed to hold in the public consciousness, I looked up to see Hank—our now resident West-

135

erner—hunching slowly across the floor with his hand at the small of his back. He came to a halt in front of us and regarded us with narrow, amused, fifty-odd-year-old eyes.

"Gawd!" He said. "Had to shit so bad, my eyeballs was turnin' brown."

"Yeah. Know the feeling." I smiled with what felt like idiotic politeness but then, for a moment, grew slightly apprehensive as I came to the realization that of the four people now in the building, I was the only one whose eyes actually were brown.

Meanwhile, Hank's thoughts had changed tack. "Ever been down to Washington?" I had indeed but was not sure that it was wise to reveal the fact so early in the game.

"Sin city!" Hank continued, his head shaking in disbelief. "You wouldn't believe some of the stuff. Yeaup, si-in city!" Jerry lit a cigarette, while I carefully unwrapped a sandwich. Hank stood and watched, then pursuing a personal logic that caught us completely by surprise, he said, "Ever mess around with them nigger bitches?" In unison both Jerry and I looked up and frowned.

Realizing that he had employed a form of slang considered offensive to most of the generation represented by Jerry and me, Hank hitched up his pants and rephrased himself, "Ever mess around with them black bitches?" Jerry shook his head, while I made busy with my sandwich. "Oh man! Watch out for them *black* bitches!"

Having tested the rhetorical waters, and having found them safe for swimming, Hank dove into his subject. "One time, I was down in Washington City. I'm just walkin' down the sidewalk, mindin' my own business. . . . I'd just come out of a bar. Well this black whore, she just comes right up to me and she says. 'Where you goin'?'

" 'Nowhere,' I says.

" 'Wanta go with me?' She says.

" 'Go where?' I says.

" 'You know.'

" 'No I do not!' " Hank feigned indignance.

" '*You* know.'

" 'Do I?'

" 'You know, you wanna fuck?'

" '*Ohhh, that's* what you meant.' " Jerry and I were starting to grin.

" 'Well, how much?'

" 'How much you got?'

" 'How much you worth?' "

136

We were breaking up into guffaws now, and I noticed Parsons stirring uneasily in his office, but Hank pressed forward. "So she says to me, 'How much you *think* I'm worth?' "

Just then big Pete came bursting in with his usual destructive energy, trailed by a worn-looking Charlie. Hank's face fell, and his narrative ended. The intimacy created by this boastful and only half-believed tale of worldliness had instantly dissipated. I returned to the mysteries of my lunch bag, while Jerry quickly snuffed out his cigarette and delved into his lunch. Hank retreated to a perch on an upturned can, and gloomily smoked.

"Well!" Pete scoffed, "We're a lively bunch, aren't we!"

31

Several days later, still occupying his throne, Pete was holding court, and bragging to us about his wife.

"Some son of a bitch calls up my wife the other day while I'm out, and says, 'Hiya baby, howya doin?'"

"Well, my wife just yells back at 'im, 'none of yer goddamn business!'"

"Yessir, my wife is a tough one alright."

Apparently, though she was not much past twenty, she'd been married before and had a kid to take care of when her husband decided to up and abandon her. That was how she settled on Pete. "Yeaup, she's a tough cookie alright. Known her all my life. When we was kids she used to beat me up." Pete looked around for signs of our astonishment.

"How'd she do that, Pete?" Jerry asked.

"Used to kick like the devil, went right for the balls."

The rest of us looked around at each other as if to say, 'charming trait in a spouse.'

"Yeaup," Pete reflected wistfully, "right for the balls."

Charlie was unable to resist the temptation to comment, and bursting forth with a devilish grin, he shouted and guffawed. "And now you're *married* to her!"

We all laughed, except Pete of course.

"She wouldn't do that now," he sneered. "She loves them things too much." Our laughter was cut short, and a repressed groan seemed to hang in the air.

Pete had a real talent for humorless vulgarity of this sort, and it seemed to amuse him to be as offensive as possible. Charlie was once describing a television drama he'd seen the night before in which a black man gets implicated in the murder and rape of a white woman in the South. Pete had been watching the same show but fell asleep before the conclusion. Though sitting within whispering range, Pete found it necessary to yell, "Did they get the nigger that did it?!"

"No," Charlie replied tersely. "As a matter of fact he was innocent. The story's true too." Pete just grunted, and crinkled up his nose, as if he'd detected a bad smell.

Jerry's mouth had dropped open in wide astonishment at Pete's pronouncement of faith, and it took him some time to form his words. "God Pete, you're really subtle, aren't you."

Pete simply nodded, and beamed with obvious satisfaction. He'd managed to shock us with his words, and so believed himself victorious.

For my part, Pete's behavior resulted in a state of gloomy and depressed resignation. Since our big blowup I had not exchanged a single word with the red-neck trucker, and as time passed I grew less and less inclined to do so. I felt like I'd been through it all before with Ray, and while my struggle with the Sarge had resulted in some sense of my own ability to survive and prosper in hostile circumstances, I didn't have the heart to go through it again. By now any feeling I might have had of really belonging at the mill, of a confident possession of my skills, and of my job, had melted before Pete's crude offense. I could no longer muster an adequate response because I no longer harbored the illusion that personal progress was possible at Parsons' mill. I knew enough by now to be sure that the old man was behind Pete's behavior and that it was his strategy to bust you down again and again, until you either surrendered or walked out.

I had begun to keep more and more to myself and rarely spoke. Sometimes at lunch I even did the rude thing of sitting on a cart somewhere, well away from everybody else, mulling over the possibilities. I'd thought of quitting many times before, but by now the thought was hitting me with such frequency that for the first time I was truly on the verge of walking out that door and not coming back. Charlie could see the way things were with me. Over the years he had been 'busted down' to an unshaven, ill-clothed, alcoholic, impoverished, and aging millhand, but he still had the strength to try cheering me up by talking about things of which Pete could know nothing.

"When I was still living in New York City," he began one day, "we were in the moving business for a while. You know, 'fly by night incorporated.' We'd rented this big big van to move this woman's stuff. She didn't have all that much in the way of furniture. You know. But the only thing the rental people could give us was this huge truck. We didn't know how to drive something like that, but that's what they gave us."

"Well, Tim," he said turning to me, "you know what the expressways down there are like; one wrong turn, and you're halfway across town from where you thought you'd be. So anyway, we're driving this big truck on the Cross Bronx—I think it was the Cross Bronx. Well, it's this huge truck, and I'm driving, and can't see behind me or anything, and suddenly we're stuck in this exit lane headed for an exit we didn't want. You know, I can see that it's the wrong exit, and my partner's shouting, 'It's the wrong exit! It's the wrong exit!' But it's too late, 'cause I can't see if there's any cars alongside me, and I'm afraid I'll kill somebody if I try switching lanes. So we kinda' rolled up this exit ramp, and like, man! we're in the worst-looking slum you ever saw! I mean this place is like a war zone. No trees, no grass, bombed out, boarded-up buildings, garbage all over the place. I mean this place was depressing!"

"So we're rolling down the street, looking for a way back to the expressway, when we hit a red light. We're waitin' there, calm as can be, when all of a sudden, somebody starts dropping bricks onto the hood of the truck from some rooftop. 'Bam! Bam! Bam!' I'm just sitting there, waiting for the light to change. 'Bam!' Finally the light changes, and I charged off like hell, roaring down the street like I was crazy."

"Jeez!" exclaimed Pete, "That was kinda dumb. If it was me, I wouldn'a waited for any traffic light. I'da been out of there fast!"

Charlie and I just looked at each other. Because just as he'd grasped the main point of the story, this big ox had managed to miss it completely. Unlike Pete, we'd actually seen the ghetto, and had some idea of what it was like. We knew that it was a war zone, a no-man's-land where people were dying violently every day. Did the Petes of the world understand that, and what it meant? Did they understand the discipline it took for a person to stay alive there? Did they understand that aside from people like Charlie and me, who just occasionally happened upon such places, there were ordinary and decent people who were forced to spend the entirety of their lives there? No. To Pete, these places were just inhabited by niggers or spics, or something else less-than-human, and in that way their suffering could be justified. Of course it seemed stupid to stay put at a red light while somebody dropped bricks on you, but short of panic, that was the just the way you did behave.

Pete wasn't going to let the matter pass. He had to let us know in his boastful way that he'd been to the big city too, and that we had nothing on him. As a truck driver, he'd been to Boston a number of times, and gotten lost. Perhaps, I began to speculate to myself, it was there that he'd been driven into the panic that caused him to ruin that load of cigarettes. He also bragged to us that as a kid he'd been—of all places—to Columbus, Ohio. "Didn't like it much," he intoned with stock rural irony and fixed me in his gaze, as if somehow I were personally responsible for the place's existence.

"I don't know," I muttered my first words to Pete in days, "never been there myself."

It was ironic, and it was the last thing in the world that I had intended when I first got there, but Charlie and I had managed to establish a secure outpost of urbanity, right there in the middle that old sawmill. This was not something we wanted to do, and up to that point, we had kept our understanding of one another to ourselves. But Pete had forced our hand and had made us act to exclude him. As petty as we may have seemed, it was not too petty for Pete, who now resorted to cracks about Charlie's drinking.

Charlie had been showing up late to work quite a bit recently, but it had been of no particular concern to anybody until Pete started making an issue out of it. "Whatsa matter Charlie," he guffawed for all to hear one morning when Charlie showed up twenty minutes late, looking a little dazed. "Little too much lemonade last night?" It was not an issue in which Charlie saw much humor, and he simply ignored the jest. Pete pressed on. "Looks like Henry could use a foreman around here, maybe you ought to apply." He was sneering now, and Charlie was looking miserable. "Why with *you* watching the clock for us, we could all take it easy."

Pete's tone was doubly insulting, because if Parsons really wanted a foreman, Charlie clearly had the seniority for it but must have been deemed deficient in some other way. It was even possible that Pete had the idea that he himself would make a suitable candidate. Though that wasn't likely when you considered how little Pete actually knew about the place. No, I thought to myself, Parsons doesn't need any foreman, more likely he's just putting silly ideas into Pete's head just to keep the rest of us in our place.

Of course it might have been that Pete thought he was really being funny. But nobody else thought so. It just wasn't considered good taste at the mill to comment on a man's tardiness, especially if it was assumed to be the result of the previous night's over-indulgence. Up until Pete's time it had been the practice to smile slyly and keep quiet about it, no matter who did it. I suppose this may have been one of the more practical applications of Christ's admonition regarding the first stone. Even Parsons failed to breach this particular brand of etiquette, though in the matter of alcohol it was widely acknowledged that—with the exception of an occassional glass of wine—he was one who did not sin.

Pete obviously wasn't winning any popularity contests by pursuing these tactics, but that was not a matter of much concern to him. There seemed to be no rebuke, short of violent confrontation, that made any visible impression upon him, and violence was not an option that any sane man would have chosen under the circumstances. So when an effective rebuke finally did come to Pete, it was not from us but from that old mill itself.

Our ox-like truck driver had come storming in at lunch with an extra measure of ferocity one day and was settling himself upon his prized cushion, when suddenly, and with a thundering crash, he ferociously slammed his arm into the wall behind him. The effect of the blow was so great, that I could feel the floor shake where I stood a good fifteen feet away. Somewhere across the mill a window slid shut.

"Goddamn wasps!" he snarled. "Been attacking me all morning!"

Once again, those righteous entomological wonders, the yellow jacketed tormentors of the now-departed army sergeant, had swung into action and brought down their terrible judgement on the hide of another transgressor! Pete was furious, and I was delighted. Perhaps, I mused, there really was some justice in the universe after all.

But the odd thing about Pete was that despite his oppressive nature I don't think there was anyone at the mill who really disliked him. There was something hopeless and frustrated in the way that he raged around the mill, and we could see that he was wounded in some way. We feared him, as we might have feared a wounded animal, but we would have rather seen him heal.

He and his wife lived in a tiny miserable shack of a place in the woods, somewhere near his folk's house. She worked the nightshift in an electronics factory, and they only saw each other awake on weekends. There were two kids to be taken care of, the older one by his wife's previous marriage, and now a new baby who had been consistently and worryingly sick since the cold weather had set in. In the meantime the older kid's father had recently reappeared out of the blue and was now shamelessly trying to gain custody. Pete was in a rage, and had to divert some portion of his income towards a lawyer in order to prevent it.

Pete's world was a very old and simple one. His folks were mountain people intimately attached to the land. They were hunters, trappers, sometime woodcutters, sometime millhands, people who had their own troubles and their own sense of justice. It was inevitable that their values would come into conflict with those of the modern world, and it was ironic that Pete had as much involvement with the courts as he did. His friend's trial for manslaughter, his own legal custody fight, his father's occasional arrests for being drunk and disorderly, these were not experiences of which he appeared either ashamed or particularly proud, but he freely related them as if they were a kind of gauge of his independence. In his world the notion of legal custody of a child just didn't make much sense. If a man abandons his wife and kid, how could he have any rights?

Pete's world was dying but not yet dead in these hills. He was building himself a house, he told us. But then allowed as how it really wasn't his house but a house on land belonging to his landlord who was this old woodsman he'd known all his life. They were working together to build the place, cutting trees from the land, hiring a fella with a portable sawmill to come and make it into lumber, and now they'd just about finished framing the place. When they were done, the old guy was going to sell the place to Pete.

To my big-city mind, it was an odd arrangement because I couldn't see what this woodsman was getting out of the deal. "That's a lot of work you're putting in, Pete. How can you trust him?" I wondered aloud. But this time it was my turn to have seized on the main point while actually missing its importance. Nobody replied to my question. Instead, Charlie rephrased the question for me. "Well now, he's not the kinda fella that'd take your help building the place and then not sell to you, is he?"

"No," Pete replied, "he's not one of those."

For people like Pete, the land was no longer a birthright. It was not something that you could expect to come into when you came of age. Ski resort owners and real estate speculators had invaded *en masse* over the last twenty-five years, inflating the dollar value of the land and putting through tax assessments that forced the poor to sell. Land that had sold for fifty dollars an acre twenty years ago was now being valued at ten to fifteen hundred dollars. Young people who'd grown up in the area couldn't afford to acquire land and were moving away. For their elders, the temptation to sell out and the difficulties of meeting the tax bill were great. But there was a willful stubborness in these people—sometimes mistaken for stupidity—that saw the whole trend as an insidious form of theft, and they refused to let go.

A lot of the people in this part of New England still held the rather antique yet radical notion that a person couldn't really own the land and that "ownership" only implied the right to make respectful use of it. That old woodcutter probably had some idea that he was just a caretaker of his land, and that before he died he had some responsibility to make sure it got into the hands of someone who really needed it. Pete had done right in marrying a woman who'd been abandoned like that, and he deserved a decent place to raise his family. That was a kind of right our highly touted criminal justice system did not understand.

Naturally Pete could not understand what someone like me was doing working in a sawmill. "Some people are so smart, they're dumb," he pronounced one day with the sure irony of genuine folk wisdom. I knew that this had been directed at me, though I wasn't quite sure why. Like many people whose experience does not inform them otherwise, Pete had the rather absurd idea that college made you smart and that being so endowed made you rich without having to work at things you hated. It was his rather vague fantasy that someday he might be able to go to college himself, and it was a blot on his ambition that anyone who'd already been to college should be laboring away at the same menial job as he.

It was a point that I did not choose to argue. Charlie would have understood because he actually had spent a year or two in college, though he liked to keep that fact carefully concealed. Instead I had to submit to the role of the "educated man" who'd actually done a little teaching and who might be trying to take unnatural advantage of working stiffs like Pete, when what I ought to be doing was making good use of my education. It was for my education that Pete had respect, and for little else. Perhaps Pete's single confession of doubt came when he informed me that he couldn't read very well.

"I mean, I'm not exactly illiterate or anything like that. I got my high school diploma. But the only thing my father ever read was comic books. And me, I can hardly pick up a newspaper and know what they're talking about." Here Pete had made himself completely vulnerable to me for the first and only time, and despite all his stupid and oppressive bigotry, I could not help feeling oddly humbled by this confession.

"I guess it's just kind of a matter of practice," I mumbled. "I'm sure if you wanted to, you could learn to do it." But whether it was true or not, I could not honestly say. This was simply an article of faith with me, and my reply came as response from my personal catechism. It put me in mind of the way the tables could be reversed, and oddly enough I began to think—of all things—about sharpening my new chain saw.

I had bought the thing, a brand-new medium-sized machine for cutting down trees because I had gotten tired of borrowing other people's when I needed firewood. The purchase had taken on a kind of mystical quality for me. Not only had it been bought with income earned at the sawmill, but it was also to be respected as the tool of a Sawyer. As such, it was an obligation of ownership that I keep the thing razor sharp, just as a logger would. Unfortunately, to this day, it is a monumental struggle for me to sharpen that bloody machine, and it requires every ounce of concentration that I can possibly muster if I am to come anywhere close to replicating the logger's skill. I know that if I really had to, or wanted to, I could become proficient at it. But I have also watched Pete sharpen the mill's log chopper, which was merely a modified chain saw and it was obvious that it came as second nature to him. Pete had been born to the woodsman's life, and I to the educator's. If there was to be any crossing over, it would take much practice. Much practice.

Thanksgiving

32

M uch to the collective incredulity of the workers at Parsons' mill, the Friday after Thanksgiving was to be a workday. There was no four-day weekend in Henry Parsons' schedule that fall. There was work to be done, a business to be run, and, in the popular political phraseology of the day, an economy to be "turned around." But despite the apparent meanness of his policy, Parsons was feeling exceptionally generous the day before Thanksgiving. He seemed to look around and about his mill and at his workers with the air of a proud general reviewing his victorious troops. It was as if on this day he was to take inventory of all the things for which he should be thankful. And given that he was a man who did not believe in giving praise, no matter how pleased he might actually be, he displayed an exceptional affection that one day.

At one point I found myself madly scrambling about with Jerry in an effort to keep up in our assistance to Parsons on the headsaw. I had just come tearing back to my place at the machine after dropping some freshly cut boards on a cart halfway across the mill, when to my astonishment I found old Henry himself on our side of the machine, helping Jerry with our work. This was something that he sometimes would do when he had only one assistant helping him, but it was unheard of when there were two of us. Normally he would stay put on his side of the machine and just keep the work piling up on us so that we had to work faster and faster in order to keep up. But on this day cooperation seemed to rule. As I dashed up I caught him smiling and looking magnanimously about at his workers, and then, finally resting his gaze on me he said, "Tim!" as if in revelation. Quite naturally I felt rather foolish for a minute, because I actually believed that this old man, who'd developed more techniques for the torture and persecution of employees than I could count, was actually acknowledging gratitude for my presence.

146

Work halted five minutes early that day, and Parsons cheerfully passed out our paychecks with enclosed bonuses. "Now eat plenty of turkey, but don't drink too much," he said, and everyone laughed. It was out of thanks to God for the bounty He had provided that those brave souls who fled oppression across the Atlantic celebrated the first Thanksgiving. It was to be the Puritans' one indulgence in the New World that they should see a little personal gain for their labors, and it was for that small gain that they were thankful. It was therefore natural that the workers at Parsons' mill should return the day after Thanksgiving, both thankful and sober, so that the Puritan Parsons might gain.

The Friday after Thanksgiving, Parsons and I showed up early, and Charlie showed up twenty minutes late. Everybody else failed to show up at all, opting instead for the luxury of a four-day weekend. As a "reward" for my obedience, I was given the job of delivering a load of firewood. And it was a sad commentary on the state of labor relations at that mill that the prospect of doing Pete's job for him gave me a great deal of pleasure. After weeks of putting up with Pete's oppressive and boorish behavior, I found myself thinking like Parsons: "Maybe Pete thinks he's indispensable, well *I'll* show him!" It was a rather foolish way for me to be looking at things, but of course it was precisely how Parsons wanted me to think. He had not been blind to the drubbing my pride had taken at Pete's hands, and in my opinion had probably helped to orchestrate it. The time had come to teach Pete a little lesson in humility, and so seeing in me the perfect tool for his ends, Parsons chose the moment to indulge me in a small measure of revenge.

Off I drove with the mill's truck, puttering down the hill through town, showing off my double-clutched flair for downshifting, riding high and feeling the rumble of the large engine in deceleration. The dawn had evolved into a bright and sunny morning, suffusing everything with clarity and warmth. Out of town and onto the concrete highway I roared, traveling through the long and spectacular views of the steep-sided North River valley. I was so absorbed in the exhilaration of the ride that I missed the little dirt turnoff I was supposed to take up along Whitney Brook and had to go back. As I climbed into the hills, taking first a right fork, then a left, another left, then right again, the road narrowed and steepened. Here winter's first light dusting of snow had arrived and had given the landscape a kind of luminous polarity that lit up the hillsides and made the dense woods that covered

147

them into transparent shadings, accentuating their shape instead of hiding them as in summer.

We had finally come into that peculiarly Gothic season between the final fall of leaves and the first arrival of deep snow. In this time hunters' shots are heard spreading through the woods, and the northern winds roar through leafless, frozen branches. It is a season that fills one with reverence for the power of nature and warns of winter's imminent arrival. But on this day it was glorious to ride high in that truck's cab, twisting and turning along the narrow path, looking out over sheer hillsides, grinding through the gears, and feeling the sure weight of the truck move determinedly through the hills.

At last I found the house, tucked away in the woods like grandmother's ought to be, although this appeared to be a more modern version. Smoke drifted lazily from a stone chimney as I drove up a long driveway, closely hemmed by straight and well-spaced hardwoods. These were orderly woods, and it was an orderly house with orderly wood sheds, and orderly stacks of wood. The place was an illustration from a child's book, and I imagined the people inside must be hearing the truck's roar and saying, "He's here, he's here. The man from the mill is here in his big truck." And it gave me great pleasure to think I was that man.

In answer to my knock, I was greeted by the frightened countenance of a very fair and pretty young woman, holding an equally fair and pretty baby. Their obvious shyness took me aback some, and I realized that I must have seemed an intimidating presence, what with my cap and sagging jeans, my beard, the truck I was driving, and the fact that I was a millhand. All of it conspired to give the false impression that I was some sort of rural roughneck. Being exceedingly polite and soft spoken, I tried to put right my deceptive appearance and turned to dump my load of firewood.

As I looked around I realized there was no car. "Where is her husband?" I wondered. I couldn't imagine what this woman was doing all the way out here by herself. Didn't she realize what could happen to these narrow little roads on the sides of steep hills when the blizzards came? "Foolish," I thought. "Very pretty, and in a pretty spot, but foolish." It was obvious that she was not accustomed to the country life. You could not live easily in such a place if you were as frightened as she seemed to be. If that baby were sick, the roads blocked, the phone lines down, did she know her neighbors? Somebody up the road had a couple of nasty-looking German sheperds I'd noticed.

I was unable to turn the truck around and dump my load in the designated space, and was forced to back slowly out the narrow drive, turn around on the road, and then back slowly up the drive again. The trees lining the drive were so close that there was almost no clearance on either side of the truck. I was exceptionally proud of my skill in successfully maneuvering the truck, but now as I backed slowly and deliberately up the drive toward the house my mind was briefly diverted by the enchantment of the place and the imagined vulnerability of its inhabitants, not by the demands of the task at hand. Bam! The truck hit something and jolted me out of my reverie. What had I hit? It couldn't be too bad because I'd been going so slowly. So I jumped out to have a look and discovered that unfortunately the entire right side of the tailgate had wrapped itself around a tree. This wasn't bad, it was terrible!

Instead of screaming, I grabbed my cap and flung it murderously to the ground. But by some perverse feat of aerodynamics it flew right under the truck and I was forced to crawl after it. My enchanted spell had broken into a nervous fit of wrenching anxiety. I angrily returned to the truck, backed it up, and started to dump. The truck's bed lifted higher and higher into the air, but the tailgate showed absolutely no interest in opening, and refused to spill the load.

I had no idea what to do. I still wanted to scream at the top of my lungs, and the effort of repressing this desire was making me shake. I could not return to the mill with the truck full because that would only make a bad situation even worse. Parsons had the view of a military man, and his attitude would be that I'd been sent on a mission to deliver wood. Failure to achieve that objective would be far worse than any casualties incurred along the way. I found a large wrench under the seat and desperately started to hammer away at one of the tailgate hinges in a crude attempt to restore the thing to working order. After five minutes of incessant pounding, during which I alternated between rage and exhaustion, I managed at last to free the tailgate and wood began to pour out.

By now my hands were bleeding, and I was covered in dirt and leaves from crawling under the truck to retrieve my cap, but I was still invited into the house, while the young woman—apparently oblivious to my torment—got me a check. The place was immaculate. Fine handwoven rugs adorned a polished floor, luxurious chairs beckoned, and in the corner sat a beautiful baby grand piano, its pristine ivory keys uncracked and untarnished, its finish like crystal, showing to perfection the deep dark grain of its exotic wood. The piano's lines were so simple, clean, and elegant that it seemed to sound a beautiful note without the depression of a single key. It was as pretty as the lady before me, and as alluring as her shining baby. Moving closer I could make out the open music books on the piano stand and saw that they were hopelessly complicated; the staffs dripped with notes and made it clear that someone around here really knew how to play. Thinking of the few pitiful chords I could play, and examining my blood caked fingers, I drew back, feeling that touching such an instrument would have been desecration.

She wrote out the check on the piano bench, while her child watched me in wonder. As she handed me the check, I wondered again who was taking care of this woman and child and almost felt compelled to ask if I could somehow join her in this piece of heaven. Instead I took the check as gracefully as possible, thanked her, returned to the dented truck and to Parsons' mill, where I would have some explaining to do.

Parsons was in the cellar working on the bandsaw when I came in. "Well," I pronounced, trying to sound as folksy as possible, "I probably cost you more than I made you today." He smiled and nodded appreciatively, never taking his eyes off his work, as if thinking that there was nothing unusual about that. But then suddenly he stopped what he was doing, looked straight ahead and squinted as if in deep thought. After a second his eyes opened wide in revelation, and he turned abruptly to see that I was not smiling, and waited for an explanation.

33

For three weeks in late November and early December the weather remained uniformly grey and cold. The sky was blanketed by a roiling mass of grey and black clouds with such an ominous look that somebody would inevitably pronounce with wise certainty, "It looks like snow." As the days went by, there did not seem to be anyone among the workers at Parsons' mill capable of resisting this particular prophecy. One by one we tried our luck, each picking a day on which certainty of the impending maelstrom struck us with such force that it was impossible to resist sharing it with everyone else. But as many times as somebody said it looked like it, or felt like it, no snow was forthcoming.

True to my rather stubborn nature, I successfully resisted this speculative exercise longer than anyone else. I'd watched with smug pleasure as one meteorological forecast after another came to nothing, and I was in no hurry to follow suit. But then one day as the sun rose, and the sky lightened to its usual gloom, I too succumbed to idle speculation, for on this day I felt *absolutely certain* that it looked like snow. Of course I turned out to be as wrong as everyone else, and now it was their turn—chastened as they were—to take pleasure in my mistake.

The whole matter was altogether too much like a game of Russian roulette. Except, instead of having only one chamber loaded, the gun appeared to have only one empty. With the exception of old Henry, all of us had succumbed to this suicide of pride. As far as we were concerned the game had ended in a stalemate, and there was little enthusiasm for a second round. We had no expectation that Parsons himself would take a hand because, as always, he carried the responsible air of a man with more important considerations on his mind.

One morning as I arrived at work, I thought I detected a slight change in the predawn darkness. As the morning progressed it became evident that we were in the midst of a brilliant gold and blue, cold and shiny day and that at last the threat of snow had passed. At morning break, birds were chirping, and the sun was streaming in the windows at our backs as we sat down, basking in its radiance, gleeful at this reprieve from eternal gloom. At 9:10 Parsons emerged from his office to stir us from our luxury, and prod us back to work with the usual incomprehensible directives. But before he set us in motion, he paused for a moment to look over our heads through the windows and make an appraisal of the street outside. Smiling broadly, he announced triumphantly, "*Now* we'll have our snow!" Considering the pristine sky, such a prediction seemed to border on the ridiculous, and I took it as just another version of Parsons' peculiar brand of sarcasm.

It snowed that night. It snowed and snowed and snowed, until by morning a full two feet of snow lay on the ground. The radio at home announced that a record of some sort had been broken and that every school in the area was closed. We were advised by the civil authorities not to go out unless we absolutely had to, since road conditions were considered "extremely hazardous." Amy, whose single greatest fear was having to drive down slippery roads, was gleeful. For my part there was only an impatient wait for the almost certain call from Parsons announcing that work was off for the day. No such call came through, and I was sure that Parsons' phone line must have been knocked out by the storm.

Somehow or other I managed to push my little wreck of a pickup truck through the snow drifts and down barely perceptible highways toward work. I arrived fifteen minutes late, to find Parsons and Charlie waiting for the rest of us to arrive. They both had the smug air of men who'd seen it all before, and—for that matter—much worse.

"Well, you two might as well get started," Parsons intoned with resignation.

Charlie handed me a snow shovel. "I'll get the deck, you better get started on the truck entrance. He likes to be able to get the truck out as early as possible." This instruction put me in a slight state of shock. It had never occurred to me that having made it to the relative warmth and safety of the mill I'd be required to go back outside and shovel snow.

The truck entrance to the cellar was cut from the steep embankment separating the mill from the street. It was reinforced by eight-foot concrete walls that joined the building itself. It is the unique property of the sort of light, windblown snow, which had just fallen in so much quantity, that it will drift along the contours of a hill, leaving an inch or so in its trail, until it finds a convenient imperfection in the form of a large hole, or depression. The snow promptly sets the imperfection right by filling in and smoothing over, until the original contour of that hill is restored. In this respect, the truck entrance was the perfect repository for vast quantities of fine, white, powdery snow, and it was my misfortune to be in the position of reimposing the will of man.

I suppose that I was grateful for the fact that the snow was light, since there were places where I had to lift great shovelfuls of the stuff over my head. It is a fact of nature that light snow is greater in volume than the heavy, wet variety. In terms of its removal, one has few options, but preference is a different matter. If your idea of happiness is to move a given weight in a large number of light movements, then you will prefer light snow, even though there is more of it. If you prefer fewer, more painful movements, you will go for the wet stuff. Of course this leaves aside attendant matters, such as the fact that light snow thrives in an atmosphere of ear-ripping, finger-killing cold, while the wet variety usually leaves you soaked from head to toe. I generally preferred lighter snow. But nature being what it is, our preferences are seldom heeded. What may begin as a nice, dry, light snow can turn warm and slushy in a matter of hours. This often leads the shoveler to curse nature and—turning to the heavens—to exclaim, "Why, why, why, have you done this terrible thing?" Whereupon nature, apparently listening with much glee, replies by suddenly turning the temperature down. And then what had been a moderately difficult slurry requiring mere patience and a snow shovel, becomes an icy crust requiring sainthood and a pickax.

It is said that nature is infinitely wise. Be that as it may, it is also infinitely perverse. New Englanders are notoriously proud of their weather. But it is not the broad reaches of a fine and stable atmosphere they treasure; that is for the Californians. No, the New Englander, reputed to be dry and taciturn, is proud of his weather precisely because it is so perverse. And therein lies the implication of wisdom.

Thus the first winter snowstorms, which had announced themselves with such a flourish, continued their extravagance for several weeks. We had quickly come through our child-like wonder at that first blanket of white and were now cursing the stuff on a daily basis. It was soon apparent that as long as these storms lasted, an inevitable two to four hours of daily labor would be devoted to the snow shovel. There were two log decks to be cleared, the truck to be got out, and a path to be cleared to the drying shed. The body of yard was cleared with a plow attached to the front of the forklift, but there were still large inaccessible areas that had to be cleared by hand.

It was during one of these marathon shoveling sessions that my embittered mind began to consider a number of alternatives, including another line of work. Apparently I was not alone in this regard because Charlie suggested that if we were to spend so much time shoveling snow for a living, perhaps we'd be better off going into business for ourselves and selling our services door-to-door.

Pete took a different approach and started grumbling about welfare fraud. "I hear they're beginning to catch some of them welfare cheats. I hope they lock 'em up!" he snarled one particularly miserable day. This was in response to a recent and well-publicized campaign by the federal government to cut the "fat" out of the welfare budget, and if Pete's comments were any gauge, it appeared to be working. The odd thing was that a few days earlier Pete had expressed almost the exact opposite point of view. He'd gone on at some length about how badly some of the old people in his town were treated by the welfare office. In order to receive benefits they would be forced to sell their cars, no matter what sort of old heap, and were then expected to commute the fifteen miles to the county seat to sort out some detail or other before checks would be forthcoming. "Bunch of arrogant bastards working in that office," Pete had groused. "Young too. Dress well. Probably went to college," he added, giving me an accusing stare.

We were all in a nasty mood as we chopped ice with our picks and blew desperately on our hands to keep them warm. Despite the fact that Pete had changed tacks and was now siding with the same "arrogant bastards" he'd earlier condemned, I knew better than to point out the contradiction. Instead Jerry responded with an enviable diplomatic skill that was fast becoming his trademark. "Yeah!" he shouted in agreement, "There's lots of work around if you're willing to look for it!" And then, as an aside to me, he muttered, "And it's all *shit* like this."

Parsons' Gloom

34

Parsons had suddenly descended into one of his blacker moods, and as usual nobody knew why. It may have been the gradual effect of weeks of continual bad weather, or perhaps a downturn in profitability, or even a cosmic misalignment, for all we could tell. But it was the absurdly trivial matter of a broken rubber belt, normally attached to the headsaw, that seemed to precipitate the matter.

One morning Charlie and Parsons came in from outside, engaged in heated argument.

" . . . Well I don't know," Charlie was whining dubiously.

"Thirty years!" Parsons snapped back, "I never had a belt break on me like that before!

The two of them strode up to the machinery in question, and as Charlie stood by, hands on hips, Parsons practically dove into the bowels of the thing and angrily started fiddling with one of its pulleys. The rest of us had gathered around to see what all the fuss was about, and before long the entire crew was standing around watching as Parsons—angrier by the minute—became more and more entangled in the offending mechanism.

"Sixty dollars!" he shouted. "Sixty dollars! It costs sixty dollars to replace that belt!" He looked out from where he crouched in the machinery and glowered accusingly at us. It was obvious that he thought one of us was a saboteur and that the belt had been deliberately broken. Not knowing which of us was the guilty party, he employed the tyrannical prerogative of parents and schoolmasters the world over and made it clear that as far as he was concerned we were *all* guilty.

To his chagrin Parsons discovered that the machine had not been mortally wounded and would run perfectly well for the time being without the belt. For the moment the wind fell from the old man's angry sails, and with a chorus of sighed relief we dispersed quietly, spending the rest of the morning tiptoeing about, trying to remain as invisible as possible.

Lunchtime arrived safely without further unpleasantness, and we began to pass around a few bits of conversation, hoping to lighten the mood. But Parsons was determined to upstage any such impulse, and before retreating into his office he performed his midday ablutions with an unusually slow and drawn out deliberateness that seemed calculated to draw everyone's attention. Washing his hands with the care of a surgeon preparing for an operation, he vigorously manipulated thin, lithe wrists and rubbed away at the germs lying in wait on his long bony fingers. Turning his attention to the clean linen provided by his wife, he patted first the front, then the back of his hands, and with effete delicacy dried each and every finger, finishing off the tips with a little toweled flourish. Folding the linen precisely, and smoothing out its wrinkles, he threw it on its bar with a careless little toss and shot us a contemptuous glance as he disappeared into his office, leaving us silent and open mouthed. Somehow one could not help feeling that we "hands" might be in for such a cleaning as well.

By now we dared not stir and could only reflect on the sins we might have committed to bring about this terrible suspicion. I thought guiltily back to the mild rebellion that I'd inadvertently caused some months before when I'd started a brief craze for apple eating amongst the millhands. I was then still anxious to make good as a country boy and had the rather foolish notion that it would impress the locals if I made a point of bringing a couple of locally grown apples to work just as the fall harvest was at its height. In this way I hoped to demonstrate just the right measure of provincial Yankee wisdom by being an advocate of the inexpensive and healthy nutrition so readily available. Drawing as much attention to myself as possible, I munched and slurped my way through these apples with great relish, loudly discussing with new-found expertise the relative merits of a "mack" versus a "golden delicious," all the while perfectly ignorant of the unfortunate dental condition that made apple eating anathema to the old man.

Apparently everyone at the mill except me had made careful note of the fact that Parsons wore dentures. I did not realize until much later that at least half the teeth he brushed so carefully after finishing his lunch were of the removable variety. Of course my fellow workers had no idea that I didn't realize what I was doing, and it was not long before the delicious cruelty of an effective—if unintended—ploy against the boss had taken root. After a week of what I considered daily demonstrations of healthful eating and a profound concern for the welfare of the local economy, I noted with pride that others were following my lead. And now, as 12:25 rolled around and Parsons emerged from his office to prepare for his after-lunch ablutions, he was greeted with the sight of four or five crunching and slurping apple eaters, all competing with each other to make as conspicuous a display of healthy gums as possible.

Unfortunately such high spirits now eluded us. On the surface Parsons seemed calm, but experience informed us that such halcyon moments probably represented the mere eye of the storm and that we had yet to pass through to the other side. Out of nowhere, the horn attached to the phone screamed and bleated through the mill, causing us all to jump in unison. This device was an absolute necessity if the phone was to be heard while the mill was up and running, but in the gloomy silence of lunch that day it was a heart stopper. As usual Parsons picked up the receiver and calmly placed it against the radio speaker, treating the caller to the reassuring voice of the President, who was just then explaining the fundamental tenets of the "trickle-down" theory of economics. The receiver was held there for a full five minutes, while Parsons continued to eat with his free hand before finally consenting to speak. "No, I'm not interested," was all he said and then hung up.

After lunch the morning's debate between Parsons and Charlie was renewed on a slightly different track. The discussion no longer concerned the broken rubber belt but an employee who had been fired the previous spring for another alleged act of sabotage.

"Well now, Henry," Charlie was saying indulgently, "you know that he and I didn't exactly get along, so I don't really have any reason to defend him. But I still don't see how he could have done what you say."

It seemed the controversy in this case centered on the cut-off saw that Charlie used every day to chop logs to length. Its cutting bar was suspended at the operator's end from the ceiling by means of a rubberized "bunji" cord. This kept the saw up and out of the way while a log was being maneuvered into place underneath it. Also suspended from the ceiling was an electrical cord leading to the power switch at this same end of the saw. The alleged saboteur had managed to sever the electrical cord while operating the saw, and the argument was over the deliberacy of his act. For a good half hour, acting like a pair of opposing lawyers arguing their case in front of some phantom jury, the two of them took turns manipulating the saw in question, each demonstrating with irrefutable logic that the accused either was or was not guilty.

"Now ya see," cried Parsons, "he'd a had to pull the bar all the way to the floor for that cable to break, and what reason would he have for that!"

"But Henry," Charlie protested, "the cable is longer now than it used to be."

"Do you have any idea how much it cost me to get this thing fixed? I had to get a whole new switch put on there."

"There must've been something else wrong with that switch, 'cause just breakin' the cord wouldn't hurt the switch."

"Well, so that just proves my point. He broke the cord, and then he broke the switch!"

And so while the debate continued absurdly, the point that seemed the most relevant remained unspoken. After all, what difference did it make when the employee in question was long gone? It began to dawn on me that it was not really a question of this particular man's guilt or innocence, but the guilt and innocence of a whole list of fired, or soon-to-be fired employees, who stood accused of working in the service of Parsons' enemies. In other words, Henry Parsons' sanity was being debated here, and both Charlie and the old man knew it.

The day passed without serious explosion from Parsons, but in probability we would have been better off if he'd vented a little more spleen. Whatever was eating that old man remained, but instead of purging it with one big eruption he turned his frustrations inward and fell into a deep depression. Over the following days his directions to us grew increasingly more vague and incomprehensible, and asking for clarification became even riskier. "Why don't you use your *brains* to figure it out?" he snapped at me. His tone seemed to imply that the brains in question were merely alleged.

We resorted to those tasks closest at hand. But these soon ran in short supply. Old Henry was finding it increasingly difficult to face the headsaw, and when no boards were being produced it was only a matter of time before it became impossible to produce anything else. When—after monumental struggle—he did bring himself to work the big saw, he did so in such a half-hearted and tentative manner that it was often hard to tell if he was actually getting set to split logs or just testing the thing out to see if it was still in working order. He'd roll a log up onto the log beam, crank up the big electric motor, and with the guarded hope that things might be returning to normal certain of us would drop whatever it was we were doing and rush over to help. But then, after working the machine for three-quarters of an hour or so, just as we would be getting into the rhythm of the thing, he'd shut the machine off and go do something else, leaving us totally flat. Such behavior was dispiriting to everyone because now his erratic work habits were imposed on us all.

Finally he began to disappear altogether. His car would be there, so we knew he was nearby, but hours passed during which nobody saw him or had any idea of his whereabouts. The mill was not that big a place, and I found myself speculating that perhaps he had the ability to metamorphose into one of those angry yellow jackets, which periodically swarmed in to attack an errant worker, and that he was now buzzing about in some hidden recess waiting for his opportunity.

But in this instance the human incarnation of the mill's wrath finally came showering on the head of a misdirected employee. As Parsons struggled his way out of indecisiveness, he decided to persecute Hank. It was obvious that Hank's tales of Washington Babylon had offended him from the start and now Parsons fixed him as a source of the moral decay at the root of the mill's problems.

I was standing by the ripsaw, pretending to be busy, when Hank ambled over. "He says I should work with you."

"Did he tell you what we're supposed to be doing?" I asked.

"Nope. What do you think we're supposed to do?"

"God only knows." I threw up my hands. "God or Henry."

"Not to be confused with one another," He replied slyly.

From across the mill Parsons caught our sarcastic looks, and his face began its dangerous journey toward the red end of the spectrum. Realizing that we could no longer idly stand by, I invented something. We were poaching work that normally fell into Pete's territory, but I didn't think he'd mind. Even he'd been intimidated by Parsons' latest funk and, sensibly, had been out all afternoon with the truck. We figured he was probably out boozing it up somewhere and that we wouldn't see him until about quarter after four, just enough time to put the truck away and go home for the day.

"I dunno," sighed Hank. "This is a bunch of shit. I could just head out to The Boom Chain and wrap myself around a brew right about now."

"*Now?*"

"It'd beat hell outa this."

159

I just looked at him. I wasn't *that* anxious to get canned, and I wasn't about to encourage him to do it by himself. After all, I figured that I might get away with it, but I could see from the way Parsons had been eyeing Hank he was just looking for a good excuse.

Later on, when I found some work for us to do together on the ripsaw and tensions seemed to have eased a bit, Hank said to me, "You know, you're all right." And when this old guy said it, you knew that for that brief moment at least, you were. The next afternoon Hank did leave for that beer. He'd been standing around for an hour with nothing to do but push a broom aimlessly, when he finally gave up. He strolled over and passed a word to Parsons, who stood dazedly making half-hearted attempts at manipulating the headsaw. The old man simply nodded, and Hank moved over slowly and deliberately to gather up his red-checked wool hunter's jacket and strolled casually out the door under the sign marked "exit."

"Hank," I thought, "you're all right too." And for that brief moment at least, he was.

It was odd and it was contradictory, but so long as the winter weather continued to make it immensely difficult to get to work, and even worse once we got there, it was a matter of personal pride to see how promptly one could show up in the morning. It became the measure of a man's skill, intelligence, grit, and general moral worth that despite the worst possible calamities of nature he could be counted on to arrive at precisely seven o'clock. The fact that once he had succeeded in arriving at work he had absolutely no interest in staying there was absolutely irrelevant. The challenge of getting there was the important thing.

After every night's storm, each man would recount the derring-do with which he had triumphed against the elements and hazards of his particular route. We would hear of the accidents he'd seen, of the fools he'd passed by, and the number of times he'd nearly lost it himself. All of it intended to point out the glorious triumph that his mere presence represented. In hearing of Pete's East, Jerry's South, Tim's North, and, until recently, Hank's West, we in that mill formed a general picture of the weather's effect upon our shared corner of the world, and how—like Shiva—each of that storm's many arms was more terrible than the next.

There was absenteeism and tardiness aplenty at Parsons' mill, but almost never did it occur on a day when there was good reason for it. Whatever the perversities of nature, it seemed that we could summon the perversity to match it. Schools could close down, the power could fail, bridges could collapse, but Parsons' mill would remain open. The ordinary considerations of profit and loss, of orders to be filled, and of productive efficiency now seemed diminished before the prideful necessity of a crew struggling to keep the shop running.

But in the midst of this struggle, and despite our best efforts, Parsons had lost faith in us. His latest fantasies about sabotage and his decision to fire Hank were but the most recent signs of a self-doubt that he could not accept and had pinned on his workers. In the six months I'd been working at the mill, I had seen five men come and go. In the previous spring four others had left, or been fired, so that within the year nine men had gone from a mill that was then only employing five people.

"It just doesn't seem to bother him that he's sending people on down the road," Charlie mused soon after Hank's departure. "He just doesn't care." He shook his head as he said this, wearing the incredulous expression of someone who wonders why he had been spared the disasters that befell those around him.

36

It was apparent that Parsons' dismissal of Hank had not proved enough of a sacrifice to the demons that possessed him. He now resolved to regain his lost initiative in running the mill by starting in on a new round of persecution. As it turned out, I was to be victim number one. From some obscure hiding place, like a sorcerer pulling an evil spirit from his mill-cauldron, Parsons sent a cart rumbling my way one morning loaded to capacity with dowel blanks for steaming and straightening. Quite naturally I was horrified. I'd been certain that we'd already eliminated all such work, and because of the nature of the new ripsaw, I knew that we'd produced very few since. But then there it was, right before my eyes, just waiting to spring its quotient of misery upon me. Parsons rarely did a thing without calculated purpose, and it was obvious that he had taken great pains to hide this cart.

Although officially no longer the superintending fireman, my return to the hated steaming tanks meant a return to the fearsome boiler itself. Parsons had long ago admitted to the need for heat in the mill, entrusting that weighty responsibility to the rough and capable hands of big Pete, skilled after a lifetime's experience in firebuilding. In the morning he would rake the coals from the previous day and quickly transform them into the inferno required to raise the substantial head of steam that sent soothing heat to the main floor. Then working with the variety of forged-iron rakes, pokers, and shovels specific to the trade, he could stabilize this inferno, and load it with the proper sizes and configurations of wooden scrap so as to provide a nice, even fire that required only occasional additions during the day. At day's end he would rake and bank the fire, throwing on many shovelfuls of sawdust, and so put the fire "to bed." In this way he would ensure the coals for the next day's quick start.

Unfortunately the twin demands of steam for the steaming tanks and steam for the radiators upstairs were much more than either Pete or I had ever been forced to provide, and I soon discovered that Pete's idea of an adequate supply of boiler fuel was not nearly sufficient for my purposes. Stepping into the breach I began to feed the thing with every scrap of wood I could lay my hands on. But no matter how much wood I piled into that firebox, I could not muster an adequate head of steam. Aside from the fact that the mill was completely uninsulated, the blower system did an incredibly effective job of sucking warm air out of the place almost as rapidly as the boiler could produce it. With the steaming tanks turned off, and with the constant and controlled diet of fuel that Pete had been feeding the boiler, it had been just possible to achieve an equilibrium that provided modest comfort to those working upstairs. But now that the steaming tanks were running full blast such an equilibrium was totally out of reach.

Thus, aside from the plain misery of having to steam myself to an odoriferous wreck while working the tanks, I was now faced with twice the usual amount of boiler tending. In the meantime, Pete had become miffed because I was fooling with *his* boiler, while everyone else upstairs was mad at me because they weren't getting enough heat. At lunchtime people started passing sarcastic remarks around about how nice and toasty it must be to work around the boiler all day. I just sat there in grim silence, feeling soaked to the skin and thinking that while it might indeed be warm down there, Hell itself also happened to be noted for its warmth.

In tending the boiler there was only one specific, absolute, and unbreakable rule that Parsons expected us all to follow. This had to do with the water inlet valve that fed water into the pressure tank to replace that which had been carried off as steam. Right next to the valve was a glass tube, eight inches or so in length, filled with varying amounts of water that corresponded to the water level in the boiler itself. As the tube approached the empty level you were supposed to open the inlet valve until the tube indicated you had filled the tank. Failure to fill the tank in time would in all probability have led to some sort of internal hemorrhaging that would have completely destroyed the boiler. At the other end of the spectrum of disasters lay the possibility that the tank might be overfilled, and it was to preempt this latter scenario that Parsons had formulated his single rule.

"Now, when you open this inlet valve, you—are—not—to—take—your—hand—off—the—valve—until—you—have—closed—it—again.

Otherwise you might *flood the boiler.*" His pronounciation was clear, and unmistakably ominous; it was not a rule I was to forget if I knew what was good for me. There was even a certain musical, almost operatic quality to the words, *flood the boiler,* and although the total implications of this possibility were left unexplained, it brought to mind visions of cataclysmic disaster. Heedful of such a terrible warning, I faithfully followed this rule right from the start. Despite a healthy measure of rebelliousness, I am not one for making a principle of breaking rules. Indeed there is a certain doggedness in me that often sees me following rules the vast majority of sensible people have long since given up as ridiculously outdated. To some, a rule is a rule, while to others, a rule is meant to be broken. But in typical, middle-of-the-road fashion, I generally see the wisdom of both propositions. Though, rather foolishly, I tend to apply one or the other in direct contradiction to the prevailing sentiment at a given moment.

So it was that on a certain day, not long after my reintroduction to the boiler, when the temperature outside was hovering steadily in the teens and I was running to and fro at an increasingly frantic pace, I decided that the time had come to break Parsons' rule. It seemed totally impractical to stand around, stupidly holding on to a valve for five minutes, when I had wood to load, dampers to check, and dowel blanks to toss into the steaming tanks. With a shrug I broke the rule.

After a few minutes spent on other chores, I came back to find that the water in the boiler had risen to a satisfactory level and shut the inlet valve off, feeling completely confident in the non-necessity of Parsons' little rule. Naturally one infraction soon led to another, and to another, until I made a regular habit of leaving the valve open and unattended while I went off to do other things.

Several days later, feeling reasonably content at how close I was to completion of this latest round of steam bending, I opened the valve, threw a few chunks of wood into the firebox, and then went off to sit on the toilet for a while. This universally popular technique for taking unauthorized breaks was particularly popular among us millhands because it was a relatively safe haven from the ever-imminent wrath of Parsons. The toilet was closeted in a little room in a dark corner of the cellar a few yards from the boiler. In a day long past, an enterprising millhand had drilled a set of strategically located holes in the walls, so that it was possible to keep a safe eye on all possible avenues of approach. For his part Parsons had responded by tacking a government sponsored poster to the door facing the toilet, which went into some detail as to a worker's right to compensation in the event that he was dismissed.

There was one further refinement to this little hideaway, which came in the form of an automatic toilet seat, the likes of which I have not seen before or since. Whenever anyone sat on the seat the weight would cause a spring-loaded valve to open so as to let a jet of water flush continually into the bowl. This was a particularly unsettling refinement; not only did it provide an uncomfortable rushing sensation beneath one's posterior, but it also meant that the *sush* of water could be heard travelling through pipes that happened to lead directly to Parsons' office upstairs. Parsons did not spend much time in his office during work hours, but he did duck in for a minute every now and again, and the element of uncertainty was always present. The knowledge that he just might be keeping track of your activity downstairs was sufficient for nearly everyone to resort to some form of subterfuge in the matter: a strategically placed block of wood, a failure to place one's full weight on the seat, or flipping the seat up and making do without it were some of the more familiar options.

I was thus fully occupied on that particular day, when I noticed that despite my precautions there was a distinct gurgle of water in the drain below me. I stood up quickly, wondering how my usual precautions had failed. The gurgling sounds continued to rise from the toilet bowl, and I was looking vaguely about for an explanation of this strange phenomenon, when at last it hit me like a shot. There, meandering along the ceiling, I could see a pipe leading directly from the boiler to the common sewer pipe. I hastily zipped up my pants and went dashing for the boiler at the precise moment that Parsons himself came tumbling down the cellar stairs shouting, "My god! You've flooded the boiler!"

Apparently the matter had not achieved the disastrous proportions it might have; these were still unclear. The only result of my inattention was that Parsons had to attach a length of garden hose to the boiler and let it drain out the truck entrance door for an hour or so before firing the boiler back up. I suppose that if this had occurred on a really cold day the lack of heat over those hours might have had serious consequences for the mill's plumbing. Actually there had been no damage at all, and the dire nature of Parsons' warnings seemed blown all out of proportion.

Of course in the matter of rules, especially ones that he himself had constructed, Parsons was not one who believed they were meant to be broken. After he'd ministered to the boiler and pronounced it well on the way to recovery, he took me aside and waggled a finger at me. "If you can't do better than that, I'm afraid we can't use you here." Then turning on his heels he strode away.

It was the first time he'd ever threatened to fire me, and I did not take it lightly. I just stood there where he'd left me in front of the boiler staring at my fingernails and trying to sort it all out. He wasn't mad at me for causing any damage because even that time I'd smashed the truck he had taken it pretty much in stride. No, what I'd done now was far worse. I'd taken a rule that had been unmistakably set before me and had deliberately gone and broken it. And no matter what the actual value of that rule, my transgression was proof positive of a disloyal nature.

Later, when I mentioned Parsons' threat to Charlie, he made light of it. "Ahh!" He dismissed the thought with a downward wave of the hand. "He wouldn't fire you for *that*. You're too valuable to him."

"I don't know, Charlie. He sounded to me like he meant it."

Mercifully I was soon relieved of my duties as boiler tender. Parsons had apparently decided that further steam bending could wait for a while. Inadvertently I had won a kind of victory. But it was not long before the old man began to relieve me of other duties as well.

Whenever the phone rang at the mill, it was custom that whoever happened to be closest would answer it. Parsons did not like to be disturbed once he'd established a rhythm on the headsaw and relied on us to carry any important messages to him as he worked. Most calls had to do with the delivery of scrap wood, which was not a matter considered worth bothering him about. So, if a call came through and he was not consulted, he generally knew what it was about anyway. Several weeks before my little problem with the boiler, I had responded to the rather irate inquiry of a woman demanding to know what had become of the load of firewood she'd ordered. "I ordered that wood way back in April, and you *still* haven't delivered it!"

I explained that we were sorry but that the waiting list of orders had been very long this year. Following standard procedure, I located her name on the list and informed her that there were only three or four people ahead of her and that we should be getting to her within a couple of weeks. This seemed to mollify her and she rang off. Unfortunately while this had been a wholly reasonable estimate, given the mill's pace of production at the time, I had not foreseen the possibility that things were going to slow down as much as they eventually did. While the mill's production slowed to a crawl, this particular customer's impatience wound tighter and tighter.

Three weeks after her first call, and only a couple of days after I'd flooded the boiler, she called again, this time demanding an explanation from Parsons himself. After settling his business with this outraged customer, Parsons emerged from his office, looking red in the face, and strode directly up to me. "Was it you who promised her that load?"

"Yes."

"Well in future, I think it would be best if you did not answer the phone."

"You mean," I hesitated uncomprehendingly, "you don't want me to answer the phone at all?"

"That is correct. I think it would be best," he snapped dryly.

I was dumbfounded. Here I was, twenty-six years old, responsibly married, a hard worker, and yet after all these months I was not even trusted to answer the telephone. I began to feel like the little boy whose parents had just taken away some petty privilege because he was not "grown up" enough to be trusted with it.

"Charlie," I later moaned, "this is getting to be serious."

"Ahh," he just waved the thought away again. "Don't worry about it. He's just having another one of his spells. You'll see, he'll forget all about it." But as I looked at him there, making busy with a broom because once again we'd run out of work for the day, I thought I caught a look of uncertainty.

His name was John, and he appeared at the mill one morning about a week after the new year had begun. Small and wiry, wearing tattered clothes and worn-out shoes, his hair was disheveled and unwashed, while his fingernails, long and curling where they had not broken, were filthy black underneath. He looked about the mill with a kind of sly expectancy that gave me a deep sense of foreboding. Nobody had been aware that Parsons was looking for a new hand, nor would anyone have expected it, since things at the mill were now moving so slowly. But I'd been around Parsons just long enough to know the minute I laid eyes on this new man that trouble was ahead. After break Parsons assigned him to me as an assistant on the ripsaw. As we worked together he maintained a grim silence, which he broke only after my suspicions and my questions grew sharper and more insistent.

"Where ya from?" I tried with nervous folksiness.

"Up north," he mumbled.

We worked on in silence for a while, he taking my direction on the ripsaw's operation with grudging little nods of the head, acting all along as if he didn't see anything too special about it.

"How come ya came down here?" I asked.

"Got laid off."

"Oh? Where'd ya work?"

"Furniture factory." He fell silent for a moment, and then as if finally deciding to lay out his trump, he said, "Used to run a ripsaw, just like this one."

I broke my pace for a second and looked him directly in the eye. A very slight smile showed on his lips, while his head dropped forward in a barely perceptible nod. We then both fell silent and remained that way until lunch. There was nothing else left for us to say to each other because in that second we understood each other perfectly.

At lunch break Charlie decided to be friendly and ask our new member where he was living. Much to everyone's surprise the man suddenly became sullen and coarse, swearing violently about the present condition of his car, an ancient boat of a Chevy, which listed heavily to one side out in the yard. "I'm stayin' in a place off South Main. Not there two days when the peckerheads steal the fucking batt'ry from m'car! Damn shitheads!" His profanity rang through the mill, shocking everyone else into dead silence. Even Pete was looking a little stunned.

Later on, as we broke up to go to work, Parsons slipped out of his office and crept up to the big truck driver to ask confidentially, "What *is* a peckerhead, Pete? Is that like a jerk?"

"Uuh. . . . " Pete hesitated, deciding how best to respond. "Yeah, that's right. Like a jerk." Parsons nodded his head rapidly, turned on his heels, and fled downcellar.

It was my custom after an afternoon of ripsawing to shut my machine down, dust myself off, and amble across the mill to the bench where my coat and the remains of my lunch were stored. There I would flip off my headphones, slowly put on my coat, stick my thermos under an arm, and walk toward the door. But before leaving my last act was always to climb part way up a large stepladder that leaned against the wall by the door and reach in among the rows of neatly labeled circuit-breaker boxes to shut off the current to my machine.

From up there I could reach most of the mill's twenty or so breaker boxes, each carefully labeled with the name of a machine. Of all those machines, the ripsaw was the only one that always had that current shut off here at the end of the day. This was for the simple reason that as one of the few truly modern machines in the mill, it had a little red jeweled light on its instrument panel, which would have gone on burning all night if its power was not shut off at the source. It was meant to be a safety measure, so that a person knew that when that light was off, there was no chance of the machine accidentally starting up. The same measure of safety might have been applied to all the machines in the mill, but none of them had that little red light. Since it would have been somehow disharmonious—not to mention wasteful—to leave that light burning all night, mine was the one that always got shut off.

Stepping up that ladder, snapping down the heavy spring-loaded lever, and then stepping back down the ladder had become a ritual to which Parsons and I mutually subscribed. As a responsibility it didn't amount to much. But for me it had become an important sign of my small authority as a Sawyer.

The day that John had shown up to take my saw away from me, my routine was exactly the same as always. But before I could carry it out, Parsons came gliding up to me as I was dusting myself off. He had the same mysterious and devilish grin as on the day he'd slipped me the envelope that stuck me with responsibility for collecting for the United Way charities. It was odd in the same way also because he almost never presumed to address an employee after working hours. I looked into those sharp and narrowed eyes as he made straight for me, and I saw that they had the focused look of a predator going for the kill. "Well Tim," his smile broadened, "it looks like we got one man too many working here, and I guess you're *it*." He handed me a little white envelope and said, "Here. I guess this'll make us about even."

As I finished snapping off the circuit breaker for the day and came creaking down the stepladder, savoring each step as best I could, Jerry was just heading out the door and said as usual, "Good night Tim, see ya tomorrow."

"Yeah," I said, "see ya sometime."

The Auction

38

A s it happened, I did see Jerry one more time. Early that spring, I was driving down the main street in town when I spotted him emerging from a block of flats and waved him over for a chat. It was a workday, but he'd taken some time off to look for a place in town to live because he was tired of living at home. "How are things at the mill?"

"Oh, you know. Same as usual. Parsons hasn't changed."

"What about the guy who replaced me?"

"Oh him!" Jerry laughed. "Didn't last the week." Then turning the questions back in my direction, he asked. "You workin' now?"

"Naw!" I waved the notion away. "Been checking out some construction jobs, but I haven't gotten anywhere with 'em." A slight look of disappointment seemed to cross Jerry's face as I said this, and it struck me how completely our relative status had reversed these last few months.

"Who's he got working the headsaw now?" I asked slyly, knowing the answer as soon as I asked.

"Uuh, well, he's had me workin' it quite a bit lately," he replied sheepishly.

"Yeah, well," I sighed, "that's about what I figured he had in mind for you."

Jerry looked a little uncertain and allowed as how he'd better be getting on his way back to work. When I next heard of Jerry it was several months later, and he'd quit, or been fired, after two weeks of chronic absences. I could easily imagine the sorts of psychological tortures Parsons had inflicted on his fledgling head sawyer and was glad never to have been part of it myself. It no longer seemed possible that the old tyrant would ever find anyone capable of replacing him as head sawyer. It was almost as if he'd looked over our generation and found it entirely lacking in the requisite qualities for such responsibility.

Jerry had no trouble finding work and was almost immediately picked up by the same local construction firm that had sent the riggers to install the new ripsaw. Pete soon followed suit, resigning his position and claiming that he was going into business for himself as an auto mechanic. By the end of that spring only Charlie was left as an employee at Parsons' mill. As I drove into town I could see him sometimes up there on the log deck, a solitary figure resting his weight on a peavey, waving as I cruised by. He seemed as permanent a fixture to that mill as Parsons himself, and I thought it only a matter of time before Parsons began to recruit a new wave of transients to fill out the gap between him and his impoverished log chopper.

But it was not yet summer before Amy reported having seen Charlie in town during the middle of a workday, and we began idly speculating as to what his business might have been. "Probably a dentist's appointment or something," I said. Then, a few days later, he was again seen downtown during a workday, and I wondered if his supposed dental work was not more serious than I'd first imagined. A week later he was seen again, and as his appearances in town became more and more frequent, it occurred to me that it had been quite a while since I'd seen him on the log deck as I passed the mill. Thus it came only slowly and gradually to me that Charlie too had been "sent on down the road."

We would spot Charlie in town once or twice a month. He was kind of a fixture on the main street and could be seen striding up the town's steep hill, where the prosperous and picturesque tourists gave him wide berth, probably thinking all the wrong thoughts about him. In July, at a local farmer's market where we'd taken to selling a little produce, we finally talked with him.

At the market the vendor's tables were arrayed in a large, straggling loop stretching across a freshly mowed field just outside of town. The day was a hot one, and the tourists from off the highway ambled listlessly from table to table, looking and chatting but holding tightly to their wallets and purses. Children ran among the tables, making friends where they could, or gingerly reaching out to pet the goat for sale, which was tied to a tree in the loop's center. The featured entertainment for that hour of the afternoon was a demonstration class which was being led by a local *tai-chi* master. His twenty students stood there in rough rank, creakily stretching limbs in semi-synchronous slow motion, carefully eyeing the effortless, graceful movements of the master. In their midst stood Charlie, who watched himself self-consciously, as he tottered, unbalanced, from one foot to the other, his pants slipping down as always, his glasses resting on the end of his nose.

"Oh yeah," he said to us later. "He really went nuts after he fired you. Everybody thought it was incredibly unfair, what he did to you."

"Everybody? I bet ol' Pete didn't mind."

"Oh no!" Charlie assured me, "Pete was the one that seemed the most angry about it."

After some initial anxiety about being unemployed, Charlie said he welcomed the opportunity of a summer off after so many years of hard work. In the fall he found himself a job with the same huge warehouse that had fired Pete for destroying a truckload of cigarettes. Ironically, after spending three winters laboring outside in the cold for Parsons, Charlie's new inside job was in a freezer compartment, and he was still required to wear layer upon layer of clothing for work. Now, instead of seeing him up on the log deck, I'd sometimes see him in the late afternoons on his way to work on the second shift. He'd acquired an old bicycle, an English three-speed, which he would ride the two miles out to the warehouse on the rapidly expanding north edge of town. He was still a solitary figure, meandering in and out among the commercialized effluvia of outskirts America, dodging the hazardous stream of cars and trucks that flowed continuously between the islands of fast-food outlets, gas stations, and shopping malls. If there was time we would stop and talk but soon found less and less to talk about. We no longer had the mill in common and no longer worked side by side. Our occasional conversations were soon reduced to a "Howya doin'" and a wave, and then after a while to a simple wave as we passed each other by.

The mill struggled on for another year. Every once in a while I would see an advertisement in the paper calling for a new hand and wonder if this represented an addition or replacement. I continued to take the short cut past the mill on my way into town and would take a long look as I passed around its embankment, trying to see how things were going. A small number of winter logs arrived that fall, and judging by the number of cars in the lot Parsons looked as though he was maintaining a crew of two or three to work through them.

After a while I began to lose interest in the place, thinking that it looked as if it would maintain itself at this low ebb of production until the day Parsons died. Charlie had claimed that the old man and his mill were inseparable, and I was inclined to agree. After all those years of hard and terrible labor, of having nursed the place back to health after its near destruction by fire, the mill seemed as if it were life itself to that old man. But the following spring, a full year after my dismissal and the dismissal of all the people I'd worked with, a notice appeared on one of the back pages of the local paper:

AUCTION
HENRY PARSONS' MILL

The notice went on to give the usual detailed inventory, listing the particulars of the mill's larger machines: Lane 00 Headsaw; Tannewitz bandsaw; Whitney planer; self-feeding ripsaw; three circular crosscut saws; large chain bar cut-off saw; other saws; forklift; Chevy C-6 truck, W/PTO dumper; 40 heavy wooden carts; blower system. Large variety: electric motors; saw blades; hand tools. Many interesting items, too numerous to mention. The time and place of the auction were given, along with the conditions of sale, the auctioneer's name, and his Boston address.

After a week in which I'd changed my mind three or four times, I firmly resolved to attend the auction that Saturday morning. In one respect I'd come full circle with the mill. After having spent years driving by it and being curious as to what occurred within it, I'd found work there. Then, after being dismissed, I had again gone back to driving slowly by the place and speculating as to what went on inside. Now, I was to see the place again after having missed it for a year, and the prospect of entering once more into the domain of Henry Parsons made me as nervous as it had on that bright and blue Saturday when I'd first gone looking for work there.

Once again, I found myself slowly moving my little pickup into the mill's yard as unobtrusively as I could manage. But now, instead of the small hills of ash logs waiting to be washed, chopped, and split, the yard was filled with vans, pickup trucks, and trailers waiting to haul the guts of the place away. I crossed the yard and stepped through the same door through which I'd always stepped on a workday morning, sure of every step and familiar with every sensation but somehow feeling as if I were a stranger to the place. Whatever sense of possession I once had about the place was long gone, and I felt a little like a ghost futilely trying to reclaim my stake. Inside the main building I found

175

myself facing the wooden stepladder down which I'd last descended and was tempted to climb back up and snap on the ripsaw circuit breaker, as if in preparation for yet another workday. But now I was in the midst of a crowd of other strangers, sixty or seventy of them, all murmuring among themselves and waiting for things to get under way. I could see that everything in that room had remained exactly in its place, and yet everything seemed different. This place was no longer Henry Parsons' mill but simply the site of a public auction, one of many that I had attended. And as I moved through the crowd it was apparent in the way that people moved aside or looked me over that I was not a ghost. In their eyes I was just another bidder, another spectator.

"Well boys," the auctioneer stood up on a little box, "we got us a fine collection of sawmill equipment right here." He looked around and smiled, as if not quite sure where this fine equipment was. "As I say, a lot of equipment to sell, so we might as well get started." The crowd pushed forward around the auctioneer, who had positioned himself next to lot number one, which happened to be one of the old jury-rigged ripsaws. In the mill it had been of immense practical value over the years. But in the auction it was worthless hardware powered by a very nice old five-horsepower electric motor. The entire contraption eventually went for forty dollars.

As the next few lots went, the crowd shifted and flowed around the mill's machinery following the auctioneer's lead. Clipboard in hand and pencil behind his ear, he peered out at the crowd over a pair of half-moon reading glasses that gave him the air of a man of wise integrity and folksy good nature. This was in sharp contrast to the rather sullen nature of the crowd. His tallest assistant was always at his side, carrying the soapbox from lot to lot, pointing out missed bids, and directing the other assistants, who worked the crowd aggressively looking for cash deposits from winning bidders.

The auction worked its way down the mill's south side, selling off another couple of the jury-rigged ripsaws and then the cut-off saw, complete with the conveyer belt that had carried scrap to the truck outside. Some eager young bucks, enthusiastic in their curiosity as to the cut-off saw's merits, rudely lifted a plywood cover off the housing that held its electric motor. Peering in, one said to the other, "What would you say, five horsepower?"

"Seven maybe," the other replied.

I stepped over to peer in the box as well. I'd last looked in there a year and a half before, when I'd spent a week by myself cleaning the place up. I distinctly remember my decision not to clean the dust out of that box and instead left eighty years' worth of accumulated sawdust lying in there around the motor as my own sort of monument to the mill's history. Now the box was empty of all dust. In fact the entire mill was absolutely pristine. There was no sign of dust anywhere, and the museum-like quality that such neatness gave to the place was a little disconcerting.

Now the auction was approaching the mill's heart. In short order the next four lots disposed of the doweler, the new ripsaw, the cut-off saw used in conjunction with the headsaw, and of course the headsaw itself. The murmurs of the crowd rose to a modest buzz, as people began to speculate what price these important machines might command and who would be carting them away. Expert in his role as showman, the auctioneer took some extra time before getting set to open bids on these lots.

"Now before we move on to these next four lots," cried the auctioneer, "I would like to point out the elevator over here." He slowly and magnanimously swept his hand over the heads of the crowd and pointed at Parsons' prized 'lanyard-type lift.' "Now Mister Parsons would like to sell this elevator for its parts. Of course you'll have to dismantle it yourself," he chuckled. "Do I have any bids?" Silence. The audience was already focused on four lots waiting to be sold and had no interest in an antique elevator. "No bids? No bids? Well, okay. If any of you are interested later on, the man you want to talk to is standing right over there." He pointed to the back of the crowd, and everybody turned to look. "Henry Parsons is the one you want to talk to." Then in a mock search, pretending to shade his eyes with his hand, he called out, "Henry? Henry? You want to raise your hand so everyone can see you?"

The crowd backed away a little, and there stood Parsons, his arm half raised like a naughty schoolboy, his face red with embarrassment. Everyone looked at him for a few silent moments of humiliation until the auctioneer, now sneeringly familiar, called everyone's attention back to the business at hand.

In ten minutes the headsaw was gone, and a certain air of relief blew through the crowd. The winning bidder was the owner of a wood products business in Massachusetts who'd managed to buy a large number of the mill's more valuable machines. This had caused minor disgruntlement among the locals in the crowd, who saw it as another

177

form of thievery by the flatlanders. "Fella might as well buy the entire mill, the way he's goin," somebody muttered.

The lots immediately following the headsaw consisted of the large variety of tools associated with its operation: a pair of axes, measuring calipers, rulers, Parsons' extensive collection of oil cans, and some drawshaves. I successfully bid on the drawshaves, getting seven of them for about a tenth of their market value. Somebody came up to me later and tried to buy one off me. But despite the opportunity for immediate profit I refused him.

Later on I was chastised by one of the auctioneer's assistants—a particularly aggressive and self-amused sort who, like his boss, put on a folksy, countrified style but was betrayed as a city slicker by his expensive clothes and the frantic pace at which he worked the crowd. He slipped by me at one point and sneered loudly enough for those close enough to hear. "Couldn't even sell one, eh?"

"*He's* not interested in speculation," came a voice from behind me that seemed familiar. I turned to see that the speaker was Parsons himself, staring straight ahead as if fully concentrating on the proceedings.

Still later, moving to the wall where one of the spare, fifty-two-inch diameter headsaw blades was stored, I anticipated the crowd and stood next to the blade, running my hand along its carefully hand-crafted, stainless steel surface. There is true art to the manufacture of such a tool. It must dissipate the terrible force of those oncoming logs over its large surface, as again and again it plunges through, never wavering, always expected to perform within tolerances measured in thirty-seconds of an inch. Perhaps the blade could even be said to represent the true heart of any sawmill, past or present. For even in the days of the mill dam, such a blade lay at the center of things, splitting its precise route through tree after tree after tree.

Bidding on the previous lot had ended, and the crowd was beginning to make its way over. Putting my foot up on a cart and leaning forward, I decided to remain there at the center of the next bid, watching the auctioneer from close up. Some fellow came over to stand beside me, looked me over from the corner of his eye, and spat horribly on the floor. I retraced the exact route from his mouth to that fat gob on the floor and made an exaggeratedly disgusted face. He continued to watch me from the corner of his eye before straightening himself momentarily and moving off.

The auctioneer made his way over, impatiently pushing his clipboard through the crowd, and then turned and waited for it to come to attention. He struck the big blade with a ring on his pinky finger, and the steel rang out with a clear, even tone that wavered ever so gently as it faded away. As he withdrew his hand he showed me the ring. It held a diamond that looked the size of an English ha'penny cut flat across to reveal a perfect and deeply hypnotic luminescence.

"It's a good one," he said with a condescending smile. And it remained ambiguous whether he was referring to the stone or to the steel it had just struck.

Just then I felt another leg perch on the same cart. The cart pitched slightly on the fulcrum of its middle wheels, and I looked up to see that it was Parsons. He was smiling that contained little smile of his and staring straight ahead at the place he'd worked all these years. There we both stood, side by side, while the auctioneer quickly disposed of the blade, and then we both went off in separate directions.

An hour later, with the auction over, Parsons had left, and those of us who'd won our bids lined up outside the old office, waiting to pay for our merchandise and leave. Behind me stood an old man, holding forth in a garrulous manner to a stocky and rough-looking man of middle age, who listened with an air of amused indulgence.

"It's too damn bad, that's all I can say! A mill closing down like this. Haddam's only ash mill. Don't seem to be any reason to it!"

I turned to get a closer look at the speaker. It was Mr. Jorgenson, the old-timer whom I'd last spoken to when I was dusting the mill, and who'd been keeping an eye on the place for Parsons all these years. "Well," he continued, "they say he was a good sawyer, one of the best. But he was a stubborn son of a bitch, I'll tell ya. If he decided he didn't like a fella, well, he'd just hold a grudge against 'im forever. Too damn stubborn!" It was odd, but given the nature of the speech, if I hadn't just laid eyes on Parsons an hour before, I would have thought it was a eulogy.

Despite my continuous attention, Jorgenson completely ignored me. Playing the innocent, I asked, "Did they ever cut anything here besides ash?"

He turned and frowned menacingly at me. "No, no! Ash! That's what they cut here! Haddam's ash mill! But no longer!" He looked me up and down, and snorted contemptuously.

I faced the front of the line. People who'd paid their money were already starting to dismantle various pieces of machinery and were carting things off. Someone had climbed up a ladder to get at the clock

179

over the office door, and now there was nothing up there but a clean round patch where it had hung. Someone else was dismantling the gray institutional drinking-water machine.

The old man behind me was still chattering away angrily,

"The place is too damn neat! No sawdust anywhere. Bad sign when a sawmill is this clean. . . . "

39

▲▲▲

I do not know the precise reasons for the demise of Parsons' mill. There were the obvious matters of difficult economic times: shrinking demand for hardwood with the rise of plastics, the increasing availability of tropical hardwoods, cheap or subsidized foreign labor. Yet that mill might still be running had there not been a peculiar failure of will on the part of that old man. It seemed as if there simply came a day upon which he no longer wished to struggle, a realization of an old age that had seen enough of change and its demands and wanted things constant from now on.

Within a year after the auction at Parsons' mill, the entire complex of buildings, mill, shed, sawdust bin, and log decks, had been demolished. All that remained as reference to its former existence was a weed-filled lot, marked off by a single, spreading oak that had stood at the fork of its two driveways. Once familiar places are surprisingly hard to identify after such drastic transformation. It would now take a special effort to walk the grounds and say, "Well, here is where the log deck stood, you can see by the way the weeds have grown up here." Or, "there you can see where the mill's foundation began, and so over here is where the headsaw stood."

Of course, most of the former hands at the mill would never bother to come back and play archaeologist. A worker might drive by and say, "Used to be an ash mill there I worked at for a while."

And where would the credit for the effort of that experience lie? With the paychecks long since cashed? On the thousands of wooden ladder rungs used without thought by thousands of people somewhere else? In that worker's mind, and in my mind, perhaps yes. But in Henry Parsons' mind it was his mill and his mill's products. And any determination as to who did and did not have a stake in it would rest with him and him alone.

There was a clipboard that used to hang on a wall of the office in

Parsons' mill upon which Parsons recorded his estimates of the quantity of usable material received when a load came in. Sometime, years before my tenure at the mill, he'd had stationery printed up, appropriately ruled for this purpose. At the top was printed, "Henry Parsons and Company." The first time I'd noticed the clipboard, the "and Company" had been crudely scratched out. At the time it was not a matter to which I attached much importance. I simply assumed that the "and Company" referred to some past partner of Parsons, now long lost by the wayside, and that the old man could see no possible justification for wasting perfectly good stationery. But as I came to know him I understood that Parsons was not a man to ignore the importance of signs and symbols. Later that fall, when business had picked up and he seemed pleased with us, I noticed that the stationery no longer had the "and Company" crossed out.

As he and his business had grown older and more tired, they had grown closer and closer to one another, and his reluctance to give way to the judgment of others grew greater with each passing season. If he was in some sort of financial difficulty, we, the hands who made his business go, would have been the last to know. We were mere appendages to him, and owed our loyalty to him, not the mill. If he could have run the place himself, he would have. But as it was, it galled him that he needed to depend upon us.

During one of the several occasions when Parsons had a steady stream of men applying to replace someone he'd just fired, a certain applicant tried to introduce himself by offering Parsons a handshake. He was rudely refused, for he was only a "hand"—not really a man—and did not merit such a respectful act.

It was not that this man was poor, because I'd seen Parsons shake the hand of a poor man. An old farmer—who obviously went years back with Parsons—came with his son to buy a load of the long scraps used as "sugar wood," the fuel used in spring for boiling off maple sap to make syrup. He drove an old wreck of a pickup truck, which he and his son slowly and carefully loaded to brimming with well-seasoned ash. Afterward he and Parsons chatted together for a moment, Parsons playing the role of simple backwoodsman before getting down to the business of payment. Here they stood, each holding his wallet open for the other to see, and carefully—almost in slow motion—picked out green bills and exchanged them, first one, then the other, as they silently negotiated their price. Then, shaking hands, as they had done when meeting an hour before, they went their separate ways, two gentlemen of business, neither—that unlucky thing—a wage slave.

It was as if Parsons could not reconcile his need for laborers with his own belief that every real man ought to be independent. He could not concede his dependency to his workers, and in his furious rush to hire and fire, he meant to show them their true worth. But in the moments when all was going well, those few weeks in the fall before the heavy snows, he had given his mill over to his workers, and they had responded in kind, jumping with spirit at the load thrown their way. His dependency upon them became all too apparent, and it was his need to establish his authority, his "right" to supremacy that finally doomed the mill.

I suppose I felt as if I were some sort of ringleader in what Parsons viewed as a conspiracy against him. But I'd come there mostly to prove to myself, and to those who cared about me, that I was capable of working long and hard at distasteful tasks for dubious reward. Many of the people I'd worked with had difficulty establishing a motive for my presence when there must be so many "easier" things in the world I could do. Parsons himself clearly wondered about it and had invented some idea that I was after some of his land. All I'd been after was a simple expiation of the guilt that all privileged people feel, whether they are willing to acknowledge it or not. "I must show," thought I, "that as a young man who has grown up with some measure of privilege, I can understand what it is to live without those privileges."

In this I probably failed. One cannot escape what one is; one can only try to understand what someone else has to go through. To see through the muck of their hard lives, and divine the humanity that is buried there and know what it is we have in common. But I did feel that as a group, we, the hands at Henry Parsons' mill, did succeed. For some brief time, we managed a triumph over those legal realities that say who owns what, to whom profit will accrue, and those provisions in state law that say a worker's arm—if lost—is worth so much, his eye so much, his leg so much, and his life. . . . No, we the hands at Parsons' mill owned the place with our hearts for a while—and for that sin we would all eventually be fired. And for that failure on his part, that lapse, Henry Parsons would forget all effort, seek no new market for his product, and destroy the ash mill.

Amy and I lived another winter in Vermont. She continued to work at a local high school as a librarian, while I returned to handyman status, adding yet another vocation to my list, that of writer. The next summer we moved back to Boston, having sampled life in the glorious mountains among phoebes, thrushes, grosbeaks, and chickadees, hard and softwood forests, mountain mowings, rolling dirt roads, surprised deer, persistent raccoons, and the genius of slow and stupid porcupines.

Now in Boston I write and live among the educated and the socially aware, the financially ambitious, and the desperate poor. The city is where I grew up, and I have much in common with the people who struggle there. But my eye is always on the country, where life is beautiful and hard in equal proportion. I aim to go back some day, maybe to work the mills—I don't know. But there will never be another mill like Parsons'. He is still around, and now and again when I visit there, I've seen him tending his properties—posing as a tree farmer now. He knows much about the land, though what he knows will probably die with him. I rarely see the people I worked with, though I see people like them everywhere. And though I am still fairly shy, the boy who went to prep school and college no longer regards them with such terror and is honored with the idea that some of them have been his friends.